One Beat of a Heart

Kay Seeley

TO MY FAMILY
WITH THANKS

Kay Seeley's books

Novels

The Water Gypsy
The Watercress Girls
The Guardian Angel

The Hope Series
A Girl Called Hope (Book 1)
A Girl Called Violet (Book 2)
A Girl Called Rose (Book 3)

The Fitzroy Hotel Stories
One Beat of a Heart
A Troubled Heart

All Kay's novels are also available in Large Print

Box Set (ebook only)
The Victorian Novels Box Set

Short Stories
The Cappuccino Collection
The Summer Stories
The Christmas Stories

Who's Who in One Beat of a Heart.

The Fitzroy Family
Herbert Fitzroy (Father) (owns the hotel)
Elvira Fitzroy, (Mother)
Lawrence Fitzroy (oldest son)
Jeremy Fitzroy (second son)
Clara Fitzroy (only daughter).
Doris Templeton (Herbert's widowed sister)

The Carter Family
Nora Carter (Mother)
Daisy Carter (Head of Housekeeping at the Hotel)
Jack Carter (Daisy's older brother)
Dan Carter (Daisy's younger brother
Jessie Carter (Daisy's younger sister)

The Hotel Staff (in order of appearance)
Daisy Carter (Head of Housekeeping)
Mrs T (Cook)
Ruby (Kitchen maid)
Matilda Mulroony (Assistant cook)
Barker (Concierge).
Hollis (Porter)
Kitty (Chambermaid)
Annie (Chambermaid)
Mr Jevons (Maître d')
Alfred Elsworthy (Porter)
Thomas (Groom)

Other significant characters
Sebastian Shawcross (Soldier Clara meets in the Park)
Sir Richard, Viscount Westrow (Friend of the family)
Dolly Deverill (Hotel Guest)
Charlie Benton (Jessie's boyfriend)
Felix Benton (Charlie's older brother)

Chapter One

London 1902

Upstairs, in her room in the twenty bed-roomed Fitzroy Hotel, owned by her father, Miss Clara Fitzroy paced the floor. It was a good sized room, one of the best in the hotel, with a brass bed, floral patterned wallpaper and carpets and lace curtains at the window. Outside, early morning sunshine filled the streets. Costermongers, newspaper sellers and traders on their way to work hurried along the pavement accompanied by the rattle of wheels and the jingle of harnesses. Inside she bubbled with excitement.

Ever since Queen Victoria's death a year ago Clara had been making plans. It was clear there'd be a Coronation. She'd clapped her hands in joy when the date in June, at the peak of the London Season, was announced. It meant London would be full of eligible young men looking for brides.

A season of her own was out of the question and she wasn't invited to the Summer Balls, not being entitled, but before her grandfather's death she would have expected at least a few invitations to the more general events. Now they lived in more straightened circumstances they no longer moved in the right social circles. What was the point of living in her father's dreary London hotel if she couldn't get out and meet the 'right sort of prospect'?

The Coronation's postponement, due to the King's illness, had been a blow, but now she chose to see it as an opportunity. The whole country was buzzing with what the papers called a 'new era of optimism'. Clara wasn't sure what that meant, but was determined to enjoy it. Many of the young military men brought into town for the Coronation procession would be hanging around with little to do until the rescheduled ceremony. A meal out in the right restaurant, a ride in the park, if she could borrow a horse, or if not, a walk, a dropped glove, a confused expression, a smile and a tilt of the head, who knew where they might lead. The sun promised to shine on a day fragrant with possibilities.

She turned her attention to the supper she planned for the evening after the Coronation. She'd wanted to hold a grand dinner dance but her brother, Lawrence, who managed the hotel, had put paid to that.

"We don't have the resources or the space," he said, so her plans, like all her other schemes, were scaled down. He'd eventually agreed to a supper party and musical evening for a few intimate friends. Although it would be a smaller event than she'd hoped, she still wanted to make an impression.

She chewed her lip as she took out a green silk gown. Several years old it looked dated. She sighed. She could do with a new wardrobe instead of having to have her dresses remodelled and wear them until they fell from her back in ribbons. If only Lawrence wasn't so mean with her allowance, she thought, handing it out in dribs and drabs. If she'd been a boy, like her other brother, Jeremy, she'd be able to manage her own money instead of depending on Lawrence to hold the purse strings, and hold them far too tight for her liking.

She held the dress against her body and gazed in the mirror. The colour complemented her auburn curls and brought out her jade green eyes. She wrinkled her nose, pursed her lips, blew out her cheeks and screwed her face into several contortions while she thought about it. Perhaps if that girl Daisy could lower the neckline, add some beading, shorten the sleeves and take some of the fullness out of the skirt it would be passable. She sighed, laid it on the bed and got on with dressing. She'd have to take her aunt with her to the park, but that wasn't a problem. Doris Templeton, her father's widowed sister, had been installed in the hotel as chaperone. She could twist Aunt Doris around her little finger.

*

Downstairs a blast of stifling heat and the smell of fried bacon and tomatoes greeted Daisy Carter as she walked into the kitchen. Mrs T, the cook, lifted the lump of dough she was kneading and banged it onto the table, sending a flurry of flour into the air.

"So, what did His Lordship want this morning?" she asked, her displeasure clear on the fleshy features of her face.

"One of the guests had an accident at last night's party," Daisy said. "She tore her dress and Mr Lawrence asked me if I could mend it."

"Hrrumph." Mrs T pounded the dough with her fists. "Over and above that is. It's not your job to mend guests' clothes. They take advantage and that Miss

3

Clara's no better. Treats you like her personal lady's maid." Her heavy breasts wobbled with indignation.

Daisy shrugged her slender shoulders. "She makes it hard to say no," she said. "Anyway, I don't mind. Miss Clara's been good to me." That was true. Daisy had been taken on as a chambermaid, but, thanks to Miss Clara she'd been made up to Head of Housekeeping with two girls working under her.

Mrs T gathered up the dough and divided it between the ready prepared baking tins. "I still say they take advantage, always putting on airs and graces. Jumped up nobodies, that's what they are." She huffed and turned to put the loaves into the already lit oven.

"You'd better not let Mr Lawrence hear you call him His Lordship. You know how that rankles."

Mrs T's features hardened. "Trade – that's what they are. Came from trade, working in trade and they'll die in trade. You can sprinkle sugar on a turd but it don't make it chocolate."

Daisy suppressed a smile. Mrs T had worked for the gentry and never let anyone forget it, but Daisy liked Mr Lawrence and his brother Jeremy. They were well educated men of the world. It wasn't their fault their grandfather had gambled away his fortune and left them to fend for themselves in a world where trade was looked down upon. Mrs T was right about Miss Clara. She was spoiled and did take advantage, but it wasn't her fault either. She'd been brought up with expectations and it was only when the old man died they discovered the real state of his affairs.

A bell sounded in the distance.

"That'll be one of the guests wanting breakfast." Mrs T glanced around. "Where's Ruby? She should be here by now." She tutted. "Rack and ruin. The place is going to rack and ruin."

"I'll get out of your way then. I only came in to wash my hands." Daisy smiled to herself as she left the kitchen. She knew the Fitzroys were struggling to keep the hotel open. If it closed they'd all lose their jobs, so she was prepared to do whatever it took to help, even if it did mean staying up most of the night making, altering and repairing dresses for Miss Clara so she could attend the soirees that brought in customers.

Mrs T may have a brusque tongue in her head, Daisy thought, but underneath that rough exterior she had a heart of gold. Everyone had been upset lately. Just six weeks ago the hotel had been full with guests arriving for the King and Queen's Coronation. When it was postponed several of the hotel guests had left early and demanded refunds for their shortened stay, which meant the takings were down and the situation even more distressing.

Now they were having to do it all over again. Mrs T was preparing meals for a hotel full of guests as well as catering for the picnics and supper parties Miss Clara had arranged for the Summer Bank Holiday weekend. On top of that, the August weather being so fine, Mr Lawrence had promised several influential guests that Mrs T would prepare picnic hampers for them too. It was only his assurance that the requests had come specifically thanks to her reputation as one of the best cooks in London that she eventually agreed to provide them.

"I'll need more help," she'd told him, "and I know just the person to ask. She's a fine pastry cook. You won't be disappointed."

"Hmm. Only until the Coronation then," Mr Lawrence said. "After that London will empty faster than a factory when the clocking off whistle goes."

So Matilda Mulroony, the daughter of one of Mrs T's oldest friends, was hired for the weeks up to the Coronation.

"Blimey," Barker, the concierge, a grey haired, grey whiskered man in his early fifties, said when he heard. "Mrs T's got friends. That's a turn up."

Chapter Two

After breakfast, just as Clara predicted, she was able to persuade her Aunt Doris to accompany her to Hyde Park. "It's such a lovely day, it would be a sin to stay indoors," she said.

Barker called a cab to take them to the park gate. As the cab dropped them off, Clara helped Aunt Doris into the warm sunshine. Patches of light trembled through trees to dapple the grass. The wide open space felt airy and bright, unlike the oppressive heat and dust of the city's narrow streets. The flowers alongside the path were vivid with colour and perfumed the soft morning air. Birds chirped and bees buzzed around the sweet chestnut trees. The sound of a brass band playing in the distance drifted across the park on the lightest of breezes.

People strolled along the paths, either as couples, with children, with dogs or just taking in the sights. Clara paid particular attention to the women, assessing their outfits, making mental notes of the most fashionable and comparing them to the pictures in her copy of *Vogue*. She judged every outfit alongside her own and found hers wanting.

Aunt Doris wasn't too fond of exercise so Clara knew she could rely on her to look for a seat before too long. She guided her towards the bandstand where an ensemble of Grenadier Guards played rousing military marches.

"Not too near the front, dear," Doris said. "Too noisy for me. Here in the shade will do." Clara found them two chairs in the shade of a line of lime trees that, despite rustling in the breeze, did nothing to dispel the warmth of the day. It wasn't long before Clara saw

Doris's eyes droop as she dozed, nodding to the music. She sat up sharply when the Guards came to the end of their session and there was a short break until the next band took their places on the bandstand.

Clara glanced around. "Should we take a walk in the rose garden, Aunt?" she said. "It's such a lovely day and the roses will be magnificent."

Doris fanned her face. "It's a bit too hot for me, but you go if you like. Just don't wander too far off."

"Of course not." Clara gave her a confident smile. "Perhaps I could get us some ice creams. Would you like one?"

"That would be lovely, dear." Doris smiled.

Released at last, Clara jumped up and wandered away, taking in the splendour of the trees, the warmth of the day and the people walking past. She made her way to the side of the Serpentine where most visitors gathered. She saw families with children feeding the ducks, young couples wandering by and elderly ladies admiring the boats and the rowers. Here, by the lake, the air felt cooler. The only sounds were the lapping of the water and the slapping and creek of oars from the boats. Sunlight shone like diamonds on the ripples spreading across the surface of the water. She took a deep breath. A perfect summer's day, she thought, idyllic, just like a picture postcard.

She walked slowly along the path, glancing around, pretending to be engrossed in watching the boats and the scenery around her, whereas her interest really lay in a trio of men in military uniform standing by the boathouse. They appeared to be deciding who should take out the boat moored by their feet.

She found a seat on a bench where she could watch them from beneath her parasol. Two of the men took

8

off their jackets, laying them in the bottom of the boat before they climbed in and shipped the oars, while the other one untied the boat and bent down to give them a push. Away they went, all laughing and waving.

She took particular notice of the tall, broad-shouldered man left standing on the path, the way the breeze ruffled his blonde hair, the mirth in his summer blue eyes and the smile on his fine intelligent features. Her heart fluttered. She twirled her parasol and stood up. She took a breath and glanced around before strolling casually towards the boathouse. As she passed him she dropped her glove. He stooped to pick it up and came after her, just as she knew he would.

"Excuse me, my dear. I think you dropped this," he said, holding the glove out to her. His gaze brushed her face and she felt her cheeks flush.

"Oh, my goodness," she said. "How clumsy of me. You're very kind. Thank you so much." She took the offered glove. "I was on my way to the cafe to buy some ice cream. Perhaps I could treat you to a reward."

His eyes sparkled and he appeared to be struggling to suppress a chuckle. "Allow me," he said placing his cap on his head and offering his arm.

He was a good half-a-head taller than her and her heart swelled with pleasure as she rested her hand on his arm. The grin on his face stretched wider. "If we're to partake of ice cream together it's only proper that I introduce myself. Captain Sebastian Shawcross of the Gloucester Rifles at your service." He raised his cap.

"Miss Clara Fitzroy," she said. "Of The Fitzroy Hotel." She dropped a quick curtsy.

"Charmed," he said.

His gaze lingered and her heart quickened. He's a little forward, I must say, she thought, but hadn't she been a bit too forward in her approach to him? It was a game and she was happy to play it.

In the ice cream parlour he bought her a pink and white ice cream sundae. Served in a tall glass with a long thin silver spoon it was the biggest ice cream sundae she'd seen in her life.

They sat at a table outside in the shade and by the time they'd finished their ice creams Clara had learned that his regiment were in London for the procession, he was a first class shot and he hated boats as much as she did. She felt as though she'd known him forever. He was easy to talk to and didn't make fun of her like her brothers did whenever she tried to make conversation with them. She felt so at ease with him, she didn't notice the time. It was only when Aunt Doris came bustling towards them, hanging on to her hat and gazing wildly around, that Clara realised how foolhardy her actions had been and the trouble she'd be in.

"I'm sorry," she said, jumping up. "Please forgive me. I have to go… my aunt." She gestured to the short chubby woman making her way, in a state of great agitation, towards the ice cream parlour.

Dismay and disappointment like a dark cloud washed over her, as though the sun had gone from the day. She'd had such a good time. If only she could stay and hear more about his adventures in South Africa, she thought. He was the most exciting thing that had ever happen to her and she didn't want to say goodbye, although she knew she had to. She suddenly realised how stupid she'd been letting him buy her ice cream. She'd been too easy and must certainly have given the wrong impression, sitting with him, making out they were friends and when they'd hardly been introduced.

She hadn't thought. Her heart fluttered. What must he think of her? It was quite improper to be sitting outside, unchaperoned in full view of passers-by. If anyone had recognised her she'd be the subject of the worst gossipmongers in town. Her reputation would be in tatters and beyond repair. She'd crossed a line. She'd allowed herself to get carried away with the heady excitement of meeting a handsome man on her own terms. She cringed at the thought of what would happen if Aunt Doris told Lawrence. She'd be confined to her room for the rest of her life and probably sent back to her mother in the country. She couldn't bear the thought of that.

"I'm sorry, Aunt Doris," she said hurrying up to her aunt. "I had to wait ages to be served and this gentleman allowed me to go ahead of him, so…"

"I wondered where you'd got to," Doris said, seemingly appeased at the sight of Clara fit and in perfect health. "We really must be getting back or we'll miss lunch." She glanced at the man sitting at the table, a look of bemusement on his face. "Who's your friend?"

"Oh he's the brother of a girl I was at school with. I just ran into him and asked how she was. He tells me she's fine and is coming to London soon." As she spoke she steered her aunt back the way she'd come. "I wonder what we'll have for lunch," she said. "I'm starving."

Chapter Three

Daisy managed to repair the guest's dress quite quickly and decided to take it back to the guest's room so it wouldn't get damaged when the rest of the staff came downstairs for lunch.

Upstairs she tapped on the door, listening for an answer. When she heard no response she unlocked the door and peered in to see if the room was empty. The sight that met her eyes made her jaw drop and her blood boil. The brass bed was in disarray, its sheets in a tangle, bottles and glasses were strewn across the floor, some of them lying in their spilled contents. Cigar and cigarette butts and ash covered the dressing and side tables. The fetid stench of stale alcohol, smoke and the after-smell of the night's obvious activities hung in the air.

Before she could go any further she felt someone behind her. He pushed her into the room, catching her around the waist and spinning her around. Shock stole her breath. Her knees buckled. She opened her mouth to protest, but the scream died on her lips when she saw it was her brother, Jack.

"Jack! What on earth are you doing here?" she gasped pulling herself out of his grasp. "And how did you get in?" Her skin bristled with annoyance.

"I walked in, through the front door, same as everyone else." He grinned. "That doorman's about as much use as a wax fireguard. He had his head in the paper checking the odds for the afternoon racing at Epsom."

"I've told you before we're not allowed visitors during working hours and, anyway, you should use the tradesman's entrance."

"And risk being turned away by that harridan Mrs T? It was you I came to see, not the help."

"Well it's a dangerous way of going about it. If you get caught we'll both be for it." Her voice rose in irritation. She had a vision of Miss Deverill, the occupant of the room they were in, returning and finding them there. What would he say then? She dreaded to think.

"What? You don't think I'd pass as a respectable visitor. Let me tell you not everything about this place is as respectable as you like to think."

Daisy blushed. She'd heard rumours about one or two of Mr Jeremy's guests, but never paid them any mind. Mr Lawrence was always going on about the hotel's reputation and how it must be preserved. In her opinion if anyone was likely to tarnish the hotel's reputation it would be Mr Jeremy and his rackety friends, who treated the place like a club for reprobates.

Daisy's irritation mounted. "So, you're here now. What did you want to see me about?"

"Ma sent me. Dad's been laid off again. She was hoping, seeing as how you've had a leg up, you could send a bit more than usual." He shook his head. "I wouldn't pay much mind. He still finds enough to go down the pub every night."

Daisy sighed. Like her sisters she'd been sending her mother money ever since she started work. She hadn't mentioned the promotion but Ma seemed to have ways finding things out. "I'll see what I can do," she said. "Now hop it before we get caught."

He kissed her cheek. "If you say so. I just wondered if you or any of the staff would be going to town to see the King's Coronation procession? I expect all the guests will."

"I imagine they will," she said. "Most of them are only here for the Coronation. But I doubt I'll find time, nor any of the other staff. Why?"

He shrugged. "Thought it might be nice to go together."

Daisy frowned. Jack had never worried about taking her anywhere before or shown any inclination to do so. He was up to something. She felt it in her bones. She stooped to pick up the dress she'd dropped when he grabbed her. It was crumpled. She started brushing the creases out, with little effect.

"Here let me do that," he said, taking the dress from her. He opened the wardrobe to hang it up. A wide smile stretched across his face. "Blimey," he said. "Get a load of this." Her eyes widened at the sight of an array of corsets and under-garments in vivid colours and an assortment of manacles, whips and boots that she wouldn't expect to see outside of a brothel, or what she imagined a brothel would look like. He picked up a pair of tall riding boots and a crop. "Lady goes riding does she?" he asked eyebrows raised.

Daisy swallowed. "She might," she said, although not very convincingly.

"And these?" He ran his hand through the rainbow row of corsets, suspenders and lurid undergarments. "It's obvious what goes on here," he said. "So much for your hotel's precious reputation."

Daisy heard footsteps coming along the corridor. She grabbed the dress and hung it on the rail. "You'd better go before we get caught," she said.

Her heart beat faster as her anger mounted. He was right. Miss Deverill was plying her trade in the hotel and she'd been completely unaware of it. She wondered if Mr Lawrence knew. Then she recalled that Miss Deverill was Mr Jeremy's guest.

Jack cautiously opened the door and peered out to see if the coast was clear. He chuckled as he left, shaking his head as he went. Daisy had the distinct feeling he knew something she didn't. She recalled Jack had a knack of getting into places he shouldn't. Once they were on a day trip to the seaside with the Pastor's Sunday School Outing when he disappeared. He was eight years old and, being two years older, she had the daunting task of looking after him. When she went to find him she saw him disappear into one of the town's grand seafront hotels. She went after him only to be stopped by an obnoxious and arrogant doorman, asking where she thought she was going. "I've come to look for my brother," she said.

"A likely story." The doorman grabbed her roughly by the arm to escort her out when Jack appeared, looking chirpy as ever.

"Sorry," he said. "Needed the khazi."

The doorman glared. He grabbed them both and threw them out.

Jack had chuckled with glee. "Look what I got." He took three bars of Knights Castile Soap and two napkins embroidered with the hotel crest out of his pocket. It was seeing inside that hotel that had decided Daisy to work as a chambermaid instead of going into the factory like her younger sister. Factory Fodder, her dad called her, but he still took her wages. One day I'm going to work in a place like that, she'd thought. And I'll be in a position so no one can throw me out.

She closed the wardrobe door and glanced around. It would take the chambermaids best part of a morning to clear and clean the room and restore it to its usual pristine condition. That would put them behind cleaning the other rooms. It was too bad. She'd have to say something. She ripped the sheets off the bed and bundled them up to take downstairs. If she hurried she could catch the boy who brought the clean laundry and took the basket of dirty linen away to be washed and pressed. The stains would need special attention. Another job she'd have to do before she could get on with her work.

She worried about what she'd seen for the rest of the day. She had a good mind to speak to Mr Jeremy about the state of the room. Then there was the chambermaids' extra work and the hotel's reputation to think about. Perhaps she should mention what was obvious to anyone who saw it, to Mr Lawrence. But then he could tell her it was none of her business what guests got up to in their own rooms. Maybe they even sanctioned it. Another facility to offer to the wealthy businessmen for their evening's entertainment. She wouldn't put it past Mr Jeremy to do something like that, but not Mr Lawrence. It would be without his knowledge. Daisy was sure of that.

The matter was forced from her mind when Miss Clara, who, according to Barker, had arrived back from her walk in the park more flushed than usual, sent for Daisy to come to her room.

"She'll be wanting you to make a silk purse out of a pig's ear," Mrs T said when she heard. "Girl's got high society tastes on a dock worker's budget. You mark my words. She'll be wanting it done for nowt an' all."

Daisy sighed. Mrs T was probably right, but she didn't see why she should encourage her.

Upstairs Miss Clara was parading in front of the mirror with a green silk dress held in front of her. "Ah, Daisy," she said. "I was wondering if you could do something for me."

Daisy knew what was coming. Another elaborate alteration that had to be done in an impossibly short time. "Of course, Miss Clara." Daisy forced her lips into a smile.

"This dress would be much improved if you could update it somewhat." She went on to explain what she had in mind. "I've done a sketch." She handed Daisy a sheet of paper on which she'd drawn a vastly different dress to the one she was holding.

Daisy's heart sank. It would take hours of work, not to mention the beading, the silks and the lace she'd need.

"I'm not sure…"

"Oh, please say you can," Clara pleaded. "It's for the Coronation Supper and Musical Evening. I can pay you for the beading and silk and I won't mention to Mr Lawrence that I saw your brother lurking in the corridor this morning on my way out."

Daisy silently cursed Jack. She loved him dearly, but he'd always been a bit of a tearaway. At nineteen he'd turned into a young man who couldn't settle to a steady job and had too much time on his hands. Ma worried about him too and now he'd got Daisy into more hot water. It was what he did. He'd worked as a bell boy at the hotel for a short while during the summer holiday a few years ago, that's how Miss Clara knew him. But Mr Herbert had been running the hotel then, and it had been a much better place to work.

"He came to tell me my father's been taken ill," she said, the lie tripping off her tongue with surprising ease. "But I'll see what I can do with the dress, perhaps if I can have some time off?"

Clara smiled. "An illness in the family? I'm sure that can be arranged," she said.

Daisy took the dress to her room. She didn't want the other staff seeing it and giving Mrs T more ammunition for her battle with the Fitzroys. In any case the alterations Clara wanted were far too extensive for Daisy to manage. Her parents' neighbour, a widow with two small children, took in stitching so Daisy thought she could pass the work on to her. The small charge would be added to the cost of the beading and silk. Miss Clara would never know about that.

Chapter Four

Once the problem of the dress was settled Clara sat at the bureau in her room writing out the Coronation Supper and Musical Evening invitations. Jeremy would be organising the music, an ensemble who could play the latest tunes from the West End shows and a singer for the later part of the evening's entertainment. She still had to speak to Mrs T about the menu but was putting off that tiresome task. Lawrence had approved the guest list. The young men she could invite were eligible, the young ladies were girls she knew from school. All came from wealthy, respected families. She added 'Carriages at dawn' to the invitation but doubted anyone would stay until then.

She had no illusions about why she was in London for the summer. Her mother had impressed upon her the importance of marrying someone who could restore the family's fortunes. Regrettably, as it was August, many of the better off families had returned to the country for the opening of the shooting season. It irked her that Lawrence and Jeremy didn't have to suffer the same indignities and have the weight of expectation placed upon them. She complained about it to her friend Amanda.

She liked Amanda, even though she was quite plain, or more accurately, because she was quite plain and presented no competition when it came to gaining male attention.

"Honestly, Amanda. They can do whatever they like. Jeremy and his friends are always out on the town, while I have to stay home and learn embroidery or knitting. It's so unfair."

Amanda shrugged. "I don't mind. I like living in the country, being able to ride out with my dear papa and my brother. I think I must be a bit of home body. A life in high society, always having to be cheerful and entertaining, wouldn't suit me at all."

It was through her friendship with Amanda Melville that she'd been invited to the summer events at all, even if she did have to spend an afternoon with Amanda's brother Rupert, who had a lisp and took great pains to explain to her, over several hours, the intricacies and benefits of dual gauge rails as opposed to single gauge, the impact on traffic load and the problem with deformation of low embankments as the railways expanded.

She'd been with Amanda one Sunday when they went to Speakers' Corner to listen to the suffragettes. They wanted independence for women, the right to handle their own money and have a voice in the way the country was run. Clara listened avidly and agreed when they said they were prisoners in a universe dominated by men.

She even shouted "Hear! Hear!" and waved her gloved hand. She wasn't going to wear white with purple and green, or parade around town waving banners, but she wished them well. She'd even dropped a half-sovereign into their collection box, smiling at the thought of how furious Lawrence would be if he'd known.

She sighed at the memory. She understood everything her mother told her, but couldn't see why she shouldn't have some fun as well. All her friends seemed to be enjoying themselves, why shouldn't she? Perhaps a mild flirtation with a soldier before I settle down to the serious business of finding a suitable husband, she thought.

Captain Sebastian Shawcross came to mind. She'd wished she could spend longer talking to him in the park. He was a man of the world, he'd travelled and seen things she could only dream about. She recalled his face, the laughter in his eyes, his honeyed voice. A shiver ran through her at the thought of seeing him again. She added his name to the invitation list, giggling as she did so. She put a note in the envelope saying that she'd be in the park earlier in the day as her brother had arranged a boating party by the Serpentine. He'd be most welcome to join them if he could get away.

The clock on the mantelpiece chimed three o'clock so she hastily put the invitations into envelopes and took them downstairs to be sent out by messenger. She was having afternoon tea with Amanda and her mother at the Savoy and didn't want to be late.

That night she dreamed of Sebastian Shawcross. She'd seen reports of the fighting against the Boers in the papers and had enjoyed hearing his exploits over ice cream in the park. In her mind she saw him, handsome and brave thundering across the veldt his body a blur of scarlet and gold with bright sunlight glistening on brass as he rode into battle, fighting for King and country. Then he'd come to her, muddied and bloodied, and kiss her with all the passion only she could inspire in him. He'd court her with the admirable restraint shown by all the heroes in the Jane Austen novels she read so avidly. He'd swear that he would die for her.

The next morning her plan to visit the park again in the hope of seeing him, was thwarted when she got a note from Lawrence to say that their parents were in town and she was to meet her mother in the tea room later that morning. Her anticipation of a day out in the sunshine and the possibility of renewing her acquaintance with a man she'd found for herself with no interference from her mother, dropped to the floor with her heart. Why were her parents in town? And more importantly, what did her mother want now?

When Clara got to the tea room her mother, Mrs Elvira Fitzroy, was waiting for her. Unfashionably overdressed in a brown wool coat that was far too hot for the time of year, she wore a worried expression on a face that had seen better days. More grey than Clara remembered peaked out from beneath her mother's satin and pheasant feather trimmed tweed hat. Despite nearly forty years of marriage to Herbert Fitzroy, Elvira had never managed to lose the lingering trace of her Scottish ancestry. It permeated her being, both through her thrifty ways and her overarching ambition. Clara always felt a tingle of apprehension in her presence.

The white-linen-clothed table was already set with tea and muffins for two. "Good morning, Mama," Clara said bending to kiss her cheek. "I trust you are well."

"As well as can be expected in this heat," she said, fanning her face with her gloved hand as though flicking away an irritating fly. "Tea?"

Clara smiled and sank onto the chair opposite her mother. "Thank you. What brings you to London? Have you come for the Coronation?"

"The Coronation? No." She shook her head. "Your father had business in town and I decided to accompany him. We're staying with Viscount Westrow. Sir Richard has been very good to us since..." She paused and picked up the Royal Worcester teapot. She poured the tea into the dainty teacups as though not wishing to think about the time before the 'since'. "You know he's the only one who didn't turn his back on us when..." She paused again before handing Clara the tea. "He's invited us all to dine with him on Saturday. Unfortunately Lawrence will be working and Jeremy is otherwise engaged, but I'm sure you will do us proud."

Clara sipped her tea. Once again Lawrence and Jeremy had got out of family duty visits. She'd hoped to go dancing with Jeremy and his friends, all of whom were lively and fun and none of whom would rate her mother's approval. She knew Sir Richard was a friend of her father's and she guessed the business he'd come to town for was to do with some sort of financial arrangement he had with him. Although the financial situation was never mentioned it hung in the air like a bad smell saturating the fabric of her family. It was the thing that had changed their lives forever, but she couldn't see what difference her making a good impression on Sir Richard would make.

Her mother looked her up and down. "What is that you're wearing? It looks like something out of the rag bag."

Clara glanced down at her olive green and cream day dress. It was an old one she'd had Daisy re-model but it still screamed of the provinces. "If I had a decent clothing allowance—"

Her mother interrupted her. "Never mind. I'll have a word with Mrs Henderson, my dressmaker. I was a good customer before..." She pouted. "She owes me several favours. When I think of the people I introduced to her services..." She drifted off into some sort of reverie.

Clara waited. The prospect of a new dress mollified her somewhat. So she'd have to spend the evening with some of her father's dreary old bore friends, but it would be worth it. Sir Richard was wealthy and well connected. He'd always been charming to her. She knew he'd lost his wife a few years ago. He had sons, but she thought they were too young to be eligible, so her mother's enthusiasm for an evening with them seemed to be misplaced. Perhaps Sir Richard had invited someone who might be of interest for her mother's sole purpose in life, which was to get her married off to someone wealthy enough to save the family's current financial embarrassment. She'd have to wait and see.

"Come along, my dear. Drink up. We mustn't tarry. Mrs Henderson awaits."

Chapter Five

When Matilda Mulroony, the new pastry cook, arrived she was a lot younger than Daisy had thought she would be. She had a pleasant face but the wariness in her hazel eyes and expressionless lips gave the impression of timid vulnerability. As her stay was to be temporary she was to share Daisy's room which Daisy didn't mind as she liked the company. It would be nice to have someone to share things with, even if it was only for a short while.

"How long have you known Mrs T?" Daisy asked as she took Matilda up to the room.

"I don't know her," Matilda said, her broad accent revealing her Northern heritage. "She was a friend of my mother's, but they lost touch when she married. My aunt wrote to her when Ma died and I wanted a change of scenery. She suggested I travel to London and see if Mrs T could recommend some employment. I'm very happy to say she did." Matilda smiled but Daisy noticed the smile didn't reach her eyes.

"I'm sorry to hear about your mother," she said. "That must have been dreadful. Do you have any other family? Father, brothers or sisters who can share the pain?"

Matilda had glanced around. "This is a lovely room," she said. "I shall be very happy here."

Daisy gazed around the drab room with its sparse furnishings. Bare floorboards, a small cracked window and a wardrobe with the door hanging off, still waiting to be fixed, was hardly what Daisy would call 'lovely'. It was very different from the elegantly furnished guest bedrooms downstairs. Daisy didn't like to pry further, but she had the feeling Matilda wasn't telling her everything. What had the girl got to hide? Even stranger still was when Mrs T asked Daisy how she'd settled in. "I promised her aunt I'd keep an eye on her," she said.

Once she was sure Matilda had everything she needed, Daisy folded Clara's green silk dress in tissue paper and placed it carefully into the carrier. When she'd told Mr Lawrence that she'd be out on an errand for Miss Clara he'd given the usual resigned huff, the one he always gave when she mentioned doing anything for his sister, and told her not to take all day. Her family lived in Silvertown, so Barker hailed her a cab. She could drop the dress off at her mother's neighbour and then have tea with her mother. It had been a while since she'd visited and she felt guilty about that.

The overpowering stench of burning rubber, rotting animal carcases and sickly sweet sugar from the factories lining the road by the river greeted Daisy long before the cab dropped her at the end of the narrow street. Not many cabbies wanted to spend more time than they had to in the area where Daisy's family lived. Built in the shadow of the Royal Victoria Docks the cramped, terraced houses were mostly populated by families of the workers from the docks or the factories that belched great plumes of smoke into the air night and day. Children played in the street and a stray dog chewed on the remains of a dead rat. She wrinkled her nose at the nauseating smell from the tanning factory as she passed and once again thanked her lucky stars that she'd managed to get away from it all.

She heard the hum of Betty Hewitt's sewing machine as she waited on the doorstep. She knocked as loudly as she could in case Betty couldn't hear her. The sound of the machine stopped, replaced by the thud of footsteps.

"Good Lord," Betty said when she opened the door. "I thought at least it was the Fire Brigade with all the noise."

"Sorry," Daisy said. "Didn't think you'd hear me."

Betty noticed the carrier. "Brought me something?" she asked.

"A dress to alter. Too much for me to do by hand, so I was hoping…"

"Best come in then."

Daisy followed her into the front room which had been turned into her sewing room. Bits of material, cottons and fibres covered every surface. The sewing machine stood in the window with a length of material still under its foot. "Let's see it then."

Daisy showed her Miss Clara's green silk dress and the sketch she'd drawn.

"Doesn't want much does she? Be easier to buy a new dress."

"I know." Daisy's heart somersaulted into her boots. If Betty couldn't do it she'd have to try herself and it would take best part of a day. "I can do the beading and shorten the sleeves. It's just the skirt."

Betty sucked her teeth. "It's a lot of work. I'm already behind with what I've promised."

"Please, Betty. I don't know who else to ask and you've always been such a good friend."

Betty softened. She smiled. "All right. Leave it with me. As it's you," she said. "I'll see what I can do and I won't charge more than a bob. Give me a couple of days."

"Thank you." Relief flowed through Daisy. The dress would be in safe hands. "You're a saviour."

The relief was short-lived. When she called next door her mother greeted her with a face like thunder. "I 'ope you 'aven't brought me bad news," she said. "I've had enough upsets for one day."

Daisy swallowed and followed her along the narrow hall into the kitchen. Nora Carter was a big woman, her once gentle nature hardened by years of struggle and hardship. Her distress became clear to Daisy when she saw her younger sister sitting at the table, tears streaming down her red, blotchy face. Jessie was bright and usually full of life so seeing her in such a state shocked Daisy.

"Jessie, what on earth's wrong?"

"Tell her," Nora said, striding past her to pick up the kettle and fill it from the tap over the sink.

Jessie collapsed in a bout of sobbing, her hands covering her face.

"Up the duff, ain't she?" Nora said. "Up the duff good and proper."

"Oh no." Daisy sank onto the chair beside her sister. "Who was it? The father?"

Jessie lifted her head, tears stained her cheek but fire glinted in her soft brown eyes. "What do you mean who was it? What sort of a slut do you think I am?"

"We can all see what sort of slut you are," Nora said, banging the kettle on the stove. "Only have to look at you to see that."

"Charlie. It was Charlie. Wouldn't be anyone else would it?" Defiance shone in her eyes. "I love him and he loves me. We're going to get married."

"Told you that did he?" Nora glared at her. "You're only fifteen."

Jessie hung her head. A curl of dark as night hair fell across her face. "Sixteen next month," she whispered.

"Wait till your father finds out," Nora said. "You'll be married all right, even if we have to wheel 'im down the aisle in a chair. Charlie Benton's got a lot to answer for."

Charlie Benton? A chill ran through Daisy making her shiver. The Benton family were bad news. If Jessie got tangled up with them... She only vaguely recalled Charlie Benton, the youngest of the five boys, but she certainly knew his older brother Felix. With their father in prison and their mother on the drink making a living the only way she knew how, it wasn't long before the boys were running wild and Felix Benton was wildest of them all. He had a mean streak about him. He'd made her life a misery when she was growing up, following her home from school making lewd remarks and threatening her. With his brothers he'd throw stones and worse at her and her friends. They weren't above picking up dog mess to throw and jeering as they did it. She dreaded to think what would have happened if it hadn't been for her brothers Jack and Dan. They always looked out for her and Jessie and her father was known to be handy with his fists too, which wasn't a bad thing if you lived in Silvertown. She only hoped Charlie was made of a different stamp to his brother.

"Don't be too hard on her, Ma," she said. "It could happen to anyone."

"Aye, anyone who's prepared to spread her legs for the price of a pie and pint down the Rose & Crown."

"It wasn't like that. Charlie loves me. We've been together for ages." Another bout of sobbing wracked Jessie's body.

Daisy's heart broke for her sister. If Jessie was mixing with that family... It wasn't the life anyone would have wanted. Now she'd have to marry and make the best of it like every woman put in the family way by a lad too green to know better.

The kettle boiled and Nora turned to make the tea. Daisy put her arm around Jessie's shoulders. "Don't worry," she said. "She'll get over it. You know Ma. Explodes like a volcano, but once she's calmed down she'll do the best she can for you." Or as best she can with the Benton family involved, Daisy thought.

Jessie sniffed and nodded. "I'm going to go and see Charlie," she said.

Daisy's brow furrowed. "Doesn't he know?"

"He knows all right. Just doesn't know I've lost me job and had to tell Ma why. Once they found out at the factory they wouldn't keep me on. He'll be right miffed about that."

Daisy thought he'd be more than miffed once their father found out about Jessie's predicament, but she didn't want to make things worse for her sister.

Once Jessie had gone Daisy helped Ma with the tea. "Do you know the lad, Charlie?" she asked. "Will he marry her?"

"Aye, 'e will if 'e knows what's good for 'im."

"How long has Jessie known him?"

Nora shrugged. "They bin seeing each other a while now. I should 'ave guessed somat was wrong with her being sick every morning a while back. I thought it was just her doings, you know. And when she seemed to get over it..."

"It'll be hard on her, being so young," Daisy said.

"I know." Nora sighed. "And it's not what I wanted for her." She huffed. "They say your kids break your heart. They're not wrong." Daisy saw the sadness in her eyes. She looked deflated, as though life had suddenly become too much for her. She took a breath. "I don't know what your father will say. I only hope to God he hasn't been drinking when he finds out. He'll kill the pair of 'em."

Daisy shuddered as she sipped her tea. "I'm sure it won't be as bad as that," she said. "He always had a soft spot for Jessie, being the youngest."

"Aye. He had plans for her an' all but I don't think they included getting up the duff and having to get married at fifteen."

Daisy sighed. She knew it happened to a lot of girls from the factory who had nothing much to occupy their thoughts other than boys and being popular. The work was boring and repetitive and their social life, what they could afford, hardly more than a once a week dance if they were lucky. There wasn't much in their future to look forward to other than marriage and children, hopefully with a man who didn't beat the daylights out of them every Saturday night when he had a tank on.

Nora sighed. "Well, I'd best be getting your father's dinner. If I'm to tell 'im he's going to be a grandfather come Christmas it's best he has a full belly first, although I'm not sure that'll stop him murdering the pair of 'em."

Daisy left with a heavy heart. She loved her mother and sister and could only imagine what would happen when her father found out. And if Charlie was anything like his brother Felix she pitied Jessie all over again.

Chapter Six

The visit to Mrs Henderson was a great success. The portly dressmaker recalled Mrs Fitzroy's visits and, business being slow since everyone had finalised their Coronation outfits, she was pleased to be able to accommodate her. She also recalled her thriftiness and willingness to take 'seconds' should they become available. "I have just the thing," she said when she saw Clara. "Two new patterns that were made up for a client, a lady of some standing, I might add. Unfortunately she was called away on business abroad before she could collect them." She eyed Clara up and down. "Yes. I think, with a little alteration, they will be just the ticket."

Clara strode up and down in front of the mirror while the dressmaker's assistant endeavoured to pin the fabric of the dresses to fit. Each had an abundance of lace above a nipped-in waist with an elegant slim-line skirt in the front and fullness billowing out at the back, flaring into a train as she walked.

"I'm not sure," Clara said, gazing at her silhouette in the mirror. "The red silk satin shimmers beautifully, but I think I prefer the pale blue chiffon. It's so difficult to decide."

"Why not take them both," Mrs Henderson, suggested. "I'm certain we can work out a reasonable discount for such a good customer."

So it was decided. Clara took both dresses, which were put on her mother's account. Perhaps it was worth missing an evening out with Jeremy, Clara thought with a smile.

Saturday evening the heat of the day still lingered. It had been quite sultry with little breeze to stir the trees or cool the air. Earlier in the day Clara had enjoyed a pleasant lunch with friends, but the thought of the evening ahead loomed over everything like a dark cloud. It was only the thought of her new dresses and who she might meet there that lifted her spirits.

Elvira arrived in Sir Richard's carriage to collect her. The carriage waited while her mother checked that Clara was properly attired and looked good enough to make the sort of impression she hoped for. "Now, remember. He's been very good to us," she said. "It won't hurt to butter him up. Like any man he responds to flattery from a good looking girl. Do your best."

Clara wasn't sure what her mother meant, but, she told herself, an evening out in amiable company, wearing a new dress in the latest fashion. What could be the harm?

A footman opened the carriage door when they arrived at Sir Richard's town house in Belgravia. Another footman took their wraps and Markham, the butler, showed them into the large first floor reception room where Sir Richard greeted them. In his early fifties Sir Richard was an imposing figure. Although grey-haired and portly he still carried the upright bearing of a man who'd spent a lifetime in the military. His eyes twinkled and he stroked his neat grey moustache as he greeted them. Clara thought he looked like a cross between a pigeon and a vulture, but she remembered her mother's entreaties to butter him up, so said nothing.

"My dear Clara, you grow more beautiful every time I see you," he said, taking her hand to brush his lips. "A pleasure indeed to enjoy your company tonight."

"Charmed," she said, groaning inwardly. Now if it had been Captain Sebastian Shawcross…

The only other guests in the spacious, elegantly decorated room were her parents and two boys nudging their teens, Sir Richard's sons. Clara glanced around expectedly but there was no one else there.

"You know the boys, Cedric and Eustace," Sir Richard said.

"Yes. Good evening," she said, surprised that they were to be included at the dinner. She had supposed it to be a dinner party for friends, not a family gathering.

"I thought it would be a chance for you to get to know them better," Sir Richard said. The boys stared at her, wide-eyed.

"How nice," she said, although nice was the furthest thing from her mind. Why would Sir Richard want her to get to know his sons better? Thoughts raced through her brain. Surely he couldn't think… her parents wouldn't want… She glanced at them; her mother's smile as false as the glass jewels at her throat and her father, who she noticed looked more frail and at least ten years older than the last time she saw him. Surely they can't want that?

"How are things at the hotel?" her father asked. "Lawrence tells me it's fully booked. Is Mrs T still there? She makes the best suet dumplings you'll ever taste." A fond smile lit his face. "Good to see you Clara. And looking so well. The London air must agree with you."

"Good to see you too, Papa," Clara said, kissing his cheek. "Everything at the hotel is splendid. You have no need to worry. Lawrence takes care of it all, even Mrs T."

He nodded, reassured.

Dinner, served in the ornate, white and gold dining room beneath glittering chandeliers, was a greater ordeal than Clara had ever imagined.

"Are you looking forward to the Coronation, Clara?" Sir Richard asked. "Great shame about the postponement and the King's illness. Still, good for your business I suppose, Herbert. All those men congregating in public houses swilling beer, eh what?"

Herbert Fitzroy nodded. "I can't complain," he said.

"What about you, Clara? Any plans?" He leaned over to tap her hand as he spoke to her. His gaze flitted from her face to somewhere slightly lower making her squirm in discomfort. She regretted asking Mrs Henderson to lower the neckline on her dress.

"I have a Supper Party and Musical Evening planned for a few close friends," she said, fearful in case he took it as an invitation.

"Quite right, my dear. Sounds delightful. More fun than the Regimental Dinner I have to attend." He sniffed. "Good news about the defeat of the Boers. I was in India you know. The days of the British Raj. Beautiful country..."

Clara glanced around the room as he droned on. She was bored already and it was only the first course. There was fish, fowl, and two kinds of meat to follow before the sorbet, dessert and cheese board. She wasn't listening. She felt out of place, as though she'd somehow stepped into something surreal like Alice in her *Adventures in Wonderland.*

"Where do you go to school?" she asked the boys, attempting to include them in the conversation. They stared at her then looked at their father who answered for them. Clara's heart sunk further. As the meal progressed she realised that Sir Richard had an opinion on everything and wasn't slow to share it.

Throughout the dinner Sir Richard oozed charm, his sons, on the other hand, were taciturn, giving each other shifty looks whenever Clara glanced at them. Sir Richard's remark about getting to know them better swirled around in her head like water circling a drain while the butler, two footmen and two maids in mop caps and frilly aprons served them course after course.

One thought filled her mind. She'd heard of well educated young ladies whose families had suffered financial misfortune having no choice but to work for the wealthier, better heeled in society as governesses. She'd gone to a good school, had a well rounded education, could play the piano and had sung at musical evenings at home for as long as she could remember. But she didn't think any of that qualified her to work as a governess to two belligerent boys. She recalled her own governess, an old maid at thirty with no prospects in her life other than to spend the rest of it teaching her benefactors' truculent offspring. Is that what her parents had in mind for her? The thought horrified her. She was eighteen and had her whole life ahead of her. There was no way in the world she was going to end up like that.

After the meal the boys went to their beds. Sir Richard showed her and her parents into the lavishly decorated drawing room for coffee. Heavy gold satin curtains hung at the long windows, the carpets were ornate and Turkish, the furniture expensive and tasteful. Paintings of earlier viscounts gazed down at them from extravagant gilt frames. Clara noticed a mahogany and rosewood piano stood as though waiting for someone to come and play.

After coffee had been served Sir Richard suggested a few hands of bridge. No one was happier than Clara when her father declined, saying they had an early start the next morning as they were going to Goodwood for the races. Her relief was short-lived.

"Elvira and I will away to our beds, but perhaps Clara would play something for you on the piano," her father said. "She's really quite adept."

Clara panicked. "Oh no," she blurted, then, quickly recovering she put her hand to her head. "I'm afraid I have a terrible headache. I think it's the heat." She fanned her face with her hand. "It's rather stuffy in here."

"Oh. I'm sorry," Sir Richard said. "Perhaps a turn around the garden would help?"

Clara grimaced. "I'm afraid it's no good. I really think I have to go. I'm sorry."

Sir Richard nodded to Markham who went and got her wrap. The hall clock chimed midnight as she passed, greatly relieved, through to the waiting carriage. She smiled. There was still enough time to go dancing after all.

Chapter Seven

Daisy couldn't get out to collect Miss Clara's dress from Betty Hewitt until late in the evening. There'd been a summer storm and the hotel was busy with people coming in out of the rain. By the time she was able to leave dusk had fallen and street lights reflected on wet pavements. She managed to find a cabbie willing to take her to Silvertown and wondered whether she should ask him to wait for her. Then she thought better of it as that would cost more than she could reasonably pass on to Miss Clara and anyway, the cabbie drove off as soon as she handed him the fare. She turned off the main road into a narrow street shrouded in darkness. She swore to herself as her foot slipped on the muddy cobbles and she staggered to keep her balance wishing she'd come earlier while it was still light.

A little further on, as she passed a passageway between two tall buildings billowing smoke into the evening air, the hulking shape of Felix Benton appeared in front of her. Jolted to a stop she swallowed and tried to collect herself. Curls of brown hair peaked out from beneath his cloth cap and meanness glinted in his dark eyes. He grabbed her arm and pulled her into the alley.

"Get off me," she yelled her heart pumping. "Get off me." She struggled to get free but she was no match for his size and bulk.

He pushed her against the wall. "Aw, Daisy. Don't be like that," he growled. "Not now we're gonna be related." He chuckled. "I always fancied you, you know. Can't I get a kiss from my future sister-in-law?"

She turned her head to avoid his slobbery lips as they touched her cheek. She felt the roughness of his thick coat as she tried to push him away. "I don't know what you mean," she said.

"Our Charlie and your Jessie. A right pair. They're getting married. That makes us real close, don't it?" The smell of his beery breath filled her nostrils. He leaned closer, his face dark as thunder and filled with menace. "An' it won't be long away, judging by the hoo ha your dad kicked up last night when he paid us a visit." He leaned even closer, his mouth twisted into a sneer and his grip tightened. "'E 'ad poor Charlie sobbing and puking 'is guts out. I'm surprised 'e could stand this morning."

Daisy squirmed to get away from him.

"Aye an' he'll do the same to you if you lay one hand on our Daisy." Jack's voice came like a beacon of fire in the darkness, bringing a swell of relief to trembling Daisy. She saw his hand on Felix's shoulder as he pulled him away.

Felix turned. Dan and two of his friends, standing behind Jack, clenched their fists and moved nearer. Felix shrugged. "Just being friendly now we're gonna be family." He grinned at Daisy, chips of hate shone in his eyes. He touched her cheek. "I'll be seeing you," he said and turned to walk away. "Don't think this is the end, Carter," he called over his shoulder. "It ain't finished, not by any means."

Relief flowed over Daisy. Jack on his own might not be a match for Felix, but with Dan along, the younger brother who worshiped Jack and followed him around like a puppy, she was safe. Jack nodded to Dan and Daisy watched as he and his friends followed Felix. "Phew. I'm glad you were here," Daisy said, still trembling. "He's got a tank on. Anything could have happened."

"What you doing round here anyways, Dais?" Jack said. "I thought you'd be safely tucked away in Holborn."

"I had to pick up a dress from Betty next door," she said. "I saw Ma a couple of days ago and heard the news about Jessie. Poor girl."

"Stupid girl, more like. As if she hasn't got the sense to stay away from the Bentons."

"She thinks she's in love," Daisy said.

"Then God help her," Jack said.

He walked with her the rest of the way to Betty's to collect the dress, waited for her and walked her back to the main road where he hailed a cab for her.

"Best stay away from here for a while," he said. "Dad went up to Benton's last night. I think it's all out war."

Daisy nodded. She didn't need telling twice.

Chapter Eight

Coronation Day dawned warm and bright, the August sun shone, pearly clouds scudded across the sky. Clara laid the blue chiffon dress on the bed in her room. She'd wear it to the Coronation Supper and Musical Evening. She pondered what to wear for the boating party Jeremy was hosting that afternoon. It would be a rare chance to let her hair down, relax and enjoy herself without the weight of expectation usually placed upon her. A convivial atmosphere always accompanied Jeremy and his friends. So unlike Lawrence who always insisted that Aunt Doris chaperoned her every outing. He'd relented this afternoon since Aunt Doris had pleaded a headache and a desire to stay in the hotel.

Clara pouted when Lawrence suggested one of the staff could accompany her. "I'll be with Jeremy," she said. "He'll see no harm comes to me."

Lawrence didn't look convinced. He finally agreed but only on her promise to stay with Jeremy and not wander off on her own. Anyone would think I was five years old, she thought, although she knew Lawrence was only concerned about her reputation.

In the end she plumped for her sprigged lavender linen dress. Stylish enough to impress but simple enough that it wouldn't cause any difficulty if she decided to go out on one of the boats. Not that she liked boats, she didn't. There was no dignified way to get in or out of a rocking rowing boat on choppy water and the young lads were far too eager to splash about with their oars.

The fine weather promised an idyllic afternoon with endless blue sky and Jeremy always seemed to find money for ample supplies of champagne and the other treats he provided for friends. He'd arranged transport too and a motley crowd arrived at the boathouse, with hampers of food prepared by Mrs T. Someone set up the phonograph and giggling girls danced with energetic young men on the grass beside the water in spun gold sunshine. Music and laughter filled the air.

*

The whole country seemed to be caught up in the euphoric optimism of the occasion, despite the celebrations being scaled down following the King's illness. The hotel staff were no exception. With most of the guests out enjoying the celebrations, Daisy and the chambermaids were allowed a few hours off in the afternoon to go to Westminster to watch the parade. Barker, the concierge, Hollis, one of the porters, Thomas the groom and Billy the boot boy were allowed to go with them.

With the promise of an afternoon off the bedrooms were cleaned in double quick time.

"What do you think it will be like?" Annie asked, starry-eyed. "Seeing the King and Queen?"

Barker huffed. "I doubt we'll see much of 'em," he said. "But it's a day out."

"Don't you want to come?" Daisy asked Mrs T. "It'll likely be a grand thing."

"Don't you think I've got enough to do with dinner for guests and Miss Clara's do? I ain't got time to stand and watch them as got nowt better to do than parade around the streets in their best finery."

"Mr Lawrence says we'll be watching history," Daisy told her.

"Aye. An' 'istory's what I'll be if I don't get these patties and pies made. Any rate me old legs ain't up to standing 'ours on end. No you go, take Tilda with you. I can manage awhile on me own." She huffed a heavy sigh. "Glad of the peace and quiet an' all," she said.

As the small group made their way towards Westminster Daisy marvelled at the decorations. Buildings were festooned with bunting, flags fluttered from windows above the shops. Illuminations stretched across the roads adding to the air of celebration. Daisy and her party joined people who'd travelled from all over the country, jostling along the crowded pavements to see the spectacle. The air hummed with expectation and good humoured frivolity. Music from street musicians playing merry tunes, hoping for a few extra pennies in their hats thanks to the large crowds, filled the air.

"It's seeing, history," Daisy said as they made their way to find a spot among the spectators. "That's what Mr Lawrence said."

"It's an afternoon off, never mind the why," Barker said. "An afternoon off's an afternoon off."

Daisy chuckled. She knew that despite Barker's indifference he was just as excited at the prospect of seeing the King and Queen as she was.

Guards in scarlet and gold tunics lined the route. The rousing notes of the marching band could be heard long before the horses and carriages of the procession could be seen. The open carriages were preceded by mounted regiments from all the British Domains as well as the marching bands of the military. As the procession approached people cheered and waved their flags. Daisy wished she'd thought to buy a flag to wave. Her heart swelled with pride at seeing the monarch and his entourage passing by. She cheered herself hoarse along with everyone else. It seemed to go on forever. Mr Lawrence was right. It was history and a sight well worth seeing.

"Something to tell your grandchildren about," Barker said, when he saw them and Daisy's heart swelled even more.

After the procession had passed they found a coffee stall to have a short break before going back to see them come out of the Abbey and return to Buckingham Palace. Daisy had brought some of Mrs T's iced buns and they found somewhere to sit and eat them.

"I wouldn't want to be togged up like that and have to wear a heavy crown every day," Annie, one the maids said.

"They don't wear it every day," Kitty, the other one said. "Silly."

Daisy sat with the chattering group and thought how lucky they were to have been able to come out and see it. She listened to their lively discussion on the things they'd witnessed and the drawbacks and the advantages of being royal.

Even Hollis, the porter, Thomas, the groom and Billy the boot boy joined in the discussion.

"Don't really matter does it?" Barker said. "Seeing as how none of us are likely to be asked."

*

Clara spent the afternoon on tenterhooks. She constantly gazed around wishing, hoping. She declined the numerous invitations to join lads in the boats for a trip around the lake in case she missed him. Would he come? Could he get away? Butterflies bounced off the walls of her stomach whenever she thought of him. She recalled his broad shoulders and the way the sun brushed his mop of blonde hair, burnishing it to gold. He'd been kind too, and so smooth she thought he'd be able to jump through puddles without making a ripple. He was someone she'd found by herself. A mystery man no one knew about. She glowed inside as she chatted to callow adolescents, all dull by comparison. She felt sorry for them too, knowing they were destined to live lives already mapped out for them by their families.

The drink flowed as the afternoon wore on. By mid-afternoon disappointment sat like a stone in Clara's stomach. She fed it with champagne and reflection. It had been too much to hope for. She'd been stupid inviting him. She'd wasted the whole afternoon pining for him.

Captain Sebastian Shawcross arrived as the sun moved across the sky casting them all into shadow. Clara's heart somersaulted when she saw him. In his scarlet and gold uniform he was even more handsome than she remembered. He had an easy grace about him and a smile that seemed to light up the sky. Suddenly the day looked brighter.

"You came," she said.

A spark lit his blue-green eyes. "I was invited," he said. "I can't stay long. I have to report back..." His words barely registered in the befuddled haze of her mind. "I'm surprised you weren't watching the parade."

"The parade?" she shrugged. "Too crowded by far." She smiled. "I'm glad you came," she said, her words slurring slightly. She leaned over and kissed his cheek. "Let me get you a glass of something." She glanced around. Some of the partygoers were the worse for drink and becoming rowdy, the ones in the boats dangerously so. The girls too were beginning to throw caution to the wind, their shrill laughter as they cavorted in a most unladylike manner grated on her ears. This wasn't what she wanted at all. She'd imagined a romantic interlude with her beau, not to share him with all and sundry.

"Is there somewhere we can go?" he asked softly, his voice loaded with speculation and the promise of pleasures ahead.

Light-headed with champagne and excitement Clara glanced around again. She wanted to be alone with him and there was only one place she could think of for that, but it would be quite improper and highly inappropriate, not to say risqué. She took a gulp of champagne to wash away the doubts. Still she hesitated.

"Well, I suppose we could... I mean... there's always... She looked coyly up at him, saw the intimacy in his eyes and her stomach churned. He looked so confident, so self-assured.

Why not, she thought. Everyone else is enjoying themselves, why shouldn't we? She took a breath and picked up two bottles of champagne and two glasses. "Follow me," she said, a thrill of jubilant exhilaration running through her. She led him to the road where they caught a hansom for the short journey to the hotel.

Anxious in case anyone saw them, Clara glanced furtively up and down the street as they slipped into the hotel. It was all she could do not to giggle at her audacity. She felt bold and brave, daring even. Clever and, of course, so devastatingly desirable that he'd made the time between processions to come and see her. This man had come to rescue her from boredom and tedious monotony and he deserved a reward.

The boy on the door didn't appear to be paying much attention to them but she held her breath as they sneaked past him and went up to her room.

The rest of the afternoon was a blur. She remembered having a few drinks, him taking the pins from her hair so it fell in curls to her shoulders. She recalled the thrill of his fingers running through it as he admired the colour and texture. The way he looked at her, making her heart tremble.

Then everything seemed to happen in a heartbeat. She recalled lying on the bed, her dress somehow coming undone. He smelled of coconut and lemon, she remembered that. Her befuddled mind wasn't sure what he was doing. She felt helpless as he lay on top of her, his lips kissing her neck, his hands touching her. It wasn't unpleasant, but, even in her dizzy, confused state of mind she knew it was wrong. She tried to struggle. She couldn't find her voice. She froze with fear. What was he doing? She felt a stab of pain. She called out, but that only served to inflame his passion further. He whispered sweet nothings in her ear and when he'd finally finished told her how good she'd been.

"I'm afraid I have to run," he said. "I have to report back to the regiment, but that was quite the loveliest time I've ever had. Pass my compliments to your brother, if he is in fact your brother, which I doubt. I mean, I wouldn't let my sister do what you do.

48

And you're very good at it. If I didn't know better I'd swear you'd never done it before." He laughed and put five gold sovereigns on the side table. He planted a kiss on her stunned cheek. "Until next time," he said and left the room.

Mortified, Clara burned with shame. Oh my Lord, what have I done? she thought. How could I have let that happen? Raging guilt and humiliation coiled like serpents inside her. She was undone. Nausea churned in her stomach. It was stupid, stupid, stupid, she thought. No one will believe me if I tell them what he did. They'll say it was my fault. I encouraged him. I shouldn't have brought him back to the hotel, to my room. I was asking for trouble. Of course he'd take it as an invitation, what man wouldn't? It was foolish beyond belief. All she could think of was the degradation and dishonour that lay ahead of her. Her head spun and a sour taste filled her mouth.

She wasn't sure how it had happened, but she'd be blamed. Everything was always her fault. No respectable suitor would want her now. Her virtue had been taken from her. The doors to respectability would be closed to her forever. She burst into tears. What had she done? Why had she let it happen?

A swell of nausea rose to her throat. She dashed to the bathroom, threw up and crumpled into a heap on the floor. Lying on the cold tiles, with her head on her arm she sobbed and sobbed until there was nothing left inside her.

She felt worthless and it was all her fault.

Slowly the events of the last week ran through her mind. Seeing him in the park and approaching him, going with him to the ice cream parlour, inviting him to the party. All highly inappropriate behaviour. Then she imagined the party when he'd walked into it: Jeremy's floozies lying around, all the worse for drink and various other stimulants Jeremy provided for his guests. She saw in her mind the way he'd have seen it; women sprawled on blankets, dressed, or half-dressed in outfits that would never grace the inside of a respectable drawing room. She recalled introducing herself as Clara Fitzroy of The Fitzroy Hotel. She could see now how that could be misconstrued to allude to a disreputable establishment, especially as she knew Jeremy's floozies entertained men there. No wonder Sebastian Shawcross thought…

Oh my God, what did he think? Burning shame engulfed her again, bringing a fresh tumult of tears and recriminations.

After a while, she took a breath. What was done was done. It couldn't be undone but it was only real if people knew about it. If Ma and Pa heard about it they'd send her home in disgrace. Probably to a nunnery, or worse an asylum for fallen women. She'd be the target of the worse gossipmongers in society. Her family's reputation would be dragged through the mud because of her foolishness. Any respect or honour Papa had managed to restore after her grandfather's gambling excesses and near bankruptcy came to light, would be gone, as sullied as her lavender sprigged day dress. Everyone would say 'well what do you expect – that family?' Then they'd shrug their shoulders and smirk and feel a whole lot better about themselves.

She shuddered as another swell of nausea rushed up to her throat.

Then there was the reputation of the hotel to think about. Without the hotel they'd all be on the street. It was bad enough they'd had to sell part of their estate in the country, but if the hotel went...

Her distress turned to rage. She swallowed the sickness rising up inside her. A deep scalding fury filled her. Fury at herself, but also at Jeremy. If he hadn't brought his floozies to the hotel, if he hadn't got them all drunk and worse at the party, if he was as respectable as Lawrence, none of this would have happened. It wasn't *all* my fault, she thought. If I can blame Jeremy...

She sat for a while thinking about what she should do next. Gradually a sense of purpose filled her. She wasn't going to let one mistake ruin her life forever. One mistake that could be glossed over, forgotten, never talked about. People kept secrets all their lives. She didn't imagine Sebastian Shawcross was going to brag about what he'd done. And if he did she'd deny it. Say he'd drunk too much, fancied himself and had a vivid imagination. He was in the army. They were only in town for the Coronation. With a bit of luck he'd be back in South Africa, or somewhere else a long way from London, in a matter of days. She'd never see him again, and nor would anyone else.

That decided she ripped off her torn, soiled dress, screwed it into a ball and threw it against the wall. I hate it, she thought. I'll never wear it again.

She washed her face and every other part of her that he had touched. Back in her room she dressed in her best blue day dress, brushed her auburn hair until it shone and pinned it up again. The mirror reflected her eyes red from crying and her face blotchy with tears. She gritted her teeth and reached for her face powder. The box was empty. She remembered she'd meant to buy some when she was in town. In the excitement of the party she'd forgotten. She couldn't go out looking as she did. Perhaps she could borrow some from one of Jeremy's floozies. She'd never seen either of them without their faces being caked with make-up.

She crept quietly along the corridor and tapped gently on Miss Dolly Deverill's door. As she knocked the door moved slightly and she realised it wasn't locked. She pushed it open. "Dolly, I wondered if..."

She didn't get any further. First she gasped, then she screamed. The lifeless, half-naked body of Miss Dolly Deverill lay sprawled across the bed, her head twisted, her neck broken.

Chapter Nine

After the procession Daisy, Matilda, the maids and men trudged wearily back to the hotel, still full of the splendour and spectacle of it.

"It's a day I'll never forget," Daisy said.

"Me neither," Matilda said with a sigh. "It were right good."

"Did you see them 'orses," Thomas said. "Magnificent. Thoroughbreds, all of them and so well turned out." His eyes shone with admiration

"I thought it was wonderful," Annie said, breathless with excitement. "So majestic."

Kitty giggled. "That's cos they're Your Majesties, soppy."

"Better than working, I suppose," Barker said, shaking his head. "It'll be all gone and back to normal by tomorrow."

On the way back to the hotel the girls dawdled, wanting to look in shop windows decorated for the occasion.

"Ooo look at that one," one said.

"This one's much better," said another.

The boys were more interested in looking at the shop girls, also given the afternoon off to watch the procession.

Daisy tried to hurry them up. "We ought to be get back before the guests," she said. "They'll want tea."

"Most of the guests will be out to dinner," Barker said. "Seeing friends or taking the chance to eat out to mark the occasion. The restaurant will be quiet tonight."

"Do you think so?" Annie said. The chambermaids worked in the restaurant from mid-afternoon to late in the evening when they were required to help out.

"I 'ope so," Kitty said. "My feet are killing me."

"Your dogs are barking," Matilda said. "That's what Ma used to say when her feet ached. 'Me dogs are barking,' she used to say."

"Woof Woof," Barker said. Matilda jumped and they all laughed. "Aye. It's grim up t' North ain't it?" he said.

The smile dropped from Matilda's face. The spark in her eyes dimmed as though struck by a sudden memory. "Aye. Sometimes," she whispered.

Once again Daisy wondered about the girl. She always seemed to be nervy and on edge. Perhaps it's working for Mrs T she thought, although she'd been especially kind to her.

As they neared the hotel they saw a crowd gathered outside around a police wagon in the road. Two uniformed policemen stood by the front door, stopping anyone entering, waving people past and moving them on.

"What on earth?"

"What's up?" Barked hastened his steps. The others followed. They went around to the tradesmen's entrance and in through to the kitchen.

"What's to do, Mrs T?" Barker asked his voice stressed. "Somat 'appened? What's police doing 'ere?"

Mrs T wiped her hands on her apron. She'd been setting out biscuits onto a plate to go on the tray with a pot of tea and four cups. "Oh it's a right to do," she said. "I'm just making sweet tea for Miss Clara. She's 'ad a shock and no mistake." She stared at them wide-eyed. "Mr Lawrence called the police. Miss Clara found a body."

"A body?" Matilda shrieked. Her face paled and she grabbed the back of a chair for support.

"Who? One of the guests?" Daisy's stomach churned.

"Well it wouldn't be one of us would it?" Mrs T said. "They don't send an Inspector and six men for one of us." She put a jug of milk and bowl of sugar onto the tray. "Here. Take this up to Mr Lawrence's office." She winked. "See if you can find out owt else."

Daisy took off her coat and hat and pushed a stray lock of her dark brown hair behind her ear before picking up the tray. She left the kitchen to the sound of raised voices, gossip and wild speculation.

In the office Miss Clara sat on a chair, twisting a handkerchief between her fingers. Her face was blotchy with tears and her eyes red from weeping. Her whole body trembled. A man in a brown overcoat leaned over her. A uniformed policeman stood behind him.

"Ah tea," Mr Lawrence said, moving towards Daisy. Worry creased his thin, intelligent face.

"So, did you see anyone?" the man in the coat said to Clara, obviously not for the first time.

Clara let out a howl and sobbed into her handkerchief.

"Inspector Rolleston. I think my sister has been through enough," Mr Lawrence said, an unexpected authority in his voice. "Please let her rest. You can speak to her again tomorrow when she's had time to recover."

The Inspector dithered.

"The other staff have returned. You may question them now. They may have noticed something."

Inspector Rolleston sighed.

"Daisy, please help Miss Clara to her room and make her comfortable. Tonight's Supper Party is cancelled. Please ask Barker to see that everyone on this list is sent a message to that effect." Mr Lawrence handed Daisy a list of names and addresses. "You can send Mrs T up. The inspector can start with her."

"Yes, Mr Lawrence." Good luck with Mrs T, Daisy thought as she took Miss Clara's arm to help her up. She'll be asking more questions than answering them.

Upstairs she helped Clara undress and got her into bed, still snivelling.

"Can I get you anything?" she asked.

"Tea please and something to eat. I'm starving." She gave a wan smile. "I found the body," she said.

"The body?"

"Miss Deverill's body. She's been murdered." She stared at Daisy. "Can you believe it? Murdered. In this hotel."

"I'm sorry to hear that," Daisy said. "Miss Deverill? How awful." A vision of the clothes in Miss Deverill's wardrobe flashed through her mind. She wondered if she should say anything then thought better of it. It wasn't her business. "Have the police got any idea who did it?"

Clara shrugged. "No idea whatsoever." She looked to be in some sort of trance.

"I'll get the tea," Daisy said.

*

Once Daisy had gone, left alone in her room having escaped questioning by Inspector Rolleston, Clara thought back over the events of the day. Finding Dolly had been a shock and the vision of her body sprawled across the bed kept jumping into her mind. It put her earlier encounter with Sebastian Shawcross into perspective. She hardly knew Dolly Deverill, only having seen her once or twice with Jeremy, but she'd liked her; liked her in the way you like an errant child or a boisterous puppy you know you should disdain. Clara had admired the way Dolly defied convention, never being tied down by it. She'd lived her life on her own terms. Clara admired that.

The anger she felt at Jeremy for bringing the hotel into disrepute so that Captain Shawcross had got the entirely wrong idea about her, had evaporated. The enormity of what had happened to Dolly dispelled it completely. She tried to think back to the party, the last time she'd seen Dolly.

She'd been there with Jeremy when Clara left. When had she come back to the hotel, and who with? A shudder ran through Clara's body. Was it someone from the party? Had one of Jeremy's friends done this? There was only one reason Dolly would leave the party and she'd never have left alone.

She felt sick at the thought. No it couldn't be. It wasn't possible. She thought of all the men she'd met there and discounted them one by one. They were lads, only a few years older than her. She couldn't believe any of them would...

The police would ask who she came back to the hotel with, but she doubted that dozy porter who was covering for Barker would be of any help. He'd had his head in a lurid magazine when she'd sneaked in. What was the boy's name? Alfred? Albert? Something like that. He hadn't even looked up when they passed him.

Then she remembered earlier and the state of the bathroom, the dress she'd never wear again. She thought of Captain Sebastian Shawcross. Her Jane Austen hero had turned into something from the Penny Dreadfuls. Still the memory of him lingered; the flop of his blonde hair, his easy smile and effortless grace, the spark in his blue-green eyes, the musky citrus smell of him and the way his lips tasted of salt. She touched her cheek where his bristles had brushed it. She'd liked him until he did that terrible thing to her and wouldn't take no for an answer. She pushed the memory away. She stared at the five gold sovereigns still stood on the table by the bed. Blood pounded through her veins and her fists clenched. Was it a justifiable misunderstanding? A mistake made when they'd both over indulged in champagne? Before she met him she'd been an innocent child. He'd taken that innocence away. Surely he should have to pay for that?

Chapter Ten

The hotel staff were questioned one by one, but none of them could shed any light on the reason why Miss Deverill should have met such a fate. If anyone did know or suspect how Miss Deverill made her living, no one mentioned it. They were all as conscious as Daisy that if the hotel got a bad reputation they would all be out on their ear and a reference from a bawdy house would do nothing to help secure another place.

"We have to take everyone's finger marks for the purpose of elimination," Inspector Rolleston told her. "You may be surprised to know that everyone leaves their mark on things they touch and everyone's finger marks are unique. I have men in the room collecting those marks. By comparing them to the ones we take here we can see who's been in the room. Then we'll know who killed the poor lass."

"Well it weren't me," Mrs T said. "I ain't never bin in anyone's room."

"So your finger marks will prove it," the inspector said. "Now let's get on with it."

The process led to a great deal of discussion. Constable Perkins, an amiable lad in his late twenties, who Daisy thought must have the patience of a saint, was delegated the task of taking them. He put black ink on their fingers and pressed them onto slips of paper with their names on, much to Mrs T's disgust.

"I don't see how putting ink on our fingers is going to help catch a murderer," she said.

"You'd be surprised how much we can tell from finger marks left at the scene of crime," Constable Perkins said.

"I still don't see why we had to have our marks taken. We were all out watching the procession or here in the kitchen preparing for the Coronation supper," Mrs T said. The rest of the staff complained too.

"They don't know what they're doing," Hollis said.

"They're grabbing at straws."

"They haven't got a clue so they'll fit one of us up. You see if they don't."

Despite their protestations Constable Perkins managed to get a full set of marks from all the staff.

Mr Lawrence took his supper in his office on the ground floor, behind the reception area. The room had hardly changed since Mr Herbert's day. He'd kept the heavy polished mahogany desk, his father's books still occupied the bookcase and the same solid metal safe stood on the floor under the window. The only changes he had made were to replace his father's paintings of his beloved horses with framed family portraits which he said reminded him of the reason he was there, keeping the hotel running.

When Daisy went to collect the tray she found him sat behind the desk, his head in his hands. He glanced up. "Oh, Daisy," he said. "They want to question all the guests. Can you imagine what that will do to our reputation? Bad news in this industry spreads faster and further than a farmer's manure and smells as bad. Questioned by the police. What will they think of us?" He shook his head, despair etched on his face.

Daisy's heart went out to him. Normally so suave and full of confidence, debonair even, she hated to see him so troubled. He tried hard to keep the hotel up to the standard set in his father's time, but everything seemed to be pitched against him. Now this. It couldn't be easy for him. "I'm sorry, sir," she said.

"Oh It's not your fault. I know you and other staff are loyal, reliable and honest, but the police won't see it that way. There's been a murder. Someone must know something. They'll keep on at us until they find out who." Deep anxiety squeezed his voice.

As she was about to leave the office someone banged on the door. When she opened it an irate woman, red in the face, exploded into the room.

"I've been robbed," the woman shrieked. "Robbed, here in the hotel, this very afternoon. I must speak to the Manager. I demand you call the police."

Lawrence stood to try to calm her. "The police are already here, Mrs Fortescue-Jones." He guided her to a chair. "What is it you've lost? How can I help?"

"I must speak to the police," she said. "It's my necklace. The one I took out of the hotel safe this morning. It's been taken. My precious necklace." She burst into tears.

"Daisy, can you fetch Inspector Rolleston. He's in the card room interviewing guests. Please tell him it's urgent."

Daisy bobbed a curtsy and hurried out. If some of the other guests had been robbed...

When Daisy returned to the kitchen she was able to tell them that the police were of the opinion that Miss Deverill had been murdered by a thief in the course of a burglary.

"A burglary? That doesn't bode well for us." Mrs T sank onto a chair, deflated, as though the events of the day were just sinking in and she could see how they'd all be affected by them. "They'll say it was one of us. If they can't find the culprit they'll settle for one of us. Always do – the police. Always do."

"You don't know that," Daisy said, although she held no great hope of Mrs T being wrong. Where she came from the police were best avoided. Everyone knew they could fit you up as soon as look at you. Her whole body trembled.

Mr Lawrence wasn't the only one who took supper in his room. Miss Clara also had hers on a tray. Late in the evening she rang for the tray to be collected. Daisy had sent the chambermaids to bed as they'd had a long day and, as Barker had predicted, the restaurant was quiet. The policeman on duty at the hotel entrance prevented anyone other than staying guests entering.

"I'll go," Daisy said putting down the cocoa Mrs T had made for her and Barker. "It'll be the tray to be collected and instructions for the morning."

"I've had enough excitement for one day," Barker said. "I'm off to me bed."

"Me too," Mrs T said. "If they want owt else they can whistle for it."

They said goodnight and went on their way.

Miss Clara was in bed when Daisy let herself into the room. "I hope you're feeling better," she said. "Is there anything I can get you?"

Clara gave an exaggerated sigh. "If only there was," she said. "I'm afraid I'm quite at a loss. Inspector Rolleston will want to see me tomorrow and ask all sorts of questions. I don't know what I shall tell him."

Daisy went to collect the tray. "Just tell him what you saw, Miss. I don't expect he'll want any more than the facts of what you saw." It was clear to Daisy that

Miss Clara was going to make as much of a drama out of this as she could.

"He'll want to know what I saw when I returned from the park, or rather who I might have seen. If I saw anyone hanging around the hotel, anyone who had no reason to be there."

Daisy stopped what she was doing. "Did you? Did you see anyone hanging around?"

"Well, I can't be sure – I mean not absolutely sure – but I thought..." She paused and took a breath. "When I returned to the hotel I thought I saw your brother hanging around outside. He looked as though he was waiting for someone, or something."

Daisy's heart crunched. "You saw Jack? At the hotel? Outside?"

Clara nodded.

Daisy's mind raced. Oh Jack, what have you done now? "Oh," she said. "I expect he came to see if I wanted to watch the procession with him. He'd mentioned it earlier." She picked up the tray as though to go.

"But the procession would have been over. I don't even know if it's relevant – seeing him I mean. He wouldn't be up to no good would he? Perhaps I've no need to mention it?"

Daisy swallowed. She knew when she was being threatened. "I'm sure it's not relevant," she said, although she did recall Jack asking if the staff and guests would be going to see the procession, thus leaving the hotel empty.

"Then I won't mention it." Clara looked Daisy straight in the eye.

"Is there anything else?"

"Yes. The bathroom. I left the picnic because I felt unwell. I'm afraid I've made an awful mess in the bathroom. Clean it up and – you'll find a dress on the floor. It's ruined beyond repair. Destroy it and dispose of it, completely and discreetly. When I say completely and discreetly I mean that I don't want to see it on some market stall or on the back of one of the tarts who frequent the Haymarket. And I don't want anyone to know about it. I have no wish to be the subject of gossip and speculation below stairs. Do you understand?"

"Yes, Miss Clara. Not one word." She glanced into the bathroom. "I'll get a mop."

She took the supper tray and returned a few minutes later with a mop and bucket. In the bathroom she opened the window to get rid of the stink of vomit and cleaned the room. She picked up the crumpled dress. As she picked it up something fell with a jingle to the floor. Daisy picked it up. A shiny metal button rested in her hand. She slipped it into her pocket. The dress reeked of vomit, but there was another smell. A strange, unexpected smell. A citrusy, musky smell similar to those found in a barber's shop. Miss Clara wanted the dress destroyed and disposed of. She never disposed of anything that could be cleaned, repaired, altered or sold on.

When Daisy got downstairs she put the dress and the button into a laundry bag, folded it up and put it in her sewing basket under the cotton reels, embroidery silks, scraps of material and the never-ending pile of mending and stitching waiting to be done. Miss Clara must have a good reason for wanting rid of it. Daisy didn't know what the reason was but she decided to hang on to it in case it became useful.

Chapter Eleven

The next morning Clara went to see Lawrence in his office. If she was to be questioned by Inspector Rolleston she wanted Lawrence to be there. He'd prevent any browbeating or undue pressure being put on her or any inquiries into anything other than what she saw when she went to Miss Deverill's room. Most people in the hotel valued their privacy and any examination of their private lives had to be discouraged.

As she approached the office she heard raised voices. She paused outside, fearing interrupting what was obviously a heated argument. She didn't know whether to knock or wait. She didn't have to wait long. After a few seconds her brother Jeremy came storming out, almost knocking her over. His face was grim, his eyes shimmered with fury.

"Oh sorry," he said, grabbing her by the shoulders to prevent her falling. He shot an angry glare at the closed door of Lawrence's office.

"What on earth's the matter?" Clara said, trying to calm him.

"I've just been thrown out of the hotel and told to take my rackety friends with me," he said, thin-lipped with fury. "Apparently I'm a disgrace to the family. I've brought shame and scandal to our door. My presence is no longer required. I'm persona non grata. I've been told to leave."

"Leave?" Clara was horrified. "But why?"

He took a breath. "The police went through Dolly's things. It was obvious that she entertained men and her life-style was other than that of the respectable widow she purported to be. They have made their views very clear to Lawrence. In fact I'd go so far as to say they see Dolly's fate as something she brought upon herself." Rage reflected in his eyes. "Absolute rubbish of course." He shook his head and Clara saw how deeply her death had affected him.

"I'm sorry," she said. She could understand Lawrence being shocked and appalled at the discovery. He would be thinking, as always, of the hotel's reputation.

Jeremy's face softened and he managed a grin. "It's all right. I wouldn't want to stay anyway. Lawrence is a sanctimonious prig who can't see further than his account book." He glanced with narrowed eyes at the closed office door. "I've never been one to stay at a party when I'm not wanted. Time to move on, my darling."

A rush of despair engulfed Clara. "But where will you go?"

"Anywhere a long way away from here." He smiled but Clara saw the hurt and sadness in his eyes. "I'll miss you," he said touching her cheek.

"I'll miss you too," Clara said and meant it. Life without Jeremy would be dull indeed.

"See you later. I have to go and pack." He kissed her cheek and left without a backward glance. Deep dread and sorrow filled her heart. The repercussions from Dolly's death would reach out like ripples in a pool and none of them would be unaffected.

She knocked and entered Lawrence's office more fired up than she'd ever been. Her heart pounded and her fists clenched. It wasn't fair. Why should Jeremy have to go? What had happened wasn't his fault, but as soon as she saw Lawrence she knew to let the matter drop. His face was thunder, his manner brusque. She saw he was just as hurt as she was at the row he'd had with Jeremy. She didn't want to make matters worse.

But they did get worse. She hadn't been in the office long when she heard a commotion in the hall outside and the door burst open. Her mother barged in waving a newspaper, followed by her father looking as though he'd just escaped death by the skin of his teeth.

Elvira slammed the newspaper on the desk, blind fury filled her face. "Have you seen this?" she shrieked. "The hotel is all over the morning paper."

"Good morning, Mama," Lawrence said, his voice cold as ice. "I don't need to ask the reason for your visit. Please take a seat. I'll order some tea and we can all calm down."

Clara rushed to get chairs for her parents. They all sat while Lawrence opened the paper. There was a full description of the murder under the dark banner headline; *Murder at The Fitzroy Hotel*. Even Clara blanched when she saw it.

"What are you going to do about it?" Elvira said. "We're ruined. All ruined by that tart's activities in OUR hotel. How could you, Lawrence? How could you let this happen?"

The door opened and a maid popped her head around it.

"Can you bring up some tea, please, Kitty," Lawrence said. "And ask Mrs T to add some of her buttered scones. I think we all need a little sustenance this morning."

The maid disappeared. Clara was shaking in her shoes at her mother's wrath, but Lawrence appeared calmer than a still sea. The calm before the storm, she thought.

"The hotel was burgled. Anyone who owns anything of value risks losing it. If Miss Deverill tried to stop a burglary taking place then she should be applauded, not sanctioned because of her lifestyle. The police are dealing with it." The tone of his voice echoed restrained reason.

"It's all very well saying that—" Elvira didn't get any further before her husband interrupted her.

"Elvira, I think Lawrence is perfectly capable of handling it," he said, his voice stronger than one would suppose from the sight of him. "He is the Manager in charge here. It's nothing to do with us."

Elvira quietened but she was not placated. "Don't you see, the reputation of the hotel – the hotel that bears OUR name – it will have consequences. Consequences far beyond your understanding."

"Consequences?" Clara stared at her mother.

Elvira took her hand. "Your reputation, Clara. Your chance of attracting the right sort of suitor. All this will be damaged."

"I think it's time we left," Herbert Fitzroy said, standing up. "These young people have things to sort out and we are in the way. Come along."

Elvira gasped, but she stood. "It'll come back to bite us, you mark my words," she muttered as she staggered out to follow her husband.

Lawrence sighed as he sat back in his chair. He looked like a balloon when the air has been let out.

"I'm sorry," Clara said, just as the tea arrived.

*

Downstairs in the kitchen the staff pored over the newspaper article. "They're calling her a 'lady of easy virtue'," Hollis said.

"They mean she's on the game," Barker said. "I knew it. Woman on her own, the way she dressed. Friend of Mr Jeremy's by all accounts. Well, that ought to tell you somat."

"It's the reputation of the hotel I'm worried about," Thomas said. "Get a name for that sort of thing, you never know what it'll lead to."

"Aye, we'll all be tarred with the same brush," Hollis said. "You girls'll have to watch out."

"You don't mean…?" Matilda's eyes widened.

Mrs T tutted. "Take no notice. This is a hotel with a good reputation. Folk will see she took advantage. Didn't deserve what 'appened to her though."

"I dunno. I heard Mr Lawrence telling Mr Jevons, the maître dé, that some of the guests have cancelled their bookings," Annie said.

"Times is 'ard enough as it is," Barker said. "Another nail in our coffins."

They all murmured.

"There's a picture of Mrs Fortescue-Jones's stolen necklace," Kitty said. "A heart shaped garnet and diamante pendant. It is rather pretty. It says here it had sentimental value, whatever that is. Apparently it was the last thing her husband gave her before he passed away. Oh. That is sad."

"Stolen? Knowing the old bat she probably misplaced it," Hollis said. "I found her trying to get into the wrong room the other day. She's lost her marbles if you ask me."

"Well, nobody did ask you," Mrs T said. "She may be a bit confused about the necklace but you can't confuse finding a dead body can you?"

"The police are linking the burglary to the murder," Daisy said. "Any one of the guests could have disturbed the burglar and been killed. Her occupation had nothing to do with it."

"Still," Hollis said. "It's what people will think."

"Shame on them then," Daisy said.

"It looks as though the necklace was the only thing stolen," the chambermaid continued reading. "No other items were reported stolen. It says here that according to Mr Lawrence, the Manager, most of the guests left their valuables in the hotel safe."

"Unusual that," Hollis said. "Some people would see it as an opportunity to say they've lost something. It'd be a good chance to get somat on the insurance."

"You're so cynical," Kitty said.

The conversation continued amid speculation about who would do what in the circumstances and what actually happened. "You can't always believe what you read in the newspaper," Barker said.

"Shouldn't some of you be back upstairs working?" Daisy said, looking particularly at the chambermaids.

Kitty dropped the paper on the table and Daisy picked it up.

"The police want to talk to Alfred," Hollis said. "'E was on the door yesterday, but 'e ain't turned up today. 'Ere. You don't think 'e did it?"

"No, I don't," Daisy said, cuffing him with the newspaper. "I expect he's having a lie in. If you haven't got enough to do…"

They all grumbled, but went back to their posts. Daisy put the paper in her pocket. She'd read it properly when she had more time. Miss Clara's words about seeing Jack outside nagged at her. What was he doing there? She recalled him surprising her in Miss Deverill's room the previous week. He'd asked if they were all going to watch the Coronation procession. She'd looked out for him when she went with the other staff but didn't see him in the crowd. Then she remembered that was the day she lost her pass key and had to borrow one from one of the maids. She thought it must have dropped off the thin chain that attached it to her belt. She found it on the floor of the laundry cupboard a few days later.

A stone of dread formed in her stomach. She'd heard from her mother that Jack had got in with a bad crowd. She said she was worried about him. It was hard to keep on the straight and narrow when you lived in Silvertown. Deep dread churned inside Daisy. She couldn't believe he'd be so stupid as to try to rob the hotel where she worked. The hotel where once he'd worked so he'd know all the in and outs of it. The more she thought about it the more worried she became. Jack had visited that room. His finger marks would be in there, on the door handle and the wardrobe at least. Even if it was a week ago they may still be present. She recalled the state the room was in. The maids would have cleared up as best they could but hardly have done a thorough clean. If Clara mentioned seeing him… if they suspected him… murder was a hanging offence.

She rushed to the bathroom where she was violently sick.

71

Chapter Twelve

After the tea and scones with Lawrence, who agreed to sit with her during her interview with Inspector Rolleston, Clara went to see Jeremy. She knew he'd be in a state about having to leave the hotel that had been his home for the last two years. She was also aware that he'd been fond of Dolly Deverill. Perhaps he'd feel better if he had someone to talk to. When she got to Jeremy's room she found him sitting on the bed surrounded by most of his clothes.

"You're not really going, are you?" Clara asked, hoping against hope that he'd stay.

"I have to. I can't stay here. Not after…"

Clara sank onto the bed beside him. "I know you were fond of her," she said. "I liked her. She was fun, lively, outgoing. It wasn't your fault, what happened to her, Jeremy. It could have happened anyone."

"I know, but that doesn't make it any easier. You didn't know her, Clara. She had such a way about her. She could have been anything she put her mind to."

"You mean she chose…?" Clara couldn't find the words to say what she meant.

Jeremy took a breath. "She wasn't always a fallen woman," he said. "Her name wasn't Dolly Deverill either. It was Hilary Grenville. She came from a respectable, middle-class family in Lancashire. When she was eighteen," he glanced at Clara, "your age – she met a man who brought her to London. They were engaged. He promised to marry her, seduced her, then abandoned her. She had a child who died. She had no money. No way of making a living. She couldn't go back to her family, not after the humiliation and disgrace."

He hung his head and seemed to buckle under the weight of his grief.

"After that she changed her name and went to the places where she'd meet men who could wine her and dine her, take her to the theatre and the opera, to the races and to mix in high society. Men who had money enough to pay for their fantasies to be indulged. Dolly knew what she wanted from life and it wasn't going into service, working fifteen hours a day for shillings. She always hoped to marry."

"Marry!"

"Yes. Why not? She was pretty, intelligent, quick witted, cultured even, with a breadth of conversation that would surprise you. She had a generous nature too, that's what I'll remember most about her." He paused as though overcome by emotion. "She'd have made any man an excellent wife and rich men don't need the approval of their peers." He gazed up, his voice filled with compassion. "I'd rather spend an hour in her company than with any one of those schooled to perfection girls, who have no more idea of the ways of the world that a feather has about the wind that blows it hither and thither. Dolly didn't deserve what happened to her."

Clara had never seen Jeremy so moved. Tears glistened in his eyes. "No, Dolly didn't deserve it," she said. Hearing Dolly's story had changed her perception. She thought about her own encounter with Captain Shawcross and the disgusting thing he did to her. What had happened to Dolly could happen to anyone. There but for the grace of God, she thought.

Later that evening Jeremy called into her room to say goodbye. "Where will you go?" she asked.

73

"I have lots of friends in town and a number of invitations. You know me, Clara. I'm bound to land on my feet."

That was true. Jeremy was popular and good company. He had a boyish charm about him. Lawrence would be cross with him now, but you couldn't stay cross with Jeremy for long. "I'll miss you," she said.

"I'll miss you too." He kissed her cheek. "Now, be good, take care and don't let Mama browbeat you into marrying anyone just because they're rich. Don't rush into anything. You're young, you have your whole life ahead of you. Make sure you're the one to choose how you live it."

"That's easier said than done," Clara said. "You know what Mama's like when she gets a bee in her bonnet."

"Yes. But Papa will be on your side. He will want you to be happy. Lawrence too will have your happiness at heart. He cares about you more than he likes to admit."

"Really? I always believed he thought me the greatest nuisance. Coming here, commandeering his staff to run errands." She giggled. "Oh I will miss you, Jeremy." She flung her arms around him and hugged him.

It took a while for him to tear himself away. When he did finally disentangle himself he said, "I'll miss you too, Carrot-top."

Carrot-top. He hadn't called her that since she was five years old and had a halo of ginger ringlets that no amount of vigorous brushing could tame.

"If you need me ask at my club. Anytime. They'll know where to find me."

He kissed her cheek, grinned and said, "Be good." Then he was gone. Clara sank onto the bed. Life was so unfair.

Chapter Thirteen

Over the next week the police kept calling with further inquiries. Constable Perkins came to take statements from the chambermaids who cleaned Mrs Fortescue-Jones's room the day of the theft. Daisy showed them into the staff sitting room. She had a job calming the girls down when they thought they were being accused of stealing. They insisted she stay for the interview.

"Did either of you see the necklace when you cleaned the room?" Constable Perkins asked.

"We didn't see nothing, and we didn't take it," Kitty, who was the more outspoken of the two, said.

"I'm not saying you did." Constable Perkins looked as uncomfortable as Daisy felt.

"What time did you clean the room that morning? Was it before or after the necklace was taken from the safe?"

"We don't know. Why don't you ask Mrs Fortescue-Jones?"

"Unfortunately she's upset and a little confused. She can't recall much about it."

"We're upset an' all," Kitty said. "And we don't recall owt either." She folded her arms and clenched her jaw. It was clear they were saying nothing.

Daisy saw the confidence ebb out of Constable Perkins. She also saw an opportunity to find out more about the finger marks left in Miss Deverill's room.

"The girls have work to do," she said. "If you're quite finished."

Constable Perkins put away his notebook.

"Would you like some tea?" Daisy asked. "Matilda, our pastry cook, has just made some jam tarts that will require tasting if you can stay."

At the mention of Matilda the constable's smile widened, his eyes lit up. It could have been at the thought of jam tarts, but Daisy recalled how he'd held Matilda's hand for far longer than necessary when taking her finger marks. Matilda had giggled, a sound she'd never heard from her lips before. Her usual expression was one of deep distress. She seemed to be constantly on edge, jumping at the slightest provocation. Daisy put it down to working for Mrs T.

She nodded to Kitty who went and fetched a tray of tea and jam tarts.

"Have you had any success with the finger marks you found in Miss Deverill's room?" Daisy asked as she passed the constable a cup of tea.

He shook his head. "It's a long, pains-taking process. They'll be examining them at Scotland Yard." He took the tea. "There's a whole department working on them. You'd be surprised." He bit into the tart and a smile spread across his face. "Lovely," he nodded. "My compliments to the cook." A flush of pink rose up his cheeks. Daisy thought it quite endearing. He went on to tell her about a case currently going through the courts where the police were expecting a prosecution based entirely on fingerprint evidence. "It'll be a first," he said, "but not the last."

Constable Perkins's enthusiasm for the efficacy of fingerprint evidence did nothing to allay Daisy's fears about Jack. "Can they tell how long the marks have been there?" she asked. "They could be old ones."

Constable Perkins took another jam tart. "But the rooms are cleaned daily," he said. "Anyway, there'll be no problem if the person identified has a good reason to have been there, which Mr Fitzroy can verify."

Daisy's stomach churned. Had Jack been in Miss Deverill's room again? Why was he at the hotel? She couldn't bring herself to think that he could be responsible for Miss Deverill's death, but if he was there to steal her jewels and she found him... She couldn't bear to think about it.

When he'd gone Daisy made an excuse to leave the hotel, saying she had errands to run. She caught a bus to the docks, then went in search of Jack. She found him in a pie and mash shop having a late lunch. Thankfully he was alone. He stood when he saw her. "Don't see you round this way too often," he said. "Must be trouble. Is it?"

She lowered herself into a chair at his table. "The police are all over the hotel," she said, glancing round to make sure no one was listening.

"I know. I read the papers. Not surprising. Do you want tea?"

She nodded. He signalled to the proprietors to bring tea. It arrived in a thick mug and was strong enough not to need it.

"They've taken everyone's finger marks." She grimaced as she sipped the tea. "They've taken marks from the room to compare them with."

"So?"

"Your finger marks will be in the room. Remember, when you came to see if we were going to watch the Coronation procession."

He paled a little but shrugged. "But they don't have my marks to compare them with."

"Not yet, no. But Miss Clara told me she saw you outside the hotel the day of the murder. What were you doing there? Why did you come to the hotel?" Anxiety and desperation raised Daisy's voice. She'd do anything for Jack, but if he'd killed Miss Deverill there'd be nothing she could do to save him.

Jack looked shame-faced. He shrugged again. He couldn't look her in the eye.

"Tell me if you did it, Jack. I won't tell anyone."

"I DIDN'T DO IT," he yelled so loudly everyone in the shop turned to stare. "But that won't stop the police pinning it on me will it?"

"What were you doing there?"

"Okay. I did think of robbing the place while everyone was out. But then I saw Miss Clara coming back with a man. They went into the hotel and I thought it would be madness to try anything. If I got caught you'd lose your job an' all. I didn't want to risk that."

"A man? Miss Clara was with a man?"

"Yes. A soldier. Looked like someone from the procession. They had a couple of bottles and some glasses. Quite obvious what they were up to."

A smile lit Daisy's face. I bet that was something Miss Clara hadn't mentioned to the police, she thought. She put her hand on Jack's arm. "Sorry I doubted you. Thanks for telling me."

The conversation with Jack did a little to put Daisy's mind at rest. He was right though, if Miss Clara mentioned seeing him that day they'd take his finger marks and if they had found them in the room... At least now she knew something Miss Clara would want kept quiet. Now we are even, she thought.

Back at the hotel Mrs T had Miss Clara's supper ready for her on a tray as she'd again asked for it to be served in her room. Daisy offered to take it up to her.

"I hope you're feeling better," she said. "Inspector Rolleston didn't upset you?"

"Oh it was awful, Daisy. Such prying into one's affairs." Clara dabbed her eyes to show how upsetting it was.

Daisy smiled. "I spoke to Jack," she said as casually as she could while setting down the tray. "Just to put your mind at rest." She rearranged the cutlery. "He told me he was outside the hotel but didn't come in as he was late visiting a friend in King's Cross. He said he saw you though. When you came back to the hotel from the picnic."

The complacent look fell from Miss Clara's face. "Really?" she said, a tinge of anxiety in her voice.

"Yes," Daisy said. "Really." She didn't need to say anymore. She was sure Miss Clara understood her reason for mentioning it. There'd be no more talk of Jack being outside the hotel or any possibility the police might question him.

*

A few days later, only a handful of people gathered at Dolly Deverill's funeral. The late August sun dappled the trees leaving patterns on the cobbled path. Daisy stood beneath the spreading branches of an ancient yew shaded from the warmth of the day. Mr Jeremy had arranged for the service at the church the family attended when they were in town. Daisy wasn't surprised he'd taken on organising it. Organisation was something he was good at and Miss Deverill had been a friend of his, but she was surprised to hear that he'd paid for it, including the burial and the grave. He'd also paid for the church to be filled with flowers.

A raggle-taggle of people made up the desultory gathering that filed in after the coffin to fill the pews. Daisy tagged on behind several women who shuffled in ahead of her. Funerals always made her feel sad, but this one was particularly difficult. Dolly Deverill's death had been sudden and violent and the shadow of it hung over the hotel like a shroud. It had affected them all. None of them were untouched by it. She took a seat at the back and glanced around.

Miss Clara sat in the front pew usually occupied by family. Miss Deverill's, or as Daisy now knew Miss Grenville's, parents had been informed but only her father, a small, insignificant, balding man with round spectacles who reminded Daisy of a grocer, had attended. He sat with his head bowed, his hat in his hands and left immediately after the service, saying that he had a train to catch. The rest of the congregation consisted of a few women who Daisy suspected followed the same line of employment as Dolly Deverill, one or two of Mr Jeremy's male friends and Daisy, representing the hotel. She hadn't known Miss Deverill, but as she'd been a guest Daisy felt obliged to pay her respects. Inspector Rolleston and Constable Perkins also attended, but only to see who else came and to try to find out more about Miss Deverill's past and her associates.

Mr Jeremy read a moving, heartfelt eulogy. He spoke about her generosity of spirit, her resilience, courage and fortitude. The bitterness he felt at her passing was clear. The small congregation struggled to sing the hymns, their voices drowned out by the organ notes rising to the rafters. There followed a rambling homily given by the elderly vicar. He went on about all sins being forgiven and all sinners being welcomed into Heaven. By the end of the service Daisy's cheeks were wet with tears.

Tea and coffee were served in the church hall, but few of the mourners stayed. Daisy guessed most of them would have been happier in the local pub. Apart from how fetching Miss Clara looked in black, Daisy had little to report to the staff who gathered in the kitchen to hear all about it.

"Mr Jeremy gave her a good send off," was all Daisy would say. It was a sad ending to what Daisy thought was probably a sad life.

Chapter Fourteen

After Jeremy left, it felt to Clara as though all the life and laughter of the hotel had gone with him. The change in the weather didn't help either. The long hot days of summer were replaced by cool September breezes. The morning sun rose later and from early evening a harvest moon surrounded by stars lit the night sky.

The memory of the Coronation faded as the bunting and lights were packed away. Everywhere had an 'end of season' feel about it. Clara's friend Amanda had become engaged and, like many of the young ladies who 'came out' that year, she was planning her wedding. She'd come to London to see the dressmaker about her bridal gown and do some shopping so she asked Clara to come with her to choose her trousseau.

"I have to go with Mama to the dressmaker this afternoon," Amanda told her, "but we will have the morning to ourselves."

Clara jumped at the chance to spend a morning perusing the most exclusive shops in Regent Street. Amanda came to collect her in the Melville's carriage.

"Wow, it's amazing," Clara said, her eyes nearly popping out her head when she saw Amanda's engagement ring. "It's exquisite." She stared at the cushion cut sapphire surrounded by diamonds. "He must love you very much."

"I don't know about that," Amanda said. "But our families have known each other for ages. I think they always expected us to marry."

"Yes, but surely you love him?"

Amanda shrugged. "I like him well enough. He comes from a good family, well educated and a promising career in the City ahead of him." She wrinkled her nose. "He's quite good looking in a rugged sort of way. I think we'll get along very well."

"Is that all?" Clara said incredulity heightening her voice. She'd expected declarations of undying love at least.

Amanda laughed. "You're a romantic, Clara. Always were. I blame those books you read. Real life isn't like that."

Clara pouted. "Now you sound like my mother," she said. Still, she couldn't help feeling sorry for Amanda who'd never be swept off her feet and feel the thrill she'd felt when she met Sebastian Shawcross, even if he did turn out to be other than she'd expected.

They spent a pleasant couple of hours in the various department stores picking out several items for Amanda's honeymoon in Paris. At every store they went into they were greeted by a hawk-eyed head sales lady who spread out the most luxurious merchandise for Amanda to peruse. Every shop offered personal attention as assistants hovered by Amanda's side, making suggestions. Everything was to be delivered and charged to her parents' account.

Clara and Amanda chatted about weddings, bridegrooms, romance and love. In one shop Clara picked out a darling of a silk blouse with a high collar and frilled lace down the front. "How about this for your going away outfit?"

Amanda took it to have a closer look. "What about you, Clara? Who would be your ideal bridegroom?"

Sebastian Shawcross's face came to Clara's mind. She could think of no one else. The first time she saw him her heart had skipped a beat, but her heart had betrayed her. She shuddered. "I don't think I'll ever marry," she said. "I'll end up an old maid like Miss Haversham, pining for lost love."

Amanda giggled. "Don't be silly. You'll soon find someone and when you do you'll want to spend the rest of your life with him."

"Like you and Gerald?"

"Like me and Gerald."

Clara wasn't convinced. She knew Amanda's marriage had been arranged by the couple's families to protect their fortunes and provide a legacy. Nothing to do with love at all. When Clara married she wanted it to be to a man she could wholeheartedly share the rest of her life with. Not someone chosen for convenience.

"What about this for the first night?" Amanda said, holding up a lace confection of a nightdress.

"The first night?" The memory of Sebastian Shawcross and what he'd done to her almost overwhelmed Clara. She knew very well that something similar would happen to Amanda. "What do you think it will be like? The first night?" she asked casually flicking through a row of undergarments. "Aren't you afraid it might be awful?"

Amanda giggled. "I don't know. Mama gave me 'the talk' even though I told her we'd covered it at school."

"You mean Miss Jefferson's Birds and Bees talk?"

"Yes. Mama said it was nothing like the birds and bees, but not to worry. Gerald will know what to do." She dropped the nightgown she was holding. "Come on. Enough shopping. Let's have lunch somewhere terribly expensive before I have to tussle with Mama over the dress at the dressmaker this afternoon."

The next day Clara heard her mother was in town and wanted to see her. She feared the worst. The season was over, the town empty of what her mother called 'prospects'. The wealthier families had returned to their country estates for the shooting season. Mama would want her to go home too. She recalled Jeremy's words about not letting Mama browbeat her. If only, she thought.

She met her mother in the tea room. The afternoon sun shone through the window, pooling on the tablecloth and sending slivers of light to bounce off the silver cutlery. Her mother poured the tea. "Your father's not well," she said her voice filled with recrimination. "The police coming to the hotel, the scandal. As if he hasn't enough on his plate." She passed Clara a cup of tea.

"I'm sorry," Clara said, although she didn't know what her mother expected her to do about it. It wasn't her fault.

"Oh I know I shouldn't bother you with these things." She sat back and looked at Clara. "Sir Richard tells me he's invited you to accompany him to the opera."

Clara sighed. She had indeed received an invitation together with a large bouquet of pink and white full blown September roses. They reminded her of the ice cream sundae she'd had in the park. Her heart had leapt. Had Captain Shawcross realised his mistake? Was he distraught at the realisation? Were the flowers an apology? Her heart sank when she read the card and her buoyant mood of the morning disappeared. She'd been trying to think of a polite way to refuse the invitation without giving offence. She couldn't afford to offend him, not when the family owed him so much, as her mother kept telling her.

"Yes, Mama. He did invite me. An invitation I intend to turn down."

Elvira slammed her cup on its saucer spilling some of the contents. "Turn down? Why? Surely you can see what an opportunity this is." She exhaled heavily. "It's clear he's interested in you which, in the circumstances, is a blessing. With our reputation sullied by that... that... woman's unfortunate demise..."

"Interested in me? I refuse to be a governess for him or anyone else, no matter how well off they are. You surely can't want that for me, Mama?"

"A governess?" A frown creased Elvira's forehead. "What are you talking about? Don't you see, you have an opportunity to be the next Viscountess Westrow."

Clara's mouth dropped open. She couldn't take it in. "Viscountess Westrow? You mean – marry him?" Her brain refused to grasp what she was hearing. "But I can't. He's old... ancient and... and... decrepit."

"And rich. When one has wealth the other things cease to be important. We owe him a great deal. You have the power to change that."

"You're mad. I wouldn't marry that old goat even if he asked me, which he hasn't. He's merely suggested a night at the opera. That's a long way from a proposal of marriage."

Elvira smiled. "He hasn't asked you – yet. But he will, Clara. And when he does you will say 'yes'."

A stone of dread hardened in Clara's stomach. Her jaw clenched. "No I won't," she said. "He's disgusting."

"All men are disgusting, dear. It's their nature. But you will get used to it. We all do."

The matter was taken out of their hands when a messenger arrived for Elvira telling her that her husband, Mr Herbert Fitzroy, had been rushed to hospital with a suspected heart attack.

Chapter Fifteen

Daisy held the invitation in her hand. She recognised Jessie's handwriting on the plain white card. She'd even drawn a picture of wedding bells in the corner and written '*I hope you can come*' on the bottom. It was clear she had made an effort to make her forthcoming wedding as conventional as possible. Squeezed between two christenings and a funeral on the following Saturday, the ceremony was to be held in the church where they'd gone to Sunday School as children. The church where they learned their catechism, their prayers and to love and respect their parents, most of which had been left behind with their good intentions when they grew up.

Daisy shuddered at the thought of spending even that short time with the Bentons. She loved Jessie and wished her well, but also thought getting involved with the most notorious family in Silvertown stupid beyond belief. She wrote Jessie a note saying she wouldn't be able to make it to the service on Saturday but would call and see her on Friday evening, after work. She sighed as she put the note into the envelope. I hope she knows what she's doing, she thought.

She'd bought some good quality cotton sheets and pillowcases for the bridal pair which she wrapped in pretty paper. She bought a bottle of sherry she could share with her mother and some bottles of beer for Jessie as she knew she preferred it. It being Friday night and pay day, she could happily rely on her father and brothers being in the pub.

She left the hotel Friday evening as dusk was falling, draining colour from the sky. It had rained earlier in the day and the streets were still wet, although the air was fresh and clear. A pale moon shone in the late September sky. She managed to catch an omnibus to the docks and walked the rest of the way. When she arrived her mother greeted her at the door.

"Jessie's just popped out to see Charlie," she said. "Last minute arrangements. She'll be back soon."

Daisy made herself comfortable, opened the sherry and poured them each a drink. "So where will they be living, after?" she asked. "Not here?"

"No, thank God."

Alarm bells rang inside Daisy. "Not with the Bentons?"

Nora chuckled. "No. Charlie's rented them a room over the fish shop. First decent thing 'es done far as I can tell."

"Good. At least that's something. Perhaps he's making an effort to get away from his family."

"Well, Felix is best man so that tells you somat." She sipped her sherry. "Ada, Jessie's friend from work, is bridesmaid. 'Course old man Benton won't be there. 'E's still inside."

"What's she wearing? Something nice I hope."

"Yes. Betty next door made her dress. It's blue and loose fitting. Quite plain and one she'll be able to wear again after, but it's new, so that's a treat."

"More serviceable than white I suppose," Daisy said thinking perhaps purity wasn't the right note to strike in the circumstances. She heard the front door open and footsteps in the hall.

"That'll be our Jessie," Nora said.

Sure enough Jessie burst in through the door, her face lit up like a beacon. It looked as though she was walking on air. She rushed up to Daisy. "Dais. I'm so glad you could make it." She gave her a hug.

Daisy stood to hug her. "Good to see you," she said and meant it. It had been too long. The last time she'd seen Jessie was when she announced she was 'up the duff'. Now she carried a slight bulge around her waist. Not a lot, but enough for Daisy to notice. "You're looking well."

"I am well," Jessie said. She unwound the scarf from around her neck. "Look what Charlie gave me."

Daisy gasped. Around Jessie's neck, on a thin gold chain, she saw a heart-shaped garnet and diamante pendant exactly like the one in the newspaper. Mrs Fortescue-Jones's necklace, stolen from the hotel.

Daisy sank onto a chair. "Charlie gave it to you?"

Jessie beamed. "Isn't it beautiful?"

"Where did he get it?"

"What do you mean where did he get it?" A scowl creased Jessie's face. "What does it matter where he got it? I expect he got it from the market. That's the usual place to get things."

Daisy didn't know what to say. She knew she was going to break her sister's heart. "It looks exactly like the one stolen from the hotel. The one in the newspaper."

Jessie stared at her, then at the pendant now clasped in her hand. "What do you mean – stolen? Charlie didn't steal it. He wouldn't."

Daisy could see it all now. The Bentons robbing the hotel where she worked. Payback for the beating Pa gave Charlie. "A woman died," she said. "Whoever stole that pendant killed someone."

Jessie looked aghast. "No. You're making it up. Charlie wouldn't."

"Are you sure?" Nora said. "Cos I'm not. I wouldn't put it past the Bentons to pull a stunt like that. Here give it to me. I'll chuck it in the river."

"NO! IT'S MINE. Charlie gave it to me." Jessie turned away, clutching the pendant.

"So it'll have his finger marks on it," Daisy said recalling her conversation with Constable Perkins. "A man's been convicted of theft this week, thanks to his finger marks being found on the stolen goods. And that stolen pendant had a murder attached to it."

Jessie's face paled. She sat down.

"You have to get rid of it," Nora said. "It's evidence."

"Charlie didn't kill nobody," Jessie said but her voice was hardly convincing. "He bought it for me. Bought it in the market."

Nora and Daisy looked at each other. "Even if Charlie didn't steal it, it's still stolen property that'll lead the police to the murder," Nora said. "You have to get rid."

"I have an idea," Daisy said. "Give me the pendant and I'll take it to the police."

"THE POLICE!" Jessie shook with fury.

"Yes. I'll say one of the chambermaids found it on the floor on Mrs Fortescue-Jones's room. She's a confused old lady. They'll believe she dropped it and that it wasn't stolen after all. That way there's nothing to connect it to Charlie or the murder. It was the only thing taken, so if there's no burglary there must be another reason for the murder. The police will start looking at the murdered woman's clients."

"Oh aye. I read in the paper that she was a tart," Nora said. Hope lifted her voice. "Could have been one of them."

Tears rolled down Jessie's cheeks.

"Take it off and give it to Daisy," Nora said. "If you don't I will."

Jessie tore the necklace from her neck and threw it at Daisy. "Why do you always have to spoil everything?" she screamed. "Everything I have, you spoil it. I HATE YOU."

"Jessie I—" Daisy didn't get any further. Jessie jumped up and ran out.

"Oh dear." Nora shook her head. "That Charlie's got a lot to answer for. I regret the day she ever met him."

Daisy washed the pendant to remove any finger marks that might be on it, wrapped it in a handkerchief and put it in her pocket.

Nora poured them each another sherry. "There's none so blind as them as won't see," she said.

Daisy sat with her mother and finished the sherry, but Jessie's words kept going round in her head. She hoped she was doing the right thing.

Chapter Sixteen

With a fluttering, empty feeling in her stomach Clara went with Elvira and Lawrence to the hospital. When they arrived they were shown into a room to wait for the doctor to come and speak to them. Clara sat, twisting her handkerchief in her hands.

"Can't we see him?" Elvira asked, deep anxiety etched on her face. "I want to see him."

"You have to ask Doctor Meadows," the nurse said. "He's looking after him."

Clara and Elvira sat while Lawrence paced the floor. "I knew there was something wrong with him," Elvira said. "He's not been well. It's all been too much for him. I blame his father, the way he left us..." She sniffed and pulled a handkerchief out of her bag.

Clara took her hand and squeezed it but any words she wanted to say stuck in her throat.

After a few minutes Sir Richard came in with a plump, grey haired, man. "This is Doctor Meadows," he said, his voice sombre, bereft of his usual bluster. "He's the best in his field."

Elvira jumped up. "How is he, Doctor? Can I see him?"

"I'm sorry. We did all we could."

"You mean... you don't mean...?"

"I'm sorry." Doctor Meadows took her hands in his and looked into her eyes. "Your husband passed away a few minutes ago."

Stunned silence filled the room.

Clara burst into tears, her dear papa gone. She couldn't believe it.

Elvira sank onto a chair, her face ashen. Doctor Meadows, his kind eyes filled with sorrow, sat beside her, still holding her hands. "I'm truly sorry," he said. "He went quickly without pain. I hope that's a comfort."

"Thank you, Doctor," Lawrence said. "I'm sure you did your best."

Doctor Meadows nodded. "I'll leave you now. He's in a private room. If you want to see him just ask the nurse." He looked at Lawrence. "I'll need someone to sign the papers, see to his property and collect the Death Certificate. I'll be in my office when you're ready."

"Thank you," Lawrence said.

Doctor Meadows shook everyone's hand before he left.

"So, what happened?" Lawrence asked Sir Richard, who'd been unusually quiet.

Sir Richard shrugged. "We were walking in the garden. He said he felt unwell, then he collapsed. I got him here as soon as I could. There was nothing anyone could have done."

"I want to see him," Elvira said.

"Of course." Sir Richard took them to the private room. "I'm so sorry," he said. "If there's anything I can do."

Clara could think of a lot of things he could do, and could have done in the past to make her father's life easier, but she didn't say anything.

Entering that room was something Clara would never forget. The scene left an indelible imprint deeply embedded on her mind. Her beloved father looked so pale and frail, a shrunken shadow of the man she knew and loved. The indomitable man she'd thought invincible was gone. How could he have been so cruelly taken from her? She recalled his smile, his affable nature, the way he formed a cushion between herself and the demands of her exacting mother. She recalled his generosity, popularity and unique way of making her see things from another perspective. How could all that be gone?

They stood for a while in silence around the bed, each with their own thoughts and memories. "He looks so peaceful," Lawrence murmured.

"Almost as though he's just gone to sleep," Clara said.

Elvira touched his face but couldn't speak. She sank onto a chair by the bed as emotion overwhelmed her. No one knew what to say so they just stood in shared sorrow, gaining comfort from each other's presence.

The silent minutes ticked away. Then Lawrence whispered, "Rest in Peace. I'll miss you, Papa." He kissed his father's forehead.

Clara pressed her lips together to save herself from sobbing. She wrapped her arms around her body trying to keep it all in. She wanted to ask him why he had to go. Why leave them now? It was too awful to bear. Tears rolled down her face. She leaned over and kissed his cheek. "Sleep peacefully, my darling Papa. I'll miss you so." Her heart clenched. She still couldn't believe he'd gone.

Elvira lifted her husband's hand and took the wedding ring from his finger. "It meant a lot to him," she said, slipping it onto her own hand. I'll wear it always." She wiped the teardrops from her eyes. "I'd like to sit with him for a while." She lifted her tear-stained face to look at Lawrence. "There's so much to sort out."

Lawrence nodded. "I'll leave the carriage for you. Clara and I will take a cab."

Clara waited, her heart in turmoil, while Lawrence collected the certificate from the office and signed the papers to release the body to the undertakers. Their father's property would be packed and sent to the hotel.

By the time they left the hospital the sun had gone from the sky, now overcast and heavy with cloud. The ride back in the cab was the most dismal Clara could remember. The darkness and dank drizzle outside added to her sombre melancholy. Her world had fallen apart and she was at a loss as to how to put it together again. Lawrence sat in solemn silence, staring ahead, his face dark as granite until she spoke. "I can't believe it," she said, her voice cracked with emotion. "I can't believe he's gone."

"Me neither."

Clara had a sudden thought. "What about Jeremy?"

"I sent him a message. He'll go straight to the hospital and stay with Mama. He always was her favourite."

That was true, Clara thought, and there was no bitterness in Lawrence saying it. A huge well of unhappiness opened up inside her. It was as if all the sunshine had gone from their lives leaving only darkness behind. "What will become of us?" The tears she'd been holding back broke through and she sobbed.

Lawrence put his arm around her. "We'll stick together and work something out, just as Papa would have wanted," he said, his face grim. His voice rang with determination.

His reassurance made her feel a little better. He was Lawrence, being practical as always. "Is there

anything I can do? I feel so useless and empty inside."
She sniffed.

"Just be your charming, courageous self," he said
and kissed her cheek. "That's all anyone can do."

Another unstoppable flood of tears assailed her.
She put her head on Lawrence's shoulder and he held
her, her body wracked with weeping until they reached
the hotel.

By the time they arrived it was late in the evening.
Barker, carrying an umbrella against the rain, opened
the door of the cab to help Clara out. He must have
seen from her face that the news was bad.

Lawrence followed her out. "Barker, please
arrange for a notice to be put on the door. Due to
Family Bereavement the Hotel will be closed until
further notice."

"I understand, sir. May I be the first to offer my
condolences. If there's anything I can do."

"Thank you, Barker."

"Should I tell the staff, sir? Some of them have
been here since Mr Herbert's day. They will be very
sorry to hear the news."

"Thank you, no. I will do that myself. It's my
responsibility." Clara saw tears in his eyes as he
struggled to contain his emotions. "Please ask them to
assemble in the lounge in fifteen minutes," he said.

"Sir."

"And Barker," Clara said, grabbing Lawrence's
arm. "Please ask Mrs T to send up some tea and a
bottle of brandy from the bar."

"Yes, Miss Clara."

Clara followed Lawrence into his office. Once the
door was closed he sat at his desk, dropped his head in

his hands and sobbed, releasing all the pent up emotion of the last few hours.

Clara and Lawrence's loss was great, but she knew her mother's would be greater still. They'd left Elvira holding the hand of the man she'd loved for over forty years. He'd been her constant companion, confidant, friend and lover. How will she survive it? Clara thought. How will we all survive it? Then there was her Aunt Doris. She'd have to be told. She didn't envy Lawrence that task.

When the tea and brandy arrived Clara took it, closed the door and put the tray on Lawrence's desk. She poured him a cup of hot sweet tea and added brandy drawing strength from his vulnerability. They were Fitzroys. They had a position to maintain and she vowed not to let her father down.

With Clara's help Lawrence recovered his composure. "I'll go and see Aunt Doris first," he said. "You know her best. Perhaps you could come with me and stay with her."

"Of course."

Lawrence took a glass out of a cupboard and picked up the bottle of brandy.

Clara went with him. As expected Doris was shocked to the core. She sat staring at them, unbelieving. "Herbert? Dead?" she said. "No."

Lawrence gently explained the circumstances of his father's passing. He poured her a glass of brandy which she downed in one swallow. She held out the glass for a refill. Like everyone else she found the finality of it difficult to comprehend. "I knew he was under a great strain, with Father's business and all, but…" She swallowed and looked at Clara. "Oh you poor thing," she said. "You poor, poor thing." She patted Clara's hand. "I blame my father. He was a waster. Thought of nothing but his own pleasure." The bitterness in her voice surprised Clara. "Herbert did his best but the odds were stacked against him." She shook her head. "He should have let that damn brewery go and to hell with it." She tossed back the rest of her drink and held her glass out for another.

"Would you like me to stay with you?" Clara asked. Aunt Doris shook her head. "No, it's all right, my dear. You go with your brother. I think I'd like to be alone for a while."

Lawrence nodded. They left her the bottle of brandy.

Despite Lawrence's assurance that he would tell the staff himself, the news spread faster than butter on hot toast so when he did eventually face the staff in the hotel lounge he was faced with uncontrollable sobbing, weeping and crying.

Seeing the reaction of the staff Clara realised how liked and respected her father was and how much he'd be missed. Again she wondered how they'd manage without him.

Chapter Seventeen

Darkness shrouded the street when Daisy left her mother. They'd sat and talked for a while, but Jessie hadn't returned.

"Do you really think Charlie killed that woman?" Nora said, fear for her daughter clear in her voice.

Daisy shrugged. "Someone did. He had the necklace stolen from another guest on the same night. I can't think of any other way he could have come by it. The killer is hardly likely to put it up for sale on a market stall, not after what he did and it being in the papers. He'd keep it, like some sort of trophy."

"Them Bentons is bad news. Always have been." Nora shook her head and Daisy saw deep sorrow in her eyes.

"It's all right, Ma," she said, putting her hand on her mother's arm. "Jessie's a bright girl. She knows how to look after herself and I don't think Charlie's as bad as the rest of them." The words sounded hollow even to her own ears. "I have to get back. I hope tomorrow goes..." She smiled. "You know what I mean."

"Aye. As well as a shotgun marriage to a villain who's committed murder can go."

Daisy left with a heavy heart. Gloom and dark drizzle filled the air, seeming to reflect her mood. No moon or stars lit the sky. Slippery mud caked her shoes and dampness moistened her coat. She hoped for Jessie's sake the next day would be better. She was so deep in thought as she walked she didn't notice the footsteps behind her, muffled by the mud. As she passed a narrow alley between two buildings she was grabbed around the waist and pulled into the alley.

Shocked, she caught her breath and struggled to resist. Her heart pumped. She tried to elbow and kick her attacker, who chuckled in her ear at her efforts. He dragged her up the alley towards a jumble of derelict buildings, his hand across her mouth, wrenching her head back, to stop her from screaming. Further up the alley, standing behind her, he forced her against the wall, the heel of his hand pushing her face into the rough brickwork. She felt a sharp pain as her cheek scraped the wall.

"Got you now you stuck-up bitch." The smell of Felix Benton's beery breath filled her nostrils.

"What do you want? Let me go." She pushed against him with all her might, struggling to free herself. He grabbed her arm and twisted it up behind her back so she couldn't move.

"No chance. Where is it? That necklace you took off Jessie? Charlie didn't steal it. I did. And that stupid bitch gave it to you. Where is it?"

"You're breaking my arm," she pleaded.

"Aye. An' I'll break your bloody neck if you don't tell me where that necklace is."

"In my pocket."

With one arm pressed against her back, holding her tight, his other hand reached into her pocket, first one and then the other. He found it and put it in his own pocket. "I stole it," he bragged. "And I killed that tart. I 'ad her an' all, before I topped 'er, just like I'm going to 'ave you."

"Get off me." The more she squirmed the harder he pushed her against the wall, forcing her arm up her back until she thought it would break.

He chuckled and she felt him lift her skirt and press his knee between her legs, prizing them apart.

She tried to scream but no sound came. She couldn't breathe.

"I'm going to enjoy this," he growled. He put his head against hers pressing her face harder against the wall while he unbuckled his belt.

Just as the last of her strength ebbed out of her she heard a loud crack and suddenly he released her as his body slumped to the ground. She gasped and turned round. In the darkness she saw her brother, Jack, staring at her, a large brick in his hand, Felix's body at his feet.

"Are you all right?" he asked.

Paralysed by fear, Daisy couldn't speak. Her shoulder ached and her heart pumped faster than a hummingbird's wings. Sweat ran down her back, she was shaking. She swallowed. "I... I think so. Thanks to you."

Dan stepped forward. He examined Felix's body. "I think he's a gonner, Jack. You've done 'im in."

Jack bent and rolled the body over. He checked for breath. Couldn't find any.

"Oh. God! What have you done?" Daisy's heart beat even faster. A sharp pain, like the kick of a horse in her gut bent her double. She felt sick. She was sick, rushing over to vomit in a corner. Gradually she regained her senses. Jack had killed Felix defending her. "What are we going to do, Jack?" Tears welled up in her eyes. She dreaded to think what would happen to Jack if anyone found out. Then another thought hit her. The wedding. "He's supposed to be best man tomorrow," she said.

Jack shook his head. "Not now 'e ain't." He kicked the lifeless body. "Tike. He'd likely have killed you,

you know that don't you, Dais?" His voice hardened with rage and hate.

"Yes. He killed Miss Deverill. He told me. He'd have done the same to me."

"Dan saw him following you from the house. He came to fetch me."

"What we gonna do?" Dan asked. "We can't go to the police. They'll never believe us."

"No," Jack said. "No police." He looked as Daisy. "Are you all right to get home by yourself?"

Daisy trembled, her heart still quaked. "Yes. But what about you and Dan?"

"Don't worry about us." He walked to the back of the alley and threw the brick over a wall into some bushes. "Come on, Dan. Help me get 'im up." The two boys lifted Felix between them, his arms over their shoulders, his head lolling forward. They kicked loose stones and mud over the bloody spot on the ground where Felix's head had been.

"What are you going to do with him?"

"Put him somewhere no one will ever find him," Jack said. "Come on, Dan."

The last Daisy saw of them was the two of them staggering back along the road toward the river, singing *Daisy, Daisy, gimme your answer do,* at the top of their voices as they zigzagged along, looking for all the world like two drunks carrying home a mate who'd also had too much to drink. Daisy couldn't help but admire their pluck and ingenuity, but an avalanche of anxiety swirled in the pit of her stomach just the same. If anyone found out they'd both hang for sure.

When she got back to the hotel she collected her nightgown from the room she shared with Matilda, filled the bath in the staff bathroom with hot water, stripped off her clothes and tried to soak away the memory of what had happened, but a vision of Jack with a brick in his hand and sharp shock on his face, kept circling in her brain.

Felix had stolen the necklace and killed Miss Deverill. He'd admitted it, but she couldn't go to the police and tell them that. Until the murderer was found they'd still be looking and once again she thought of Jack's finger marks in the room. She couldn't tell anyone how she knew Felix was the killer, or she'd have to tell them what had happened to him and again Jack would be in danger. Then she wondered what would happen when Felix failed to show up for his brother's wedding. Who would go looking for him? Jessie's wedding would be spoiled and it was her fault. Once again she'd been involved in spoiling things for Jessie. Everything was her fault. If she hadn't taken the necklace none of this would have happened. Jessie would never forgive her and if Jack and Dan were caught and hanged her mother would never forgive her either.

The water was as cold as Felix's heart when she got out of the bath. She put her nightgown on and crept into bed, trying not to disturb Matilda who was already sleeping. The last thing she thought about before she drifted, exhausted, off to sleep was what would have happened if Jack hadn't been there. She'd be dead for sure.

Chapter Eighteen

"You were late last night," Matilda said the next morning.

"I'm sorry if I disturbed you," Daisy said. "My sister's getting married today, so we were up late celebrating."

"You wouldn't have the heard the bad news then? About Mr Herbert?"

"No."

"He's dead. Mr Lawrence told us."

"Mr Herbert, dead? How?"

"They say his heart gave out. Mrs T says we're all done for. They've closed the hotel. We could all lose our jobs."

"Closed the hotel?"

"Yes. Mr Barker put a notice on the front door. You wouldn't have seen it, being so late. Ain't it awful?"

Daisy bit her lip. After the trouble last night she couldn't take it in.

Matilda dissolved into tears. "I can't lose this job. I've got nowhere else to go."

Suddenly it struck Daisy that she had nowhere else to go either. She'd lived in the hotel since she was sixteen. She wasn't going back to Silvertown. She couldn't. "I'm sure it's not as bad as you say. Mrs T always thinks things are worse than they are." She tried to comfort Matilda in case the worse did come to the worst. "What about your home? Your aunt? Your family? You must have somewhere to go."

"You don't understand. I ran away from home when Ma died. I can't go back. I'm safe here, but if I lose this job they'll likely find me. Then they'll drag me back and I can't go back. I won't."

Between sobs Matilda managed to tell Daisy about running away on the day of her mother's funeral. "I had to give up me job in the bakery when she got sick. I did all the cooking, cleaning, washing and housework looking after Ma, Da and me six brothers. Treated me like a skivvy they did. I didn't mind looking after Ma, she was me mother, but they were like pigs. They expected me to take Ma's place and all I could see ahead of me was years and years of the same. The only thing I had to look forward to was a beating on a Saturday night when they'd had a skinful. I had no money of me own. I was never allowed out of the house. Aunt Enid knew how badly I was treated." She paused, her face a picture of misery at the memory. "Soon as Ma was laid to rest and the men were at the pub getting a tank on, Aunt Enid got a cab to take me to the station. She put me on a train to London. I have a cousin living in Clapham, but they know about her and it's the first place they'd look. I could only stay there for a couple of days. Aunt Enid wrote to Mrs T and she got me the job here. She saved my life." The words tumbled out like the Thames in flood.

Daisy recalled how Mrs T had got Matilda the job. A job that was supposed to be temporary but had somehow turned into a permanent arrangement. She could see why Matilda wouldn't want to go home, any more than she wanted to go home to her family. But a father and six brothers to keep? She felt for Matilda. No wonder the girl had been so guarded and on edge all the time. She took a breath.

"I'm going to speak to Mr Lawrence," she said. "I'm sure they'll reopen the hotel after the funeral. It was Mr Herbert's business. They'll want to keep it going for him." She wished she could be as positive about that as she sounded.

*

Clara saw very little of Lawrence over the next few days. He spent all his time in the office either with their father's solicitor, or accountant, or poring over ledgers and books. Every day he looked a little grimmer. He insisted their mother move into the hotel so he could keep an eye on her.

"Oh, Lawrence, it's not necessary," Elvira said, but Clara could see how grateful she was.

Jeremy took on the task of arranging the funeral which would take place in the church where their grandfather was buried, where Herbert and Elvira were married and their children christened. It was where Herbert had grown up and been happiest, before his father's gambling, mismanagement and huge debts were discovered. He'd be laid to rest in the family grave.

Jeremy put a notice in *The Times* and sent out black-edged cards informing friends and business acquaintances of the death. Under the circumstance, the family being in deep mourning, Mrs Henderson, the dressmaker was sent for to provide suitable mourning outfits for Clara and her mother.

Once the notifications had been sent out and an obituary published, well-wishers, friends and businessmen who'd known Herbert came to express their condolences. Cards and flowers arrived daily. Clara sat with her mother to receive visitors and their expressions of sympathy, to open cards and find vases for flowers.

"People are so kind," she said to her mother. "He was well liked and respected. That must bring some comfort."

Elvira smiled and patted her hand but tears quivered in her eyes and Clara saw her struggle not to shed them.

Sir Richard arrived late one evening, after Elvira had retired. Clara went to see him in the tea room. He stood by the window, his hat and cane on a table next to him. Her heart lurched a little when she saw the bunch of pink and white roses he carried.

"It's good of you to call," she said, trying to keep the revulsion out of her voice and the meeting as formal as possible. "I'm afraid my mother's already retired. She's had a long and tiring day."

He smiled. "It was you I had hoped to see." He handed her the flowers. "I bought these for you. Your favourite flowers I believe."

A shiver of discomfort ran through Clara. "Thank you." She laid the flowers on the table next to his top hat. "As you can see, Sir Richard, the family are in deep mourning. I can't imagine why you would want to see me at this difficult time."

"Can't you? Surely you're not unaware of my feelings towards you? You and your family need friends at a time like this. I had hoped we could become more than friends."

Another shiver of dismay ran through Clara. She wished that Lawrence or Jeremy were with her. It was beyond foolish to have agreed to see him alone. She hadn't thought. He was an old friend of her father and grandfather. "I understand you've come to pay your respects, Sir Richard. I'm sure my mother and brothers will be most appreciative of your kindness. I will pass your condolences on to them." She smiled in what she hoped was a dismissive way.

He stepped towards her and touched her cheek. His gaze burned into her. "As if I care one jot about them. It's you I want. I understand from your mama that she's keen to get a ring on your finger."

Aghast, Clara could hardly breathe. Her eyes sprang wide with astonishment. "You mean – marriage? You're proposing marriage?"

He chuckled. "Why not? Of course I would need to taste the goods first, if you know what I mean."

Clara knew very well what he meant. He was the sort of man her mother and teachers had warned her about. Her heart beat a tattoo in her chest. "I'm sure I don't know what you're talking about. We are a family in mourning and I find your manner highly offensive." She turned away from him, her heart racing. "In fact I find you offensive and quite disgusting. A gentleman would respect our need for privacy and reflection at our time of grief."

He laughed. "Well, my dear, we've already established that I'm no gentleman." He stepped up behind her and slipped his arm around her waist. He whispered in her ear, "I have a place in the country where we can be alone. It's very discreet."

She pushed his arm away. "I think you should go, Sir Richard. Thank you for your condolences. We are mourning the loss of my father."

"A father who owed me a great deal of money." She didn't miss the harshness in his voice and the emphasis on 'a great deal of money'. He grabbed her shoulder and spun her around, his eyes narrowed, his face twisted into a sneer. "I own you. The house, the brewery, this place – all mortgaged to me. You can be sure I won't be slow to collect." Then he let her go and laughed. He picked up his hat and cane ready to leave. "There's no escape," he said. "You will be mine." He grinned as he left.

That night Clara hardly slept. The exchange with Sir Richard kept running through her mind. She recalled her family's indebtedness to him, but she'd never really been aware of the extent of it. Her father and Lawrence took care of business. She'd never given much thought to where the money for her schooling, her dresses and outings had come from. She knew of course that when her grandfather died their lifestyle had been dramatically changed. A smaller estate, Lawrence taking over the hotel while her father managed grandfather's brewery, but for her life went on just the same. She bought dresses, though not as many as she wished as Lawrence held her allowance, she went to parties, she dined out. Was it really so bad?

The next morning she felt even more unwell than usual. Every morning lately she felt nauseous. She'd rush to the bathroom and vomit, then feel washed out and have to lie down. She put it down to the grief of loss, but another thought kept niggling at the back of her mind. Her skin was pale and dark shadows ringed her eyes. She couldn't eat. She felt dreadful and worst of all she hadn't seen her period since well before the Coronation weeks ago.

"You look terrible," Elvira said to her over breakfast in her room. "You must eat. Making yourself ill won't help anyone." She pushed a plate of kedgeree in front of Clara. Clara put her hand in front of her mouth, stood up and rushed into the bathroom to be sick.

"I'm sorry, Mama," she said when she returned with tears staining her face. "I miss him so."

Elvira patted her hand. "Me too," she said. "Me too."

Chapter Nineteen

Daisy first became aware of Clara's condition when one of the chambermaids complained about the smell of vomit in the bathroom. "If they didn't drink themselves silly every night we wouldn't have to do the cleaning up," she said. "I have to spend extra time doing Miss Clara's room every morning. As if we haven't enough to do."

The truth was that, with the hotel closed, the maids had far less to do than usual. Daisy worried about that, so, when she went to the office to offer her condolences to Mr Lawrence she suggested that the guest rooms in the hotel be given extra cleaning while the rooms were empty. It was her way of keeping the staff engaged and saving their jobs.

"It'll be a chance to do an inventory of the linen, bedspreads and curtains," she said. "See how many need to be repaired or replaced. They haven't been done since Mr Herbert left and it'll give us a chance to make the rooms look their best for when the hotel reopens."

Mr Lawrence, distracted by the enormous task of sorting out his father's and late grandfather's businesses, waved his hand and said, "Whatever you think needs doing, Miss Carter. I'll leave it in your capable hands."

"The kitchen staff could do the kitchen too," she said. "Some of the china, crockery and cutlery needs replacing as well as the pot and pans. I could ask them to make a list."

"A list? Yes. Very good. Make a list. Thank you for your help."

Daisy knew enough about morning sickness to suspect something was not quite right with Miss Clara. She recalled her mother telling her about Jessie's sickness every morning. Now, hearing that Miss Clara was being sick every morning...

"Look. I think it would be best if you and Kitty concentrate on the guest rooms and giving them a really good going over," she said to Annie. "I'll do the family rooms if you like. With the hotel empty I'll have the time."

Annie the maid looked as though all her Christmases had come at once. "I'll tell Kitty," she said. "She'll be right chirky."

Over the following days, with the hotel empty of guests each day felt as though it was suspended in time. Nothing could be done, no arrangements made, nothing progressed, until after the funeral. The chambermaids cleaned and polished, until the whole hotel smelled of soap and beeswax, the kitchen staff washed and scrubbed until every pot and pan shone. After the guest rooms they did the restaurant, tea room, card room, lounge, anything to keep busy and earn their pay until the hotel opened again. The grooms cleaned out the stables and exercised the horses, Barker and the porters helped the maître dé in the cellar and pantry.

Daisy thought about Jessie and the wedding without a best man and wondered what had happened. What had the Bentons made of it? What was the gossip along the street and in the pubs and workingmen's club? Felix's sudden disappearance would set tongues wagging. What were they saying? She wanted to find out so, one morning, she took the opportunity to visit her ma.

The day was quite pleasant and warm for October, so she caught an omnibus to Blackwall and walked the rest of the way.

Her mother let her in and they walked through into the kitchen where her mother had been busy preparing the evening meal as usual. "How was the wedding?" Daisy asked as brightly as she could. "Was Jessie all right?"

He mother spun round. "Wedding? Fiasco more like. It were a shambles. Charlie never turned up, nor did his wastrel brother, the best man. Your dad had to go up there and drag 'im to the altar. Poor Jessie sobbed her 'eart out."

"Oh dear. I'm sorry to hear that. But they did get married – in the end?"

"Oh aye. Charlie said he was waiting for 'is brother but he never turned up and no one's seen 'im since." She filled the kettle and put it on the stove. "Oh yes, they got married all right not that it'll do 'er much good. None of them Bentons is any good."

"So does anyone know what happened to Felix? Why he didn't turn up?"

"Probably lying drunk in the gutter somewhere," Nora said "Or 'e's been arrested. Poor Jessie." Nora sighed. "She were a bright girl. Apple of her father's eye. She could've been somat."

Daisy wondered what the 'somat' was, but said nothing. "Have you seen Jack lately? Is he working?"

"Jack's gone. Him and Dan. Working up North, he said." Her brow creased into a frown. "He left you a note." She went to a drawer and took out an envelope. It had Daisy's name on it. "Don't know why he wanted to write to you," Nora said, "but I said I'd give it to you when I saw you."

"Thanks." Daisy smiled but her stomach churned. A lump formed in her throat. She opened the letter and read:

Dear Daisy, I'm writing this to let you know that me and Dan are going away. I've got us both on a ship to America. I told Ma we'd be working up North as she wouldn't understand why America, but I'm sure you do. What I did was my responsibility. I can't regret it. I don't want you to feel bad about it. It wasn't your fault. I love you and Jessie and Ma more than you will ever know but I can't stay. It's best that I go as far away as possible. Dan's coming with me. You know he always was my shadow. I promise I will look after him and try to make a fresh start in America for both of us. None of this was his fault either.

Look after Ma for me and look after yourself. Try to forget what happened and forgive me for everything. It's for the best.

Your loving brother, Jack

A great hole opened up inside Daisy, as though someone had plucked out her heart and left nothing but emptiness. A tear dropped onto the paper. Jack and Dan were gone and it was all her fault.

"What is it?" Nora asked. "You look like you've been slapped in the face with a wet fish."

Daisy sniffed and wiped away a tear. "It's nothing. Just a summer cold." She forced a smile onto her lips. "It sounds as though he's got a good job up North. Wants me to send him some of those barley sugars he likes. Doesn't think he can get them up there. Any biscuits to go with this tea?"

Nora got up to get the biscuits and Daisy put the letter in her pocket. "So it's just you and Dad now. Like a couple of old lovebirds."

"Lovebirds my backside," Nora's eyes shot wide. She plonked the biscuit barrel onto the table. "With Jessie and the boys gone and your dad spending all 'is wages in the pub, I don't know how I'm going to manage." She nodded at Daisy's pocket where she'd put the letter. "I don't suppose he said owt about sending somat back from 'is wages did 'e?"

Daisy shook her head.

"No. I'm thinking of letting out the rooms. There's always people looking for lodgings around the docks." She poured Daisy another cup of tea. "I might even make enough to give up me cleaning job and stay 'ome nights. Now wouldn't that be somat?"

Daisy smiled, but her heart wasn't in it.

After saying goodbye to her mother she decided to walk back to the hotel instead of waiting for an omnibus. She needed time to think. It was all messed up. Jack and Dan were gone. If she hadn't taken that necklace from Jessie, if Jessie hadn't gone and told Felix, if Felix hadn't stolen it in the first place, if, if, if...

Lost in thought she kept walking, not paying any heed to where she was going. She walked quickly, agitation churning inside her, thoughts buzzing around her head. Felix's body pressed up against hers, the sound of the brick hitting his head, the way his body slumped to the ground, the surprised look on Jack's face – all went round and round like a merry-go-round in her head, haunting pictures on a never-ending carousel.

She walked blindly on for over an hour, thoughts rushing through her head. Eventually, as her anger and frustration wore itself out, she saw a bench ahead of her. It overlooked the river. Feeling more wretched than she had in her whole life she sank onto it and, head in her hands, wept. She cried and cried until she was all cried out. Then she sat and gazed out over the river. The only sound was the lapping of the water as it swirled and eddied against the sides of the boats moored at the bank. A seagull dived onto one of the boats and rose up again with a piece of bread in its beak. She watched it fly high into the sky until it perched on a rooftop the other side of the river.

Jack and Dan were gone. She saw Jack's face, his smile, the laughter in his cornflower blue eyes, his mop of dark curly hair. Her irrepressible, devil-may-care brother was gone, as surely as Charlie had lost his brother, she'd lost hers. Then she thought of gentle Dan. Three years younger he was devoted to Jack and would follow him to the ends of the earth. He hadn't a mean bone in his body and wouldn't hurt a fly. She saw them in her mind's eye as they were growing up, playing in the street, loud, boisterous and full of life.

Then she thought of Felix. All through school he'd taunted her. Calling her names, throwing mud and stones at her as she walked home. She'd asked her mother why and she'd said, "It's because they're jealous." She thought of Felix's family, his violent, abusive father, his drunken mother. His four unruly brothers. What chance did Felix have of turning out a decent human being? Still, throwing mud and name-calling were a long way away from rape and murder.

She drew a breath. Living by the docks, boats came and went every day from all over the world.

People coming and going, life going on. Jack would survive, he always did. He'd take care of Dan too. That was his way. She was still sitting there when her attention was drawn to a man stopping next to her. She looked up.

"Are you all right, Miss Carter?" Constable Perkins towered over her.

"Oh, yes. Thank you. I was just sitting here having a philosophical discussion with myself."

"Ah," he said. "One of those. Don't be too hard on yourself, Miss Carter. We are all doing the best we can in the circumstances."

She had to smile. He was just what she needed. Someone to distract her. "And what about you, Constable? What are you doing here?"

"I'm on my way back from visiting a friend. Thought I'd take the scenic route. It's always quiet and peaceful here and I enjoy watching the river."

He sat beside her in comfortable silence watching the boats passing on their way to the docks. "I hear you've been spending some time with our pastry cook," Daisy said after a while.

He blushed. "I am rather taken with her," he admitted, "but I'm not sure how she feels about me. Perhaps you could put in a good word for me?"

Daisy recalled what Matilda had told her about her family and could understand her reluctance to get entangled with a man in any way. "I don't suppose she wants to get involved just now," she said. "She hasn't had an easy time."

"I know. She told me about her family." He frowned and shook his head. "I don't know. Love 'em or hate 'em you can't escape your family can you? You

119

have to make the best of what you're given. Sometimes we all wish we could be someone else."

Daisy smiled. "And who do you wish you could be?" she asked.

"Me? I wish I could be the Police Commissioner." He grinned.

Daisy chuckled. "Keep wishing, Constable. You never know, one day you might be."

He laughed, stood and wished her good day. Sitting there she'd seen a different side to Constable Perkins. There's more to him than meets the eye, Daisy thought when he'd gone. He'd helped her put her problems into perspective and she felt better for having seen him. Perhaps she could put in a good word with Matilda.

Chapter Twenty

Late October brought autumnal days and misty nights. All over the countryside leaves on trees turned copper and bronze, pale sunlight broke through pearl grey clouds to dance on open meadows. Fields of golden wheat waived in the breeze waiting for the late harvest. In the small village of Nettlesham, the Fitzroy family's home, a wide variety of mourners filled the church for Herbert Fitzroy's funeral.

Transport had been laid on for the hotel staff who wanted to attend. Barker, Mrs T, Mr Jevons and Daisy went out of respect for Mr Herbert. Hollis and Billy the boot boy went as it was a day out in the country. "Better than working," Hollis said. Thomas, the head groom, went out of curiosity to see what sort of stables the Fitzroys kept in the country.

The organ played softly as the funeral procession made its way into the church. Daisy sensed the calm tranquillity of the old church and the memories it held as they entered. She noticed the plaques on the walls charting members of the parish who'd passed away, several Fitzroys among them. Pale sunlight through the stained glass windows threw rainbow patterns on the opposite wall. Garlands of lilies placed at the end of every pew scented the air. Overall the atmosphere was one of peaceful reconciliation.

Mr Lawrence and Mr Jeremy helped carry their father in, followed by Miss Clara, her mother, her Aunt Doris and her children, Verity and Henrietta Templeton. Then there were other family members.

After them the more prominent citizens of the town filed in together with the lesser businessmen and their wives. Some of them coughed and muttered as they filled the pews. The hotel staff sat at the back of the church alongside the butler, housekeeper, maids and Mr Herbert's valet from the house.

Daisy sat between Barker and Mrs T and was glad of their robust support.

"Who's the old geezer with the fancy tash?" Hollis whispered.

Mrs T shushed him, but Barker said, "That's Viscount Westrow. Well known in the gambling clubs and less salubrious joints around town. Friend of the family."

Mrs T shushed them again. "Show some respect," she whispered.

Although it was a sad occasion Daisy took pleasure from the huge turnout. "He was well liked, wasn't he?" she said looking around. Mrs T nodded and squeezed her hand. Daisy saw tears glistening in her eyes.

The service seemed to go on forever, with several readings, hymns and reminiscences from Mr Herbert's closest friends. Stirring word were spoken about his early years, his achievements, his goodness and his lasting legacy. Several people mentioned that he had a special place in their hearts and said he'd never be forgotten. After the committal and the vicar's homily a rousing rendition of 'Immortal, Invisible, God Only Wise' lifted everyone's spirit. As they left the church after the blessing, Daisy thought it a fitting tribute to the man she knew to be the most honest, trustworthy, good natured man she'd ever known. She'd have liked to tell everyone how much she'd enjoyed working for him, but when she mentioned it to Mrs T afterwards, she told her not to be so soft. "As if they'd even care what we thought," she said.

After the service the staff were treated to tea, coffee, sandwiches and cake in the church hall. The other guests were entertained at the house.

"Nice bit of ham and cheese in the sandwiches," Hollis said. "There's egg an' all."

Mr Jevons turned his nose up. "I'd have expected tongue and brawn," he said.

"What do you think the toffs are having?" Barker asked. "Bet there's more than tea and cake for them."

One of the housemaids passed around the sandwiches, while the cook poured the tea. Barker added a few drops of whisky from a half-bottle he'd slipped into his coat before they left. "A bit of extra sustenance," he said.

Daisy was glad of it. She noticed that Mrs T never strayed far from Barker's side with her teacup either.

The cake was Victoria sponge and Mrs T was gracious enough to compliment the cook. "I don't expect you have much trouble getting eggs and butter out here in the country," she said.

The cook blushed. "I'll put you some by before you leave," she said. "Nice bit of brisket too."

Overall it was a long tiring day and by the time they boarded the omnibus for the journey home they all agreed, "They done 'im proud – Mr Herbert."

"Aye," Mrs T said with a sigh. "I doubt we'll see 'is like again."

Inside Maldon Hall, the family home, Lawrence and Jeremy stood by the door waiting to greet guests as they arrived, thank them for coming and receive their condolences.

"It was a lovely service. Thank you," Elvira said to Jeremy when she arrived home. "Didn't you think so?" she asked Doris who followed her in.

Doris, who carried the scent of lavender with her, sniffed and dabbed her eyes with the crumpled handkerchief she'd carried all morning. "Lovely. Herbert would have been proud." Her face crumbled. "Excuse me," she blurted, overcome with emotion, and hurried away. Her daughters followed her.

Clara took her mother's arm and guided her into the large plush drawing room.

She led her to the most comfortable chair and helped her to settle. "Sherry, Mama?"

Elvira nodded. Glasses of sherry were laid out ready on a long white clothed table. Clara picked up one for herself as well as one for her mother. Soon mumbled comments, 'a sad day', 'a good do', 'a nice service', 'he had a good life' merged into the buzz of conversation filling the room.

Clara sat for a while with her mother receiving expressions of sympathy and chatting with people who made a point of coming over to offer some consoling words and say how much knowing Herbert had meant to them. Elvira smiled and nodded through it all, although Clara thought she looked worse than she'd seen her for some time.

"Are you sure you're all right?" she asked. "We can make our excuses if you prefer."

Elvira shook her head. "It's been an ordeal, but one mustn't let the side down. It's what your father would expect." She smiled and chatted to a few more people. After a while, as the flow of people eased she tapped Clara on the arm and said, "I saw Sir Richard in church. He was watching you. Obviously nothing can be arranged at this time, but it wouldn't hurt to let him know that his advances wouldn't be unwelcome."

"His advances? What on earth do you mean?"

"His proposal of marriage."

Clara froze. She gripped the glass she was holding. "But they wouldn't be welcome." She fixed a smile to her face and, through gritted teeth said, "I've told you, Mama, I won't marry him. Not today or any day."

A man in a broadcloth coat approached to pay his respects. When he'd gone Elvira gripped Clara's arm. Her voice and her gaze were steely. "I don't think you quite understand the position we are in," she said. "You hold the future of this family in your hands. Don't let it slip away because of some churlish idea of yours of refusing him."

Clara yanked her arm away. Tears filled her eyes. Today of all days she didn't want to fall out with her mother. She saw Sir Richard making his way towards them through the groups of mourners standing around the room.

"Excuse me," she said and dodged away in the opposite direction. Bunch of arrogant hypocrites, she thought as she wove her way through clusters of people chatting until she could escape into the lobby. None of them had called round or offered to help when her grandfather died and all their hopes of a comfortable future died with him. Now they were fawning over her mother like vultures picking over bones. Sir Richard in particular reminded her of a vulture. He even looked like one.

She sucked in great gulps of fresh air when she reached the lobby, glad to be out.

As she was making her way to the front door, hoping to escape into the garden, Jeremy came out of the cellar carrying a bottle of brandy.

"Reinforcements," he said, holding it aloft. His brow creased into a frown. "Are you all right, Clara? You look dreadful." He put his arm around her and led her outside to a bench overlooking the twilight-dappled lawns and gardens. "Tell me what's troubling you. I know it's a difficult day for all of us, but I sense there's something more than that. What is it?"

"It's Mama. She sees me at the next Viscountess Westrow. She says Sir Richard is going to propose to me and I have to marry him whether I want to or not. My feelings have nothing to do with it. It's the family fortunes that matter. If I don't we'll be destitute and it'll be all my fault. I'll be letting everyone down."

"Sir Richard's going to propose to you? I don't believe it. Why? I mean he's old enough to be your... grandfather."

"I know. But apparently he has his eye on me for his next wife. He told me so." She burst into tears. "Oh, Jeremy, he was awful. I hate him. He said—" she sobbed again. "He said he owned me. The brewery, the house, the hotel, it's all mortgaged to him. He'll take it all unless I marry him."

Jeremy's face turned to granite. "He said that?"

Clara nodded.

"Let me guess. I bet he said he wanted something else first. Something like, wanting to see what you had to offer, taste the goods, whatever?"

"He said he had a place in the country and... well you know... If I don't go with him he'll take it all from us and it'll be my fault." A swell of nausea washed over her and her heart crumbled.

"Filthy, degenerate pig." Jeremy spat the words out. "He'll never marry you. He has no intention of doing so. He only wants to seduce you, then he'll leave you and your name, the Fitzroy name, will be mud."

Clara stared at him

"That's what he did to Dolly. He was the man who ruined her. He promised marriage, brought her to London, seduced her and left her penniless to make a living the best way she could. He wants to do the same to you." His eyes filled with bitterness. "I wish I could ruin him."

Clara was stunned. "Sir Richard ruined Dolly?"

"Yes. And he'll ruin you too if he gets the chance. He won't marry you, Clara. Whatever he says."

"But what about the brewery, the house, the hotel?"

"He'll take them anyway, if he can. It's what he does."

Clara gasped. "So, we'll be ruined anyway?"

Jeremy patted her hand. "Don't worry it's not as bad as you think. Lawrence and I won't let that happen. It's not your fault and it's not something you should worry about."

"That's not what Mama thinks. She thinks everything's my fault. That I have the power to save the family fortunes but I'm not doing it because of some foolish notion I have about being in love with the man I marry."

"Don't worry about Mama. I'll put her straight about Sir Richard." His voice was cold and sharp as a knife.

"Really?"

"Yes. Not today. I think we've all had enough for one day, but rest assured I'll leave her in no doubt about his intentions."

She leaned over and planted a kiss on his cheek. "Thank you. You're the best."

Colour rose in his cheeks. "Are you going back in?"

She shook her head. "No. They're a bunch of toadying old hypocrites in there. I wish I could just run away. Get away from all this... this... hypocrisy."

Jeremy sighed. "Me too, love. Me too."

Chapter Twenty One

During the weeks after the funeral time seemed to stand still. The autumnal weather turned wintry, trees shed their leaves to lay a golden carpet on the ground. The mornings were heavy with dew and pewter clouds filled the sky.

Daisy found time to do some sewing she'd been meaning to do for a long time and the other staff were allowed to visit their families, or friends more frequently than had been possible while the hotel was open.

Nothing much changed. Mr Lawrence was still tied up with paperwork and settling his father's estate. Apart from a few small bequests to loyal servants at the house, the majority of Mr Herbert's estate was left to Lawrence with the provision that he look after his mother and sister.

He spent a great deal of his time out of the hotel while Miss Clara and her mother, being in mourning, rarely ventured out. Mr Jeremy visited and Aunt Doris often joined them for afternoon tea in their private dining room. Kitty and Annie who served them reported that they appeared very subdued.

"I don't think they know any more than we do about what's going to happen," Kitty said. Below stairs life still felt as though time had been suspended as the staff continued their normal day to day work, waiting for Mr Lawrence to decide their future.

"We'll all be thrown on the scrapheap," Barker optimistically predicted.

"The Fitzroy Hotel has always been run by Fitzroys," Mrs T said. "No reason it will change now."

Daisy wasn't so sure. She'd seen the lines of red in Mr Lawrence's ledgers when she took him his tea and collected the day's instructions. With no bookings and no rooms to get ready there was very little she could do. "If there's anything I can do," she said so often she felt like the proverbial parrot.

His answer was always non-committal. The staff pressed her to find out what his intentions were.

"You'll know when I know," she said, although she wasn't sure she wanted to know. The Fitzroy Hotel was the only place she'd ever felt at home and she couldn't anticipate a future without it.

Matilda was the only one who seemed to be a bit brighter throughout the difficult days, which Daisy guessed, was probably due to Constable Perkins's frequent visits. She noticed that Matilda took more care with her dressing and had changed her hairstyle to something more modern. She'd blossomed. About time, Daisy thought. She'd been such a timid mouse when she first came.

"He's asked me to the theatre," Matilda told her. "He wants to walk out with me. What do you think?"

Daisy smiled. She could see how excited Matilda was. "I think he's a jolly nice chap and you could do worse," she said.

"Is it all right if I go then?"

"Of course. Enjoy yourself while you can," Daisy said. You never know when it might end and we might all be chucked out, she thought.

That was the beginning of their 'walking out'. One day, when he came to call for Matilda she wasn't quite ready, so Daisy offered him tea. "Do they still think it's a burglary that went wrong?" she asked hoping to hear of any progress on the case.

"There's no reason to suppose otherwise," he said.

"What about suspects then? Do you have any idea who might have done it?"

He pouted. "There are a few regulars we're looking at, but it's the finger marks, see. They don't match. Finger marks don't lie."

"Well, I hope you catch him soon," Daisy said. And I hope you can prove it was Felix Benton, she thought.

*

October turned to November and morning mist shrouded the streets. Frost laid a coat of white on bare branched trees and the air was sharp with cold. Clara stood watching the wind blow raindrops against the window pane when she got a note from Lawrence asking her and Elvira to join him in the tea room. He'd sent a note to Jeremy too so Clara knew it was important.

"I expect he's going to throw us all out," Elvira said as they were getting ready. "I have a bad feeling about this." She put her hand on Clara's arm. "Such a pity about Sir Richard. Jeremy told me of his past, but I really can't believe—"

"Mama. Please don't. I told you he propositioned me. Surely you can see that his intentions are far from honourable. He's a despicable human being and we're well rid of him."

"If only it was as easy as that," Elvira said. "Thanks to your grandfather…"

She didn't get any further. Clara picked up her skirts and walked to the door. "Are you coming?" she said as she swished out.

Downstairs Lawrence and Jeremy were waiting. Tea had been served with a stand of cakes, and the staff dismissed with instructions that they were not to be disturbed. Jeremy held a chair out for Clara, Lawrence did the same for his mother.

"I suppose it's bad news," Elvira said, seeing the pile of papers Lawrence had laid on the table.

"Well, it's certainly not good," Lawrence said. "I've done my best but the fact is that, thanks to Grandfather Fitzroy, the family owe far more than we can pay."

"Bankruptcy?" Elvira's face turned an exotic shade of puce. "Don't say that, Lawrence. I shall never be able to hold my head up again. Everyone will be talking about us." She closed her eyes and shuddered visibly. "I can't bear it. Please say it isn't true, Lawrence."

Lawrence sighed. "I'm going to sell the brewery and possibly the house," he said.

"Sell the house?" Elvira's eyes sprang wide. "Sell Maldon Hall? You can't do that. It's my home, your home, our home. Your father would never have let you do that." She burst into tears. "What on earth have we come to?"

"It might not come to that," Jeremy said, putting his arm around his mother's shoulders to console her. "I have friends. I've been lucky and I have a bit put by." Clara knew he'd won a half-share in a gaming club but anything won can just as easily be lost so she'd hadn't paid much mind to it.

"Sell the brewery. It's about time," Jeremy said. "I never could understand why Papa hung on to it. But I think we can save the house."

"Really?" Elvira lifted her head and gazed at her youngest son with admiration. "Thank you, Jeremy. You are a wonder."

"Selling the brewery won't cover all of the debt," Lawrence said. "That's why Papa kept it as a going concern. Thanks to his hard work turning it around, I may at least be able to find a buyer. I've spoken to the brewery manager. He's a good chap. He thinks he knows someone who will give us a fair price, but there's still a lot owing to Sir Richard, who, as we know, will want his money or take whatever assets we have left."

Elvira looked at Clara.

"No, Mama," Clara said with a shudder. "I don't know how you can even think what you're thinking."

"Sir Richard was a good friend to your grandfather," she said.

"No he wasn't," Lawrence chipped in, his voice cold enough to freeze sunshine. "And Papa knew that too. What kind of friend loans you money when they know you're drowning in debt? Sir Richard encouraged Grandfather's worst excesses. He spurred him on to spend more and more money on cards, horses and dogs. He wasn't a friend, he was a unutterable cad and a relentless predator. He plays on people's weaknesses for his own benefit. I will do everything in my power to pay him back and be rid of our indebtedness to him."

"Can you save us, Lawrence? Can you?" Clara pleaded. Her voice sounded thin and squeaky, anxiety curled in her stomach.

"With Jeremy's help and if we all cut back a bit…" He shrugged. "I can try."

"What about the hotel?"

"Well, that's the good news. Papa bought the hotel outright and it's mortgage free. Despite the murder people are still writing to make bookings. It seems our notoriety has spread. Some people even ask if they can stay in the murdered girl's room." He shrugged. "Every cloud…"

"Can you raise a loan against the future bookings?" Jeremy asked. "From the bank?"

"I think so."

"Enough to cover the brewery losses?"

"Yes."

"What about the house? What's outstanding?"

Lawrence passed a sheet of paper over to Jeremy, who studied it for a few minutes, his brow creased. "I think I can raise enough to cover this," he said. He passed the paper back. "I wish I could get Sir Richard into my club and give him a good thrashing."

"I'd settle for paying him back every penny and getting him off our backs for good," Lawrence said.

"I'd settle for never seeing him again," Clara said, much reassured by her brothers' words.

Elvira sniffed. "I still think a good marriage for Clara is the most important thing we have to focus on," she said. "A wealthy suitor could turn this whole thing around."

"And you'd sacrifice your daughter's happiness to achieve it?" Jeremy said.

Elvira gasped. "It's the way it's always been done," she said. "In my day—"

"Tea anyone," Clara said, half-rising and picking up the teapot. "Should I pour?"

Chapter Twenty Two

The next day Mr Lawrence appeared a little brighter when Daisy took his morning tea. "Ah, Daisy," he said. "Mrs Fitzroy will be leaving today. Please could you arrange for someone to pack her things. Mrs Templeton is going with her. They'll need a porter this afternoon for the luggage. Mr Jeremy is arranging for a carriage to collect them at three pm."

"Yes, sir. Will Miss Clara be going with them?"

"No. Miss Clara will be staying. Please ask the staff to gather in the dining room at eleven. I have an announcement to make."

"Yes, sir. Thank you, sir." Daisy's heart raced. This was it. The announcement was bound to be about the future of the hotel. If Miss Clara was staying, was that a good sign? Or was she staying to help pack things up when they close for good? Daisy couldn't wait to tell the others and see what they thought.

The news of the coming announcement spread faster than wild fire on dry bracken. Speculation ranged from: 'He'll be wanting shot of all of us' to 'He's going to announce some rebuilding, a newer, bigger hotel now his father's gone.'

Daisy thought something in between. She had great affection for the place as it was and didn't see the need for anything different. Just before eleven she made her way nervously with the others to the dining room.

The hum of muted conversation stopped as Mr Lawrence and Miss Clara walked into the room.

"Good morning. Thank you all for coming," Mr Lawrence said. "I appreciate how difficult and distressing the last few weeks have been for all of you and I want to thank you for your continued loyalty and support. Since I took over running this hotel from my father I've seen how crucial you all are to the smooth running and ultimate success of our joint endeavours."

"How about a raise, then?" someone called out but he was quickly shushed.

Mr Lawrence smiled. "I'm sure you are all aware of the problems and realities we have all had to face recently," he said. He held his hand out to Miss Clara who stepped up beside him. "Miss Clara and I would like to express our thanks to you all for your sterling service at this harrowing time and assure you that we intend to reopen the hotel to visitors as soon as possible."

A muffled cheer ran through the audience. People nudged and nodded to each other. Palpable relief filled the room.

"Together we hope to make it one of the best and most illustrious hotels in London, just as my father would have wanted," Mr Lawrence said. "I know I can rely on you all to help."

Mrs T stepped forward, a huge smile on her face. She turned to address the gathered audience. "As you know I've been here since the hotel first opened. I think that entitles me to speak on behalf of us all when I say, we will do our best to make sure Mr Fitzroy never regrets his decision. Thank you."

She stepped down and the audience cheered again, as much from relief at hearing they were to keep their jobs as to applaud Mrs T's contribution.

The buzz of conversation followed Daisy as she filed out with the others. Their jobs were safe, at least for the time being.

The following weeks went in a flurry of activity and excitement. Daisy spent her time checking that the rooms were the cleanest and brightest they'd ever been. Mrs T tried out some new recipes and, for once, didn't complain about the extra work. Barker read up on all the latest entertainments in the capital so he could advise guests on their availability. Mr Jevons drilled the waiters and waitresses to ensure service in the restaurant and tea room left no doubt about the superiority of the quality of amenities they offered.

The only changes to the hotel came with Mr Lawrence's decision to close the stable yard. The hotel no longer boasted its own carriage and horses, but the grooms had been kept on to service the needs of guests arriving with their own livery. The number of such guests had dwindled and keeping the stable yard open was no longer a viable proposition. The staff were let go, but provided with excellent references to enable them to take up employment elsewhere. Thomas, the head groom, was found a position at Maldon Hall.

The Fitzroy brothers together produced a list of the most eminent businessmen to invite to a Grand Reopening Dinner to be held on the Saturday night. The first of the staying guests would also be arriving on Saturday.

"We could do with another porter," Barker said, as they finished breakfast in the kitchen. "Seeing as how young Alfred hasn't been seen since the Coronation. 'E never was very conscientious but leaving like that, without a word…"

"I don't think the work suited 'im," Hollis said. "I never saw 'im without 'is 'ead in a paper. Probably looking for another job."

"But to leave without references, or even 'is pay?"

"Yeah, it does seem odd. I thought perhaps 'e took off when 'e saw the police arrive about that murder. May 'ave 'ad somat in 'is past we don't know about."

"That's true," Barker said. "'E weren't 'ere long enough for us to get to know owt about 'im." He sighed. "Best get back to work."

Mrs T had done an inventory of the larder and made a list of the supplies she needed. When the order arrived it was several items short. She sent the delivery boy away with a flea in his ear and a string of cuss words for his employer.

"I'll need someone to go to the shop if I'm to get on with making pies today."

"I'll go," Matilda said. "I'll be glad to get out and I have some letters to post."

"Aye. Then take Ruby with you. She can help carry."

Ruby stared saucer-eyed at Mrs T. "Me? You want me to go to the shops?"

"Aye. You can help Matilda. It'll give you a chance to prove you're not as gormless as I think you are."

A startled Ruby went to get her coat.

"An' take your apron off," Mrs T yelled at her as she struggled into her coat.

A quiet, industrious silence filled the kitchen as they all went back to work, each trying to do their best for the sake of the hotel. The only sound was Mrs T muttering to herself as she mixed the pastry and the clatter of dishes being washed up by Annie, who was doing her bit helping out.

Half-an-hour later Daisy came back to the kitchen with the breakfast tray she'd collected from Miss

Clara's room. She'd just put the tray down when Ruby came bursting in, red in the face and breathless.

"Mrs T. Somat awful's 'appened to Matilda. She's bin took."

Mrs T glared at her. "Bin took? What on earth are you talking about, girl? How d'ya mean took?"

"Took right off the street." Ruby burst into tears.

Daisy rushed to guide her to a chair and gave her a glass of water. She managed to calm her down. "Now, tell us what happened."

"It were awful. Two men stopped us in the street. Matilda must've recognised them 'cause she tried to run away. One of 'em grabbed her. I tried to grab 'er back, but 'e pushed me away. Then a man came to 'elp, but the first man said he was Matilda's brother and she was a runaway. 'E was taking 'er 'ome." She sipped the water. "There was a right ruckus in the street. People shouting and Matilda screaming. Still, the men said they were 'er brothers and there was nowt anyone could do about it." She shivered and started sobbing again.

Daisy bit her lip. She recalled Matilda telling her about her father and brothers and the future they had planned for her. "Where was this?"

"Outside the shop."

"Which shop?"

"Meredith's, the butcher."

"Right. Come with me." Daisy grabbed her coat and pulled Ruby to her feet.

"What you gonna do?" Mrs T asked.

"Find Constable Perkins," Daisy said. "I think it's a job for the police."

Chapter Twenty Three

Daisy dragged a reluctant Ruby along the streets until they found Constable Perkins. He was at the end of his beat on his way back to the station.

"Good morning, Miss Carter, Ruby. What brings you out this chilly morning."

"Matilda's bin took," a breathless Ruby gasped.

"What!"

"Tell the constable what you told us," Daisy said. "And slowly."

Ruby gulped but managed to coherently relate the happenings of the morning.

"Her brothers, you say?" Perkins's brow creased.

"Yes. But she didn't want to go with them." Ruby was gaining in confidence now she was sure of her story.

Perkins shook his head. "I can't do much if it's a family matter. Matilda's a minor. There's no law against taking runaway children home, in fact the law never interferes with family disputes."

"There must be something you can do," Daisy said. "She'll be twenty-one in a couple of months. Surely that makes a difference." She could see from the look on Constable Perkins's face that he was as upset and troubled about Matilda being taken as she was.

He took out his notebook and wrote something, tore out the page and gave it to Ruby. "Take this to the police station. Ask for Sergeant McBride. Tell him to meet me at King's Cross. Can you do that?"

A look of deep consternation and alarm crossed Ruby's face. She nodded. "Sergeant McBride, King's Cross."

"Off you go then."

"And hurry," Daisy called after her. "What do you have in mind?" she asked.

"If they're taking her up North they'll be going by train. I'll see if I can make them change their minds."

Constable Perkins was right. When they got to King's Cross station about ten minutes later, they found Matilda in the tea room sitting between two burly men Daisy guessed were her brothers. When Matilda saw them she tried to get up but was pulled back into her seat by one of the men, deep fear filled her eyes.

"Good morning, gents," Constable Perkins said. "I believe you are taking this young lady away against her will. We can't have that now, can we?"

"We're her brothers," one of the men said. "We're taking her home where she belongs."

"I'm not sure I can let you do that," Perkins said. "Not if she doesn't want to go."

"She's a minor. No law against it. You can't stop us."

"You have evidence of that do you?"

One of the men produced a paper from his pocket. "Here's her birth certificate. You can check if you like. She's under age."

Perkins took the paper, folded it and put it in his pocket.

"You say you're her brothers. Can you prove it?"

They looked at each other. "Who else would have her birth certificate?" the older one said.

Constable Perkins shrugged. "Anyone can get a birth certificate, especially if they intend to abduct an innocent young lady for immoral purposes."

The man gasped. "Ask her. We are, aren't we?" The man who spoke elbowed Matilda viciously in the ribs. She squealed but didn't speak.

"Is that true. Miss Mulroony?"

Matilda shook her head gaining her another vicious jab from the elbow of the man next to her. She yelped like a whipped dog. Constable Perkins stepped forward, anger flushing his face.

"Leave her be," he said sharply. "You probably don't know this but Matilda is my fiancée. We're going to get married as soon as she's twenty-one. So, you see I really can't let you take her away."

The men looked at each other. Matilda's jaw fell open. At that moment the tea room door opened and Ruby appeared with a broad-shouldered police sergeant.

"I don't believe you're her brothers," Perkins said. "You've produced no evidence to prove it. I'm going to arrest you both on suspicion of abduction." He moved towards them. "Then I might make sure the papers get lost for... what do you say, Sarge? Two maybe three months?"

"Papers lost? Oh yes. Happens all the time and what with Christmas coming..." Sergeant McBride stroked his chin. "A good two months."

The men stared at each other. Their previous confidence ebbed away as their faces crumpled in uncertainty. "What you talking about? Arrest us?"

"Oh yes." Constable Perkins got out his handcuffs and stepped even closer to the men, just as the train pulled into the station.

"That's our train," one of the men said. He looked at his brother. "She's not worth it," he said. "Not bloody worth it. You can keep the cow and good riddance. Come on, Harry." He turned to go out of the door.

The other man spat on the floor and went to follow him. "Stupid cow's not worth our bother," he said.

Sergeant McBride held the door open for them.

Everyone breathed a sigh of relief when they'd gone. "Well done, Constable," Daisy said beaming all over her face. "You've saved the day."

"Call me George," Perkins said with a huge grin on his face. "And I meant what I said. I want to marry you, Matilda, if you'll have me."

Matilda threw herself at him flinging her arms around his neck. "Oh, George," she said. "Of course I'll marry you. I can't wait."

The sergeant and Daisy looked at each other. "All's well that ends well," Sergeant McBride said. "If I can quote Shakespeare."

Daisy linked her arm in his. "You can quote whoever you like," she said. "I'm just glad you were there." He blushed.

Ruby jigged on the spot. "Does this mean Matilda's staying?" she asked. "I do 'ope so."

"She'll be staying for now," Daisy said. "Until she gets married."

"Whoo hoo! A wedding," Ruby said. "I love weddings."

They all laughed, possibly with relief, but certainly with great delight.

Chapter Twenty Four

With the hotel reopening, her mother returning to the country and the prospect of a grand dinner to mark the occasion of the reopening, Clara's mood lifted. Although still in mourning she was able to get out and visit friends, as long as she dressed appropriately and they were discreet. However, there remained one pressing worry. As time went on it became increasingly clear that she was in a certain condition, one she didn't want to be in. Didn't even want to think about.

It didn't seem real. It couldn't be. But the more she tried to convince herself it wasn't the case, the more she became afraid that it probably was.

She had no married friends she could talk to. All the girls she'd gone to school with, who formed most of her social circle, were all, like her, single and unattached. One or two had secured a suitor during the season, but the weddings had yet to take place. Clara suspected that the potential brides were just as naive and ignorant as she was about such matters. She thought of Amanda Melville, and her wedding to a man she had known since childhood. She was still as in the dark about her wedding night and its possible repercussions as the other girls would be. What she wanted most was for it not to have happened. She wished she could turn the clock back and make everything all right again.

She couldn't do that, so the next best thing was to stop it going any further. She'd heard there were ways. Ways to put everything back to normal, the way it was before... if only she knew how.

There wasn't even anyone she could ask. Then she thought of Dolly Deverill and the men she entertained. She wondered if she'd ever had cause to resort to some sort of remedy for the unwanted condition. Her musings led her to think of the other girls who plied the same trade. Had any of them ever had reason to make use of anything to avoid an unwelcome result of their employment?

As much as she tried to push the thoughts out of her mind, they kept resurfacing, usually at the most inconvenient moments: when she was out shopping with a friend or having tea. Even when she was reading. She wondered at the ability of Jane Austen's heroines to avoid such inconveniences, although they were of course pure as the driven snow. Then she'd slam the book shut and take up some more engaging activity.

At least the anticipated grand dinner might provide a distraction.

Clara woke early on the day of the reopening. She lay in bed watching the cold November morning inch its way round the curtains. The sickness that assailed her daily seemed to be easing. Her breakfast would be brought up soon and the fire in her room poked back to life. She'd noticed the dry biscuits added to her breakfast tray. Had Daisy guessed her condition? Difficult not to notice the acrid stench of vomit that permeated the bathroom, despite her efforts with her perfume spray. If so she'd have to rely on the girl's discretion and she wasn't sure she wanted to do that. The thought of being the subject of kitchen gossip horrified her. Perhaps she'd ask if she'd seen her brother Jack recently. A reminder that she too had things she wanted to keep quiet. She sighed.

Breakfast. A slice of toast was about all she could manage, although she had become quite partial to a mouthful or two of the grilled kippers Mrs T had added to the breakfast menu. At the thought of the salty taste her mouth filled with saliva and she found herself rushing to the bathroom. When would it end?

Afterwards she crawled back to bed. For a fleeting moment the memory of Sebastian Shawcross flitted through her mind. She wondered where he was now, then she pushed the thought aside. She had the day to get through before dinner, the menu to check with Mrs T and the arrangement for the reception to check with Mr Jevons. Lawrence had made it clear that if she wished to stay she'd have to pull her weight. Tonight she would play hostess and show them all that they'd underestimated her. She wasn't the empty-headed dilettante they thought she was.

She spent the day checking the arrangements, writing letters and overseeing the staff, determined to show Lawrence he had been right to allow her to stay despite her mother's pleading to send her home where she said she belonged.

"We're a family in mourning," Elvira said. "Clara should be with me. There are certain formalities to be observed. Her continuing to carry out duties at the hotel is most inappropriate."

"But her presence here will show everyone that we are open for business as usual," Lawrence said. "A hotel like ours needs a good hostess to bring in the customers. We're a family hotel. People need to see that."

Elvira huffed, but Lawrence couldn't be moved and he was head of the family now.

"This is a new beginning for all of us," Clara said. "I'll do my best to make sure everyone knows it." Anticipation curled inside her. The evening was about making an impression and that was something she excelled at.

Lawrence had allowed her a new dress for the dinner. Midnight blue, rather than black, with a nod to her state of mourning by the addition of black lace and jet beading. She'd worked with Mrs Henderson to make sure it was the latest fashion and would impress all who saw it.

The staff had new uniforms too, which she'd managed to get Lawrence to provide after much haggling.

"It's what people will expect," she said.

On the evening of the reopening dinner, Clara wanted to look her best. She got Daisy to pin her hair up with black ribbon and black net roses. Memories of her father swirled in her brain, she felt his presence. It was his hotel and they were doing their best to keep it open. She missed him so, but wanted to be brave and not let him down.

The drizzly rain that had persisted all day turned to misty fog. Lamp lights glowed amber reflecting in wet pavements as darkness descended. People passing by huddled into their coats and scarves against the cold night air.

In the hotel Lawrence and Jeremy greeted guests at the door as their carriages arrived. Hollis took their coats and hats and, immaculately groomed, Kitty and Annie served sherry in the lounge. Given that the family were still in mourning it was to be a muted affair with the emphasis on the quality of the food and service rather than any entertainment that could be provided.

Clara chatted to the wives as they arrived, putting them at ease and trying to push a mosaic of memories to the back of her mind. She was unprepared for the emotions that assailed her. The stress of the day and weight of expectation took their toll. She did her best to hide the quiet despair she felt, but Jeremy must have noticed her discomfort. "Is something the matter?" he asked, sidling up to her.

"I can't help thinking about the last time I saw so many people gathered together," she said. "For Papa's funeral."

Jeremy squeezed her arm. "I know, but it's the future we have to think about now, not the past. If we're to make a success of the hotel these are the people we need to impress. Try not to show your resentment."

She took a breath. This was a good deal harder than she thought it would be. Then she thought of all the girls she knew forced into marriages or lives not of their choosing and realised how lucky she was.

Determined not to let Jeremy and Lawrence down, she stepped towards a woman standing on her own, looking bored. "It's Mrs Waverly, isn't it?" she said brightly. "Your husband is...?"

Mrs Waverly responded with a smile. "He's station master at Farringdon," she said, pride shining in her eyes. "It's a change to be invited somewhere where they're not all railway men."

Clara chatted to her for a while and then introduced her to another woman, who looked like she could do with company.

Soon after that, much to Clara's relief, dinner was called and they filed into the restaurant. Clara could hardly eat anything, despite the generosity and deliciousness of the food. Mrs T had done them proud. The guests tucked into rich game and vegetable soup, followed by oysters. The main course consisted of an abundance of roast beef or lamb with fresh vegetables sent up from the country. Lemon sorbet was served to cleanse the palate before desserts of pastries and Mrs T's best apple and rhubarb crumble served with custard or cream, or chocolate truffle cake followed by a variety of cheeses. After a decent interval the ladies retired to the lounge for tea or coffee while the men enjoyed port, cigars and business discussions.

The party broke up after midnight. Clara was exhausted. Her jaw ached from the smile she'd forced to her lips all evening. She'd found the conversation parochial. All the ladies cared about was their husbands' status. They vied with each other for supremacy in that department. It soon became clear to her that the status of one employed by the railway fell well below the status of a proprietor of one's own business. At one point, in defence of Mrs Waverley, Clara found herself pontificating on the strategic importance of the railway to everyone's prosperity. She even quoted Rupert Melville, delighted that the afternoon spent with Amanda's brother hadn't been a complete waste of time.

"I'm surprised you know so much about railways," one woman said.

"Oh. I think we should all keep abreast of progress," Clara said. "After all it's our future."

The women nodded and sipped their drinks.

The evening seemed to drag on forever, but eventually the guests made their way out to the waiting carriages, calling goodbye, thanking them for the invitation and confirming their support through recommendation.

"Thank God that's over," Lawrence said. "Thank you both for your sterling efforts. With a bit of luck we'll see an upturn in visitors thanks to this evening's endeavour."

"You put on a good show," Jeremy said. "Couldn't have organised it better myself."

"Praise indeed," Clara said, almost bursting with pride. Perhaps it had all been worthwhile.

"There's still the paperwork to finish," Lawrence said. "I'll see you both in the morning."

They all said goodnight. Clara was glad it had gone so well. Lawrence at least was pleased. Both he and Jeremy were thinking of the future: the Fitzroys back running the hotel, just as their father had done. She wished her future looked half as certain, which brought her back to thoughts of what lay ahead for her and the predicament she was in.

"You look done in," Jeremy said. "Would coffee and brandy help?"

Jeremy's concern brought tears to Clara's eyes. Whenever he showed his compassion she was transported back to their childhood. He'd been her protector then, now she needed him more than ever. "I think I'm beyond help," she said. A tear trickled down her cheek.

"My dear girl, whatever is the matter? Sir Richard hasn't been plaguing you again has he?"

"No. Nothing like that. It's something else." She gulped back the lump that rose in her throat. "Can I talk frankly to you?"

"Of course. Anything."

"I think I might be pregnant."

The smile dropped from his face. Bewilderment filled his eyes. "Pregnant? You mean?" He glanced at her middle. "You can't be. You haven't..." His brow creased as he took her words in. "I thought you were..." He couldn't say any more. He sank into a chair like a fluttering goose coming to rest.

"I'm at my wit's end," Clara said. "I don't know what to do."

"I know what to do," Jeremy said. "Find the bastard who did this to you and thrash him to within an inch of his life. You'd better tell me what happened. Who?"

Clara screwed up her courage. She could see from Jeremy's face the direction his thoughts were taking. That wasn't what she wanted. "I can't say. I won't say. I just want it gone. I've heard there are things you can do." She sat down beside him.

Anger replaced astounded perplexity on Jeremy's face. "You can't mean... You mustn't. No, Clara. Don't even think about it."

"I thought you might know of someone... your friends... the girls... they must sometimes need..."

"No, Clara, no. People have died doing what you're suggesting."

Clara stared at him willing him to understand. "I can't... I can't go through with it." Sobs overtook her.

Jeremy took her in his arms and held her until the weeping abated. "Just tell me who it was and I'll see that he does the decent thing. He'll marry you. I'll make sure of that."

She swallowed back another sob. "Don't you see? I don't want to marry him. Not like that. I just want my life back the way it was. I don't want this... this... THING!" She waved her hands over her stomach. "I thought you might know someone. What do your girls do when they have this problem?"

"My girls!" Fury blazed in Jeremy's eyes. "They are not 'my girls'," he corrected her, his tone one of heartfelt rebuke. "I'm not a pimp whatever you might think. I'm just a friend who treats them like human beings instead of something the dog dragged in off the street." He swallowed and shook his head. "Most of them are decent people who're in the position they're in thanks to some feckless, over-indulged, arrogant, good-for-nothing man like the one you're trying to protect." Clara saw the outrage in his face.

"I'm sorry. I didn't mean to upset you or make you angry." She felt more miserable than ever.

Jeremy sighed. "Honestly, Clara. I only want to help. To do what's best for you and finding the man responsible is the right thing to do."

Clara shook her head.

Jeremy relented. "Tell me what happened. When?"

Clara hesitated. She felt so ashamed she found it difficult to find the words, but eventually she managed to tell him about the events following the Coronation Boating Party. "Then I found Dolly Deverill's body." She shuddered as the memory filled her mind. "The thing is that the man I was with mistook the hotel for a brothel," she said. "And who can blame him after seeing… you know."

"So it's my fault? Me and my disreputable friends?" Jeremy's tone was one of incredulity.

"No. I didn't say that." Clara immediately regretted saying it. "Anyway, the harm is done. I just want it to be undone. If you can't help I'll keep trying until I find someone who can."

Jeremy looked aghast. "No, Clara, not that. Don't do that. Don't even think it. Like I said, people have died. I mean it." He pondered for a moment, shaking his head, the light in his eyes dimmed. "I do know someone, a doctor…"

Clara brightened. "Will he get rid of it for me?"

"No. He won't do that. It's highly illegal and extremely dangerous. But what he will do is arrange for you to have it in a clinic somewhere far away from here. We can say you're visiting friends abroad and, afterwards, he'll see it's taken to a good home."

Clara pouted. Jeremy put his arm around her. "Honestly, Clara, it's for the best. Unless you want to tell me who the man was and I make him marry you."

Clara shook her head again. "Never," she said. "I don't want to marry a man who thinks I'm a prostitute and treats me like one."

Jeremy took a breath. "Very well. Practicality. August, so due…" he counted on his fingers, "May. I'll get in touch with my friend and he'll get in touch with you."

Reluctantly Clara nodded.

"He's a good man. He won't judge or moralise. You'll be safe in his hands." He took Clara's hands in his. "Please, Clara. Promise me you won't do anything silly. I don't want to be attending your funeral too."

Clara bit her lip, but she nodded. She could see he still thought beating someone to a pulp was the best solution.

"Say it, Clara. Promise me."

"I promise." She never could resist Jeremy when he pleaded with her. Now she'd committed herself to something she hadn't wanted and had no option but to see it though. She thought of Captain Sebastian Shawcross, blissfully unaware of the turmoil he'd left behind. I hope I'm doing the right thing, she thought.

Jeremy planted a kiss on her cheek. "Good girl." He pulled her into his arms. "You know I'll always be here for you don't you?"

Tearfully Clara nodded.

Chapter Twenty Five

With the hotel reopening the gloom and despondency that had hung over the kitchen for the last months disappeared to be replaced by good natured optimism. The staff soon fell back into the routine of guests arriving and departing. Gradually things got back to normal. As the days went by the weather turned colder, leaves from the trees lay damp in the gutter or fluttered along the road carried on a brisk wind. Some days sleet and rain dashed against the windows and the hotel staff were glad to be inside in the warm. Fires were lit in all the occupied bedrooms, adding to the work of the chambermaids. Another porter was taken on to replace the missing Alfred.

Barker still found time to read the morning papers. "There's some more pictures of the King," Barker said turning the page of the newspaper he was reading. "At least he's seen out and about. Not like the old Queen, forever in mourning."

"Them upstairs reckon he's good for business," Hollis said. "People want to come to London to see 'im."

"Well, we're certainly busier," Barker said. "Not that I'm complaining."

"Not complaining about the extra tips, eh Barker?" Hollis grinned.

"Well earned tips," Barker said. "Nothing I don't deserve."

"With Christmas coming it'll likely be busier still," Mrs T said. "I wouldn't be surprised if we all get a bonus."

They all nodded, glad at least that their jobs were safe. The talk among the female staff in the kitchen was mainly about Matilda's engagement and the circumstances of George Perkins's proposal.

"I wish a man would rescue me and propose," Annie said dreamily over breakfast.

"That's as likely as pigs flying to the moon," Kitty said.

Matilda beamed and glanced at the ring George had bought for her. "We won't be getting married until next autumn," she said. "Then I'll be a policeman's wife. Who'd have thought?"

Daisy smiled. "You'll make a lovely couple. Now if you've all finished…"

Daisy was happy for Matilda. Marriage to George would ensure her future away from her violent family. She liked George too, even though he was a policeman. She even thought Sergeant McBride might be a decent human being. She joined in the light-hearted frivolity of the kitchen but a nagging worry was never far from her mind. She hadn't seen her mother since Jack and Dan left. Guilt gnawed at her inside about that. It was all her fault, her and that damned necklace.

She hadn't been to see her mother because she couldn't bear the recrimination in her eyes. I expect Ma blames me, she thought. She usually does. The events of that night ran through her mind. Then there was the other fear. What would she hear if she did visit?

The worry was always on her mind, nagging away like a toothache impossible to ignore. As the days and weeks went by she'd pick up the papers left in the lobby and flick through looking for news. How long would it be before people realised the reason why Felix wasn't coming back? Would his family report him missing? Would they even notice?

Whenever she managed to catch Constable Perkins when he came to visit Matilda, she'd ask about progress on the murder investigation. Did they have a suspect? Was there any news of the missing necklace? He'd sigh and say, "These things take time. Slow but sure. Don't worry we'll get our man in the end. We always do."

That wasn't as reassuring as it sounded either.

One drizzly, misty morning she was on her way down from the top floor, carrying some ashes to put on the path outside, when a small boy arrived with a note for her. Her heart plunged when she recognised her mother's scrawly handwriting. Thoughts tumbled helter-skelter through her brain. It must be bad news. Why else would her mother write? Something was terribly wrong. Had they found Felix's body? Had someone remembered seeing him with Jack and Dan? Were the police looking for them? Had they gone to the house? She gave the boy tuppence and took the note to the sitting room to read it. A cauldron of fear churned inside her.

The note was short. Nora wasn't one for unnecessary words. *Please come when you can.* It was signed *Ma.*

Daisy gulped back the bile rising in her throat. She'd have to go. Ma wouldn't write unless it was urgent and important. She wasn't given to panic or drama either. If she wanted Daisy to call there'd be a good reason. Daisy swallowed, put the note in her pocket and grabbed her coat, hat, boots and umbrella. If she hurried she could catch the omnibus and be there before lunch.

Mist curled in the air as Daisy made her way along the street, her mind racing. A neighbour on her way to the shops nodded as she hurried on. Daisy glanced up the street as she knocked on the door. Everything looked normal. Her mother opened the door.

"Our Jessie's 'ome," she said. "Go on through."

"Jessie home? How is she?"

"See for yourself."

Daisy undid her coat as she walked to the kitchen, the warmth of the room seeping along the hallway. She gasped when she saw her sister. Jessie sat at the table, her dark hair lank around her face and a bruise turning yellow and purple over her eye. "What on earth happened to you?" she said, staring.

"Tell 'er." Nora moved to fill the kettle.

"Walked into a door, didn't I?" Jessie said sourly.

"Walked into somat," Nora said. "I doubt it was a door. More like a fist."

"Charlie did that?" Daisy's gut tightened, her mouth dried.

"Tell 'er the rest," Nora said, moving to the stove.

Shamefaced, Jessie shrugged. She bowed her head, not wanting to speak.

"Fell down the stairs," Nora said. "Or was pushed." She banged the kettle onto to stove and lit the gas. "At least 'e 'ad the grace to call an ambulance. Lost the babby."

"No!" A knot formed in Daisy's stomach. "That's awful. Oh Jessie, I'm so sorry." Overwhelmed, Daisy sat on the chair next to Jessie and put her arm around her shoulders. "Have you seen Charlie – since – you know." She nodded to Jessie's middle.

Jessie sobbed, her hands covering her face. She shook her head, then, as though it was all too much for her, she jumped up and rushed out. Daisy stood to go after her.

"Leave 'er be," Nora said. "She'll cry it out. Best thing for 'er. Poor lass. I always knew that Charlie was no good." Bitterness creased her face.

"Have you seen Charlie? What does he say about it?"

"I ain't seen Charlie. No one's seen Charlie. 'E's done a disappearing act, just like 'is good for nothing brother."

A stab of guilt, sharper than steel, struck Daisy at the mention of Charlie's brother, Felix. The kettle boiled and Nora made the tea. Daisy sat stunned while Nora clattered about getting out cups and saucers. "Dad's been out looking for 'im. I reckon it's best 'e stays disappeared," she said, "'cause if Dad finds 'im…" Nora shook her head.

"What will she do now?" Daisy asked as Nora poured the tea.

"She'll stay 'ere a while, till she sorts herself out. Then she'll 'ave to get a job. Back to the factory probably." She handed Daisy a cup of tea. "Which is why I sent for you."

"I'm glad you did," Daisy said. "If there's anything…"

"Well, you can let Jack and Dan know for a start. Tell 'em a bit of wages wouldn't go amiss. With Jessie 'ome and in a state…" She took a gulp of tea. "I'm expecting 'em 'ome for Christmas. Then we'll see if we can sort somat out for our Jess."

Daisy's heart crunched. She sipped her tea, playing for time. She had no idea where Jack and Dan were or how to contact them. Ma was right. Christmas was a few weeks away and she'd be expecting them home. What on earth could Daisy tell her? Not the truth. She couldn't tell her that. She put her tea down and emptied out her purse, the coins clattered on the table. She withdrew enough for her bus fare and left the rest. "I'll try and send a bit extra," she said. "I know it must be difficult with them away. I thought you were going to take in a lodger."

Nora grinned. "I 'ave," she said. "A nice clean gentleman. Clerk or somat. 'E's only staying till Christmas. Then with Jack and Dan 'ome the house will be full again." She put her tea down. "I'm not sorry that Charlie's gone, good riddance, but I do feel sorry for Jessie. It weren't 'er fault."

"No," Daisy said. "It must be a bitter disappointment."

"Aye," Nora said. "She'll be heart-sick, grieving 'er loss, but I can't 'elp thinking it may be for the best in long run."

Daisy sighed. Her heart went out to Jessie. Why was it that some people got all the good luck and others all the bad? It didn't seem right.

She stayed with Ma drinking tea and later had some bread and cheese. It seemed that everything else in the world carried on as usual. There was no news of the Bentons, but then she hadn't expected any.

On the omnibus on the way home Daisy thought about Jessie. She'd be heartbroken at the loss of her baby. It was clear that Charlie had a lot to answer for, not that Jessie would admit it. She wished she could do something to help. A nagging guilt about the row they'd had last time she saw Jessie over that damned necklace circled round and round in her head. It was her fault that Jack and Dan had gone too.

She thought about her mother's disappointment when they failed to appear at Christmas. Then she thought of Mrs Benton. Two of her sons wouldn't be

160

home for Christmas either. She fought back the anguish writhing inside her. It was, as usual, all her fault.

Chapter Twenty Six

December frost froze the ground and edged the bare-branched trees with a layer of white. Ice grew up windows and chimneys belched black smoke into the air. Despite the fire in her room being lit before dawn Clara shivered and pulled her wrap closer around her. She stared at the letter in her hand with increasing anxiety. Her mother wrote that she quite understood why Lawrence needed to stay in town for the festive season, but she could see no reason for Clara and Jeremy to stay.

It will be good to have you home, she wrote. *I know how much you mourn your father, indeed, I myself am in deep mourning, but life goes on. Rest assured you will have no time to brood. I have been busy organising entertainment for you. I have arranged a few discreet cocktail parties and a bridge party on Christmas Eve. Henrietta and Verity will also be joining us so you will not lack company. Christmas Day we will all attend church together in deep mourning and the rest of the day will be spent in contemplation. However, I have some good news. You will remember Brenda Villiers and her brother Percy. He is now Master of the Hunt and has agreed that, despite being in mourning, you and Jeremy can join the Boxing Day hunt and attend the Hunt Ball. Isn't that exciting?*

I know how trying mourning can be for you young people and in this case I'm sure exceptions can be made.

Clara huffed and threw the letter down. Just like Mama, she thought. We must observe mourning, unless there's an opportunity to further her ambition to marry me off to a wealthy local yokel. She recalled Brenda and her brother. She thought him a supercilious prat, even when he was ten. What would he be like now, heir to a vast estate and not a thought of his own in his head? At least Lawrence had been more relaxed about this mourning business. He didn't see it as disrespectful to have a little fun. Her dear papa wouldn't have wanted her to be sad or miss out on life's entertainments. The thought of spending Christmas in the country, draped in crepe made her shudder. As for riding to hounds. She hadn't ridden since last spring, then only a gentle trot in the park with Amanda. The hunt was a different thing entirely. Of course it might be worth it to bring on the solution to her problem she craved, but then everyone would know of her condition and her whole family would be shamed. Her mother would never forgive her. She couldn't risk that. She'd have to speak to Lawrence about it. If anyone could persuade Mama that she needed to stay in town he could. But then she'd have to tell him why and she couldn't face that either.

She got up and paraded in front of the mirror, turning this way and that, looking for any changes in her body. There were a few, but very subtle. Her face was fuller, her bosoms heavier, her waist thickening, but not so much that anyone would notice. She could get away with it for another month or two, especially wrapped up in heavy winter clothing.

She picked up her mother's letter. At one time she'd have been thrilled by her plans, the endless round of parties, the eligible suitors lined up to woo her. How shallow it all seemed now. Then, nothing would have delighted her more, but now, since Sebastian, she'd changed. Her life had changed. One moment of madness and suddenly your life wasn't what you believed it would be, she thought.

She'd read one of the scripts handed out by the suffragettes about determining their own future. That's what she wanted now, the chance to decide for herself.

At least she'd heard from Jeremy's doctor friend, Doctor Adrien Woodleigh. He'd written to say that he'd heard she was suffering some ill health and advocated sea air as a remedy. He suggested she spend some time with him at *his place by the sea from late March or early April, a time of new birth, when the earth springs into bloom and things look brighter.* She appreciated his careful wording and the fact that he didn't want to commit to paper any of his plans for her. He'd even suggested it as an antidote to depression brought on by her deep mourning. She appreciated that too.

It wasn't something she looked forward to, but she had promised Jeremy and she wanted it over with as soon as possible.

*

The weeks leading up to Christmas were busy at the hotel. Everyone pitched in with the work of decorating the hotel and getting it ready for the festivities. Barker and Hollis put up chains of holly, ivy, yew and laurel with coloured baubles and paper angels hanging from them. Mr Jeremy supervised the dressing of the tree in the lobby. All the rooms took on a festive air with candles, ribbons and floral garlands. Even Billy the boot boy did his bit, turning out to be a dab hand at polishing silver. Mrs T and Matilda were kept busy plucking geese and pheasants sent up from Maldon Hall and making cakes and puddings.

"We 'ad people to do this when I worked for Lord Pembury," Mrs T complained while plucking her tenth brace of pheasants.

The restaurant was fully booked, thanks to recommendations following the grand reopening dinner and local companies making reservations for their Christmas dinner parties. The rooms filled with visitors coming to town to see the shows, the galleries, the opera, or to shop in London's famous department stores.

Light from shop windows, the jingle of horses' harnesses, music from barrel organs, bells rung by street vendors and costermongers' cries filled the streets. People hurried along, their breath vaporising in the frosty air.

In the hotel staff who had family living close by were allowed time off to visit them and Daisy found herself busier than ever as she filled in for Annie and Kitty. On Christmas Day they would attend the morning service before returning to their posts. Daisy had put off visiting her mother until Christmas Eve. Then she'd been delayed that morning as Mr Lawrence had asked her to help Miss Clara pack for her trip to Hampshire for Christmas.

"I'll be going with her on the ten o'clock train," he said, "and coming back in the evening, but Miss Clara will be staying until after Boxing Day."

"I don't know why I'm bothering to take a change of clothes," Miss Clara said when Daisy went to help her. "I'll be spending the whole time in this dreary black dress." The black silk dress hung in pleats from her waist to the ground, all perfectly straight except for across her abdomen where the pleats were stretched a little. She'd pouted and Daisy guessed the reason for her reluctance to go.

Once Miss Clara's trunk had been dispatched Mr Lawrence asked Daisy to prepare two rooms for his guests. "A young lady and her mother," he said. "Miss Whitney will go in Mr Jeremy's room and her mother can use Mrs Templeton's room as they're both currently vacant. Please make sure the rooms are ready and put a bouquet of fresh flowers in each." He'd blushed when he said it.

Daisy had to send out for the flowers and when she mentioned it to Mrs T she said, "She'll be in the room next to Mr Lawrence then. I hope 'is guest is in a different line of work than Mr Jeremy's guests. We all know where that led."

When Miss Clara saw the flowers arrive she wanted to know who they were for.

"A Miss Whitney and her mother," Daisy said. "Mr Lawrence asked for them."

Miss Clara's eyes flared. "Lucinda Whitney's coming here for Christmas? She's got some nerve." From the look on her face Daisy guessed Mr Lawrence would be given a hard time on the train all the way to Maldon Hall.

It was late afternoon by the time Daisy left to visit her mother, taking gifts for the family. The streets were emptying of shoppers, save for a few stragglers still hoping for a bargain before the shops closed. One or two street vendors rang their bells and the buzz of excitement that had hung in the day earlier gradually ebbed away.

Sitting on the omnibus the sounds and light faded and darkness descended. Her footsteps rang on the cobbles as she walked to her mother's door. Her heart hammered. She felt bad about not visiting for so long but fear and guilt had kept her away. Fear of what her mother would say about Jack and Dan's absence and guilt about her part in it. She only hoped that Christmas spirit would prevail and she would be forgiven.

When she arrived her fears were allayed. Betty Hewitt was in the kitchen with Nora and another neighbour, having a Christmas Eve drink. Jessie had gone out with some girls from the factory where she used to work.

Nora greeted her with a kiss on the cheek and a glass of sherry. Her face was flushed and Daisy guessed she'd already had a few herself, or perhaps the warmth of her welcome was to impress the neighbours.

"I've brought you something," Daisy said and produced some of Mrs T's sausage rolls and mince pies to add to the cheese, crackers, nuts and finger sandwiches Nora had put out.

"How lovely," Nora said and kissed her again, her face growing even redder than before.

"How are things at the hotel now it's reopened?" Betty asked, helping herself to a sausage roll.

"Fine," Daisy said. "We're very busy."

Thankfully Jack and Dan's absence wasn't mentioned and Daisy was able to leave the gifts she'd bought for the family without comment, other than thanks.

She sighed with relief when she caught the omnibus home after wishing them all a Happy Christmas.

Daisy woke early on Christmas Day, looking forward to the afternoon party when the staff would get together for Christmas dinner, followed by parlour games, tea and cake. After the Christmas service the day would be informal and they could relax. Breakfast for the family and their guests was to be served in the private dining room. There being so few hotel guests their breakfast would be served in the tea room, rather than the restaurant. The chambermaids' first job was to see that the fires were lit and the ashes raked and emptied. Before they'd even got started Daisy had a call to go to Mr Jeremy's old room. The woman who greeted her sat on the bed wrapped in the eiderdown.

"The fire's gone out," she said, "and my morning tea was cold."

Daisy glanced at the fireplace. A bucket of coal and wood stood next to it. The reason the fire had gone out was that no one had thought to add fuel and bank it up for the night. "I'm sorry," she said. "I'll see to it right away and pass the message about the tea to the cook." Even as she said it she knew it was more than her life was worth to tell Mrs T of the complaint. The tea would have been hot when it was brought up. She'd be up the stairs like a raging bull to put the lady straight.

Miss Whitney sniffed. "I expected better service in the hotel run by my intended. When I…" She smiled but her eyes were cold. "Never mind. There will be changes you can be sure of that."

Shocked, Daisy didn't know what to think. Mr Lawrence's intended? Surely not. She'd never heard of him even stepping out let alone anything further. Her heart pounded as she raked the ashes, re-laid the fire and lit it. She put the ashes in the now empty coal bucket and left without another word. By the time she reached the kitchen she could no longer contain her anger. "Mr Lawrence's intended," she said. "That Miss Whitney in Mr Jeremy's room reckons she's Mr Lawrence's intended. What do you think of that?"

Mrs T's eyes sprang wide. She chortled. "Is that what she's telling you? Ideas above 'er station that one."

Daisy relaxed. "Do you think so? You mean she isn't? I mean, we would have heard wouldn't we?" Daisy was trying to convince herself let alone anyone else. "But she could be, couldn't she?" Sudden fear gripped Daisy's heart. She admired Mr Lawrence and, for some reason she couldn't fathom, the thought of him being tied up with the sour-faced, bitter woman upstairs, horrified her.

Barker came in, stamping his feet and rubbing his hands together. "Cor, ain't 'alf cold this morning. Any tea going?"

"Daisy's just told us Mr Lawrence's intended is upstairs. What do you think of that?" Matilda said. "You know him better than anyone. Know who he sees. Has he been seeing a lady lately?"

Barker picked up the teapot and poured himself a cup of tea. "Mr Lawrence seeing a lady? No fear. He's in mourning for his father. Takes it very serious does Mr Lawrence, unlike 'is brother who's just arrived. Nah, Mr Lawrence ain't been out in… erm… weeks to my knowledge." He sipped his tea. "This is grand," he said.

"She told me she was his intended." Daisy's heart dropped again.

"I could say I was the Queen of Sheba," Mrs T said. "Don't make it so."

Daisy was relieved when the general consensus of the kitchen was that said woman had hopes that were unlikely to be justified. She still wasn't convinced so asked Hollis, who'd been commandeered to serve the family breakfast, what he thought.

"Oily as a polisher's rag," Hollis said. "All over 'im like a rash she was, all smarm and charm. The mother weren't much better. Mr Jeremy saw through 'em right away. Gave 'er a hard time. But Mr Lawrence didn't seem to notice. Things on 'is mind I suppose." He picked up the tea Matilda had poured for him. "Pity Miss Clara's not here. She'd have made short work of 'er."

Daisy didn't know what to think. The whole thing unsettled her. She didn't know why. Perhaps it was the threat of changes to be made. Did Miss Whitney think she was going to marry Lawrence and take over the running of the hotel? If so, Daisy decided, it may be time for her to re-think her future.

Things came to a head at the dinner later that day. Kitty helped serve and each time she returned to the kitchen with dirty dishes Daisy asked her how it was going. "They all seem very jolly," she said. "Mr Jeremy's being outrageous as usual. He's brought one of his 'ladies'. Mr Lawrence doesn't seem to see the joke. He's taking everything very seriously. Honestly, you'd never think they were brothers, being so different."

"And Mr Lawrence's guests?" Daisy asked.

"She blows hot and cold. Frosty as ice to Mr Jeremy, but you'd think the sun shone out of Mr L's backside."

Daisy wasn't reassured so, as the meal came to an end, she decided to go up and see for herself under the pretext of collecting the finished dishes. She heard laughter even as she approached the room. Inside everything appeared normal, people were smiling, leaning back in their chairs, Jeremy smoked a cigar and blew smoke across the table. Miss Whitney shuddered but didn't voice her obvious disapproval. Kitty was serving the lemon meringue souffle dessert when she leaned across Miss Whitney to place the plate in front of her just as Miss Whitney lifted a glass of red wine. Their arms clashed and the lemon meringue souffle slipped from the plate and landed in Miss Whitney's lap. She screamed.

"You stupid girl." She jumped up, spun round and slapped Kitty, sending her off balance. As Kitty stumbled Mr Jevons was approaching from the opposite direction carrying a decanter of red wine. They collided and the decanter fell from its tray, spilling the wine over Miss Whitney's back. She screamed again.

"What sort of menagerie do you keep here, Lawrence?" Her eyes blazed. "They'll all have to go when…" She stopped short and sank onto her chair as she realised she'd said too much.

Mr Lawrence's eyes narrowed as he stood. "Miss Whitney," he said, his voice icy enough to frost glass. "I'll thank you to remember that you are a guest in this hotel and if any of my staff are to be reprimanded I will be the one to do it." His eyes sparked like a summer bonfire. "From what I saw that accident was as much your fault as the maid's. I won't have you attacking my staff." He glanced at Kitty who was in tears and being comforted by Mr Jevons. Then he turned his steely gaze back to Miss Whitney. "I can see that accepting your offer of help at this difficult time was a mistake and I'd appreciate it if you would pack up and leave as soon as possible."

"Hear! Hear!" Jeremy raised his glass in a toast. Silence fell over the room, as though everyone was holding their breath, as they took in his words.

"Very well," Miss Whitney said, gathering up her skirts. "Come, Mother, we're better off out of this zoo." She sent daggers in her glance directed at Lawrence. "I was a fool to ever think that you…" she huffed. "People are right. You and your family. You're a busted flush." She turned and stomped towards the door, followed by her mother.

Mr Lawrence sat. "You can send me the bill for the dress," he called raising a glass as she left. Everyone breathed again.

Daisy, suppressing a smile and full of admiration for the way he handled everything, rushed to comfort Kitty and clear up the mess created by the accident.

"You can leave the rest," Mr Lawrence said. "And I hope your dinner party downstairs turns out better than ours."

"Thank you, sir," Daisy said, bobbing a curtsy. Couldn't possibly be better than this, she thought, her heart lifting.

Chapter Twenty Seven

Clara spent most of Christmas avoiding her mother's attempts to introduce her to eligible young men. At the cocktail party Elvira arranged on Christmas Eve Clara found she was right about Percy Villiers. He was just as awful as she remembered and his sister wasn't much better. At least cousins Henrietta and Verity provided some distraction. Henrietta was engaged to be married in the new year to a vicar and Clara was impressed with her enthusiasm for good works.

"We shall fill the vicarage with happiness and children," she said, starry-eyed. Clara could think of nothing worse, but at least Henrietta was fun. Verity, although a little more serious, was good company too. Even Aunt Doris blossomed, seeing her children, and was persuaded to play the piano. Her repertoire being limited to hymns and carols, Clara took over and played some songs from the music halls. Henrietta and Verity joined in, singing along, until Elvira reminded everyone that they were in mourning.

"Sorry, Mama," Clara said, "but I'm sure Papa wouldn't mind in the least. I think he'd enjoy it."

On Christmas Day, after the church service, Elvira introduced Clara to a landowner who had recently taken over a large estate nearby. "That could have been you," she whispered when he introduced them to his heavily pregnant wife. I'm glad it's not, Clara thought.

At least the dinner was a family affair although Clara had no appetite. She pushed the serving of pheasant around the plate and hid a good deal of it under the green vegetables. The smell of the mince pies and Christmas pudding almost made her retch, so she excused herself.

"I think I have a head cold coming on," she said. "All this bracing fresh country air, I'm not used to it."

Elvira scowled, but suggested she rest for a bit and perhaps join them later for a rubber of bridge. "I said living in that hotel wasn't good for your health," she remarked with a satisfied smirk as Clara left the table.

Clara did join them later for tea, followed by charades with everyone taking part. Once their enthusiasm for that had been exhausted, Clara played Ludo and Tiddlywinks with Henrietta and Verity, there being no appetite for bridge which, Clara declared, Elvira took too seriously.

Later in the evening Clara played the piano while Henrietta and Verity took turns to sing their favourite songs. As the clock struck nine Aunt Doris said she was going to bed as it had been a long day.

"I'll leave you young people to it," Elvira said at ten o'clock. "Good to see you've regained your health, Clara." She sniffed pointedly as she left to retire.

The next morning Clara managed to avoid the Boxing Day hunt, pleading a bad head.

"That convenient cold again?" Elvira asked, but softened when Clara sniffed and held a handkerchief to her nose. "You have been looking a little peaky since you arrived," Elvira admitted. "I still think living in that hotel, as nice as it is, is doing you no good. It's totally unsuitable for a young lady looking for a husband. I'll speak to Lawrence. He'll see I'm right. You should be home with me."

Clara sighed. "I'm fine really, Mama. And I do get to go out now and then and meet people. I'm not locked up." She had another thought. "In fact I've had an invitation to stay with a family by the sea. He's a doctor and thinks the sea air would do me good. You're right, I have been feeling a bit off colour lately."

"There! I knew it. A mother knows best. A doctor, you say. From a good family?"

"The best."

Elvira brightened. "Well, that's a step in the right direction. You have my blessing."

"Thank you, Mama." If only you knew, Clara thought.

After lunch she went for a walk with her cousins. "Put a bit of colour in your cheeks," her Aunt Doris said.

They wrapped up warm and, despite the cold, it was good to get outdoors. They walked out of the grounds, down the lane and past empty fields still iced with frost.

"Where do you think we'll all be in five years' time?" Henrietta mused. "I'll be married with children, but what about you, Clara? What's your ambition?"

"Ambition? I don't really have one. My mother has enough ambition for the both of us." She laughed, but it did get her thinking. There would be life after… Perhaps she should think about what she wanted to do. There were opportunities for women opening up in business. Perhaps she should think about that.

Verity ran ahead and climbed up onto a gate. "I shall be a lady of leisure," she said, grandly. "With servants and a man who adores me."

"And where exactly will you get him?" Henrietta asked. "Out of thin air?"

Verity laughed. "A girl can dream can't she?" she said, and Clara remembered when she'd been young and innocent enough to have dreams.

The next day Clara was packed up and ready to go home by the time Jeremy arrived to collect her. He stayed for lunch with his mother before escorting Clara home. Elvira insisted they take the carriage. "I have some things to be collected in town," she said, "and travelling by train simply isn't done."

Clara was relieved at this concession. She was beginning to find travelling quite tiresome and appreciated the privacy the carriage afforded them.

"And how was Christmas?" Jeremy asked. "I hope you took it easy and didn't overdo it."

"I behaved impeccably," Clara said, "and if you mean the Boxing Day hunt, I managed to get out of it thanks to Henrietta and Verity. Can you imagine, she's engaged to a vicar."

"I know. I've met him. They'll do well together. They won't be rich or have an enviable lifestyle but they'll be happy with each other. That's what counts isn't it?"

"And what about you, Jeremy? Talking of matrimony. Any plans in that direction?"

"Who me? No fear. I've seen too many unhappy people to be fooled by the rhetoric. Lawrence had a close shave though. Miss Lucinda Whitney came for Christmas, with her mother."

Clara grimaced. "I heard she was coming. Wicked Witch Whitney's been after him since they were at nursery school together. I wish I'd been there, I'd have put a spoke in her wheel." Clara's voice was laced with spite. "How did it go? He didn't succumb I hope."

"Well, thanks to a ghastly encounter between a lemon meringue souffle and a glass of red wine she showed her true colours. I think I can honestly say I've never seen Lawrence so flabbergasted."

"How delicious. I'm sorry I missed it."

"You would have enjoyed it, except when she slapped the girl."

Clara's mouth fell open. "She slapped someone? Who?"

"One of the maids."

"No! How dreadful. What did Lawrence say?"

"Asked her to leave. He was furious. Mad as I've ever seen him. Mind you, I think it'll be a close thing when he finds out about your condition."

Clara's heart crumbled at the reminder. "Do we have to tell him?"

"Oh I think so. He deserves to know the truth, don't you think? Especially if he's to countenance you going away for a couple of months."

She sighed. "I suppose."

"He is head of the family and as such is responsible for you. You know how seriously he takes these things, his responsibility and all that."

Clara nodded but her heart sank. She dreaded Lawrence's reaction. He'd trusted her and she'd let him down. He'd never forgive her for that. "We don't have to tell him yet, do we?"

Jeremy shrugged. He gripped her hand and squeezed it. "Let me know when you're ready and I'll come with you." He smiled at her. "He's not the ogre you think he is."

Clara groaned. Why did life have to be so difficult?

Chapter Twenty Eight

January brought the first snow, clothing everything in winter white. The world seemed to slow and breathe again after the hustle and bustle of Christmas and New Year. Cold clear nights full of stars brought an icy chill to the air. Morning light crept slowly over roof tops, barely warming the streets. The muffled jingle of harnesses and the rumble of wheels reached Clara as she gazed out of her window at the flurries of snow drifting and settling. She'd need to speak to Lawrence. She couldn't go on pretending everything was all right, not when she'd see him day after day, working, worrying and making plans designed to keep the hotel running and restore its reputation.

She knew her mother had asked him to send her home to live with her in the country. *It's a daughter's place*, she'd written. She'd also referred to what she called *The Dolly Deverill Affair* and intimated that Clara wasn't safe living in the hotel when a murderer was still at large. Over Christmas Henrietta and Verity had wanted to hear all about the murder and Clara's part in it, finding the body.

"I will not have that disgusting affair discussed in my house," Elvira said. "I'm sure it was to blame for hastening Herbert's death. The press hounded him. Like vultures they were, always circling ready for the kill. I hope they catch the culprit and string him up."

Clara thought if anyone was a vulture circling it was Sir Richard, Viscount Westrow, but she didn't say anything.

Today Lawrence had asked her to meet with him and Jeremy after breakfast. "Plans for the future," he'd said and her heart dropped. She hoped her entreaties to

Lawrence to let her stay had worked and she wasn't being called in to hear bad news. Her feet dragged as she made her way to the office.

They took their seats in front of the desk, piled high with papers and ledgers. "We're not out of the woods, yet," Lawrence said. "The sale of the brewery will help, but there are the other mortgages to consider. Our financial position is far from secure." He passed them each a sheet of paper with figures on. Jeremy nodded, but it might as well have been Chinese as far as Clara was concerned.

"I'm trying to restore the hotel's reputation," Lawrence said. "But it's difficult to do after the events of last summer."

The vision of Dolly Deverill's body lying on the bed flashed into Clara's head.

"There are no further reports in the paper," Jeremy said. "It seems the world has moved on."

"Yes, but the murderer is still at large. Do men want to bring their families to stay in a hotel where a murder was committed? We still get carrion crows, picking over the bones of the case, but it's not enough to pay the running costs."

"Are the police any nearer to solving the case?" Jeremy asked.

"They have found nothing," Lawrence said, "despite endlessly questioning the staff and guests who were present in the hotel that day." His irritation was clear in his voice. "Someone must have seen something. It's hard to believe otherwise."

Clara had a vivid recollection of that day. She had good reason to remember it. It played constantly in her mind every day since and it haunted her dreams. "I saw something," she said and immediately regretted the words that had slipped unconsciously from her mind to her mouth.

Lawrence pounced on her words like a lion pouncing on its prey. "What! What did you see? Have you told the police?"

She shook her head. "No, nothing. Sorry... didn't mean..."

"If you saw something you should tell the police. You could be shielding a murderer."

Lawrence's words were scorpion stings. She was flustered. She couldn't lie to Lawrence, but she couldn't tell him the truth either. "I don't know... I saw..." her face flamed. "I thought I saw... someone..."

"Someone who could have been the murderer?"

"No. Just someone... hanging about... outside... not in the hotel..."

"She didn't say because she returned to the hotel with a man," Jeremy said, a matter of fact tone to his voice. "Am I correct, Clara?"

Clara's breath seemed to leave her body of its own accord. Her head swam. Heat flashed through her. She'd let Lawrence down, let her family down. Now she had to face Lawrence's wrath. She pressed her lips together and nodded.

"A man who took advantage of her and has left her with child," Jeremy said.

Lawrence's eyes nearly popped out of his head. His face twisted in disbelief. He had the startled look of a rabbit caught in torchlight. "Clara, this can't be true. I don't believe... You mean he...?" He stared at her as the minutes ticked by. "No. I don't believe it. I won't believe it. It can't be true."

Clara hung her head. "I'm sorry," she whispered. "It's true. I am with child."

She'd never seen him look so wretched. He shook his head, still unable to believe what he was hearing. "When? When did this terrible thing happen?"

Tears streamed down Clara's face. "The day of the Coronation," she whispered, wishing the ground would open up and swallow her.

Lawrence looked aghast. She could see the thoughts running through his brain like wild hares. He looked perplexed. "He did that and you never said anything. You never said anything to the police?"

A stillness fell over the room, like the silence before the storm. Clara heard Lawrence's breathing and her own heart pumping in her chest. She saw confusion, anger and betrayal on his face as he realised the enormity of her predicament. He dropped his head in his hands.

"It's all my fault," he said. "I've been too busy with the hotel to pay attention to you. Father trusted me. I promised to look after you, be responsible for you, and I've let him down, let you down." He raised his head. "Who was it? It's not too late. Tell me and I'll find him…"

"No need," Jeremy said. "Arrangements have been made."

"Arrangements!" Lawrence jumped up. "What arrangements?" He stood, towering over Jeremy. "You knew and you didn't tell me? You let this happen and said nothing?" His fists were clenched and Clara could see them coming to blows.

"Clara asked me not to," Jeremy said. "And I respected her wishes. It doesn't mean that I don't feel the same about it as you do. I'd like to thrash the living daylights out of him, but it's Clara's reputation that's at stake. So it's her choice what happens next."

At the mention of Clara's reputation Lawrence relaxed a little. He unclenched his fists as he paced the room. "Arrangements, you said. Perhaps you'd be kind enough to tell me what these arrangements are. Or am I to be kept in the dark about them too?" His voice, icy calm, rose with his anger.

Jeremy looked at Clara. He reached out and squeezed her hand. "Clara has more courage, integrity and good sense than the both of us," he said. "She's agreed to go into a retreat where she can have the child in safety and it will be taken care of. Afterwards she can return here, her reputation intact, and no one will be any the wiser."

"Unbelievable!" Lawrence roared still pacing the room. "You two are unbelievable. Did you really imagine that I would agree to this… this… subterfuge? To see my sister so badly used and say nothing? Whoever did this must be made to pay. Who was it, Clara?"

Jeremy stood to face Lawrence. "Get off your high-horse, Lawrence. I don't give a fig for the family's reputation, but I thought you did. If this gets out the Fitzroy name will be fodder for the most salacious gossip in every pub and drinking club in London. Do you think Papa would approve of that?"

Clara watched her brothers facing off against each other. She felt on firmer ground now. Lawrence knew the worst and he was just as inept at dealing with it as Jeremy had been. Their male pride had been wounded, their vulnerability exposed and they wanted revenge. She felt the power of her position. She'd keep her secret and there was nothing either of them could do about it. "I won't tell you who," she said, "but I will tell you who I saw hanging around the hotel that day. I saw Jack Carter. Daisy Carter's little brother."

"Jack Carter?" Lawrence dropped into his chair. "He's just a lad. You think he…?"

"No. Like I said. I saw him hanging around outside the hotel. He saw me and I thought keeping quiet would save my reputation, but it's a bit late now."

"They haven't found that lad who was on the door yet, then?" Jeremy asked. "He'd know who went into the hotel."

"No," Lawrence said. "The police have been looking but they can't find him."

Relieved at diverting their attention Clara rose from her chair. "If that's all," she said.

"Wait a minute." Lawrence sat up. "You need to tell the police what you saw. It won't go away until the bastard is caught and hanged."

Clara sighed. "I don't think so," she said. "I promised someone I wouldn't, but I can't stop you if that's what you want, bearing in mind what I said."

She saw Lawrence thinking it over, thoughts clicking through his brain. Her reputation put against the unlikely chance that Jack Carter could turn out to be a killer. No contest. Lawrence valued reputation above anything.

*

The next morning Daisy went to the office to collect the schedule of arrivals and departures so she could give instructions to the chambermaids. "Can you stay, please, I want a word," Mr Lawrence said.

Daisy's heart fluttered. As far as she knew she hadn't done anything wrong and there'd been no more complaints about the chambermaids since Miss Whitney left. She sat and waited. Mr Lawrence looked uncomfortable, but not as uncomfortable as she felt.

"I just wanted to ask you about Miss Mulroony, the pastry cook Mrs T took on before the Coronation."

"Matilda? Yes."

"I understand she's engaged to the police constable err Perkins isn't it?"

"Yes, sir. Constable Perkins and a lovely couple they make. They're not intending to marry until the autumn if that's what you're worrying about. Mrs T already has her eye on a girl she can train up to take her place, so everything will carry on as usual." Daisy smiled with relief.

"Thank you, but that wasn't what I wanted to ask. I understand you often speak with Constable Perkins and I wondered if he had any further news about the terrible events of the summer. Inspector Rolleston hasn't been very forthcoming on the subject. I wondered if you'd heard whether there are any other suspects, or people seen in the area at the time who had no purpose being there."

"I'm sure I don't know what you mean, sir. Constable Perkins has been the soul of discretion. I've heard nothing that you wouldn't read in the newspaper, sir." She did of course know exactly what he meant. Miss Clara must have said something. And her with the biggest secret of all.

Mr Lawrence took an exasperated breath. "To put it bluntly, Miss Carter – Daisy, I understand that your brother Jack was seen outside the hotel on that day."

Daisy took a breath. She had to remain calm. "Indeed he was, sir. As I told Miss Clara, he was passing on his way to visit a friend in King's Cross. He didn't come into the hotel as he knew I would be watching the parade with some of the other staff. Mrs T would have said if he'd come in."

"Mrs T? Ah yes. I see."

"Oh. You were wondering if he saw anyone hanging around, or anyone who shouldn't have been there? Well, he did see Miss Clara going into the hotel with a gentleman, sir. A soldier I believe. A man in uniform anyway."

That perked Mr Lawrence's interest. "A soldier, you say. Err any idea which regiment?"

"No, sir. Jack didn't mention it to police either, sir, him being aware of the damage that would cause to Miss Clara's reputation."

Mr Lawrence looked more discomforted than ever.

"You can rest assured that I won't say anything either, sir. A fragile thing, reputation, isn't it, sir? Once lost it can never be regained." She stood up ready to go. "If that's all?"

"Yes. Thank you, Daisy."

Daisy opened the door, then turned and said, "Oh, sir. I do hope Miss Clara is feeling better now. She's been quite poorly lately. I hope it's nothing serious."

From the expression on his face Daisy knew he'd got her meaning. One up to me, Miss Clara, she thought as she closed the door.

Chapter Twenty Nine

February, herald of spring, brought warmer weather. The snow melted and heavy rain sent people scurrying along streets huddled beneath umbrellas, jumping over puddles and rushing past shops not even stopping to pass the time of day with neighbours. Even the endless construction around the docks came to a halt as the Thames broke its banks and flooded the marshes.

The newspapers were filled with reports of troops returning from Africa. Reports that Daisy noticed were read by at least two of the Fitzroy family. She wasn't surprised to see Mr Lawrence reading *The Times* before breakfast, but Clara asking to see the paper when she took tea in the tea room did surprise her.

"I want to see if my cousin Henrietta's wedding is in there," she said by way of explanation when she saw Daisy's surprise.

The chatter in the kitchen was mainly about the cold weather, the rain and Matilda's plans for her wedding.

"That Inspector Rolleston's been in to see Mr Lawrence," Hollis said when he came into the kitchen. "I just saw 'im leave. I wonder if there's been any developments."

"Developments? I doubt it. Probably came to tell 'im they're closing the case. It's been months and they don't pull out all the stops when it's someone in 'er profession," Barker said. "Probably one of her clients."

"Kitty took 'em tea," Mrs T said. "Couldn't tell owt though."

"I'll go get the tray," Daisy said. "I've got to go up there anyway."

When she reached Mr Lawrence's office it was empty. The tea tray sat on a side table, cups still in their saucers on the desk. She went to retrieve the cups. The newspaper lay on the desk. Her heart jumped into her throat when she saw it folded open at a page with the headline *Body in Thames linked to Fitzroy Hotel Murder.*

She almost dropped the cup she was holding. She picked the paper up and scanned the text. Near the bottom of the column the name Felix Benton jumped out at her. Alarm surged through her veins. Thought whirred through her brain. A body in the Thames. Felix Benton. That necklace. Jack and Dan…

She tried to read more but, hearing footsteps outside, she quickly put the paper down and picked up the tray, almost colliding with Mr Lawrence as she made for the door.

"Sorry, sir," she said trying to recover despite the storm raging in her chest. "I hope the inspector had good news, sir. About the… err… events of the summer?"

Mr Lawrence looked at her and her heart fluttered. She'd overstepped the mark. He sighed. His face crumpled, She'd never seen him look so defeated. Her heart went out to him.

"Well, it's in all the newspapers so I might as well tell you." He swung into his chair. "They've found a body in the river. Apparently the necklace that was stolen from Mrs Fortescue Jones was in the dead man's pocket. Inspector Rolleston asked me to confirm that it was indeed the necklace that had been stolen. I merely said it looked like it." He shrugged. "There's nothing conclusive, but it will open the whole can of worms again and the name of the hotel, our name, will be plastered all over the newspapers. As if we didn't have enough to contend with."

"I'm sorry, sir," she said.

As soon as she'd taken the tray back to the kitchen she went in search of a newspaper. She found one abandoned on a table in the tea room with the remnants of someone's breakfast. She turned to the page with the item on it, sank onto a chair and started reading. As she read her heart beat faster and faster. When she heard someone coming she quickly folded the paper and shoved it under her apron. She picked up the remains of the breakfast on the table ready to clear it away.

"You shouldn't be doing that," Ruby said. "Mrs T sent me up to clear plates."

Daisy smiled. "I just happened to be passing," she said. "But I'll leave you to it."

"Thanks," Ruby said. "Mrs T'd be at me again if she finds you doing my job."

"Sorry," Daisy said and hurried out. She dashed upstairs to one of the rooms she knew would be empty, sat on the bed and read the rest of the news report. It said that the police thought the body had been washed into the Thames as a result of the recent flooding. *A preliminary examination has revealed that, thanks to the peat contained in the marshes, the body has been reasonably well preserved, despite the man having died sometime ago.* Then there was a bit about the preservation of bodies in peat being a natural phenomenon due to the pH levels of bog acids. She skipped that bit.

She read on: *The deceased has been identified as Felix Benton of Silvertown, a man well known to the police. A full post-mortem and a thorough investigation will be carried out to ascertain the nature of his injuries and the cause of death.*

A bit further on she read: *An item of jewellery found on the deceased person could link him to the burglary and murder of Miss Dolly Deverill at The Fitzroy Hotel, in London on Coronation Day.*

Inspector Rolleston, who headed up the investigation, was at pains to point out that there was no conclusive evidence to support that fact and inquiries were ongoing. He urged anyone with any information about the murder of Miss Dolly Deverill on Coronation Day or the death of Mr Felix Benton to come forward. The supply of such information would be treated with utmost discretion and in the strictest confidence.

The police were also interested in the whereabouts of Alfred Elsworthy, 16, formerly a porter at The Fitzroy Hotel who they think may be able to help them with their inquiries.

She dropped the paper into her lap, her hands shaking. She struggled to find breath. *A full post-mortem and thorough investigation.* The words kept going round and round in her brain like an everlasting carousel. What would they find? *Well preserved.* Did that include fingerprints? Whose fingerprints would they find? Would Jack have left any prints on the body? Would anyone remember seeing him and Dan carrying Felix along the road on the day before his brother's wedding? No one had asked any questions when Felix disappeared, but now he'd turned up dead would memories surface? Would people talk? They'd try to trace his last movements. Would Jessie remember seeing him and telling him about the necklace, that damned necklace that she'd given to

Daisy? Questions ran through her brain like stampeding horses, until she could stand it no more.

She took a breath and tried to calm her racing heart. She needed to keep calm and carry on as though nothing untoward had happened. Jack was gone. They'd never find him even if they wanted to.

She struggled through the rest of the day, avoiding people as best she could. She didn't think she'd be able to cope if they started talking about it, which they were bound to do eventually. The events of that evening played in her mind, over and over. She'd have to go home and see Jessie. Find out what she remembered, what people in Silvertown who knew Felix were saying. Jack was gone. She couldn't do anything about that, except hope and pray that he was safe and living a good life and looking after Dan.

That night she dreamt about him, seeing him and Dan walking across a golden prairie. The sun was setting. He turned and smiled at her, then he disappeared and she woke up in a cold sweat.

Oh Jack, she thought. Be safe.

Chapter Thirty

Inspector Rolleston arrived the next morning with Constable Perkins. They each had a photograph of Felix Benton. They questioned all the staff again about their memories of that day and whether anyone had seen Felix Benton hanging around the hotel.

Daisy pouted and shook her head when Constable Perkins showed her the photograph. "No. Sorry. Never seen him," she said. Then he asked about Alfred Elsworthy, the porter who was on the door that day.

"You can't think he did it," Daisy said her voice filled with righteous indignation. She tried to recall the lad who'd been on the door. He hadn't been with them long so she hadn't got to know him at all. She recalled he was fond of horses – or was it horseracing? She couldn't remember. "He was a nice lad. He wouldn't hurt a fly. Wanted to get on in the business."

In the kitchen speculation was also rife.

"I liked Alfred," Kitty said. "I can't think ill of him."

"I've yet to meet a young lad you didn't like," Hollis said, which earned him a sharp nudge in the ribs from Kitty. "But I agree. Alfred wouldn't kill anyone. Hardly said boo to a goose. I do wonder what happened to him though."

"I can't think why they'd be looking for anyone else if that dead chap did it. They say he had the goods on 'im. Good riddance to bad rubbish, I say."

"Yes but it's not conclusive. He could have bought the necklace from the killer. Doesn't mean he stole it."

"Possession is nine tenths of the law," someone else said. And so it went on, the arguments going round and round until Daisy sent them all back to work.

*

Inspector Rolleston himself interviewed Clara, who wasn't in the best of moods. She'd had a letter from her mother telling her she'd be visiting and expected Clara to return home with her, *Where it would be appropriate for them to entertain people at the house while they were in mourning.* Obviously Mama thought her remaining in London was not only inappropriate, but also a missed opportunity to meet eligible young men in the county who would call on the pretext of offering their condolences.

Clara glanced at her refection in the mirror. It wouldn't take her mother more than five seconds to realise her condition. She didn't go out these days as it was becoming difficult to disguise the thickening of her waist and the extra weight she was carrying. She'd had Daisy let out all her dresses, but, now six months gone, it was impossible to deny it much longer. She'd have to go to the coast before her mother could come to London.

She couldn't travel alone; it wouldn't be, in her mother's words, appropriate. So she'd have to speak to Lawrence to make arrangements for someone to travel with her. She couldn't think either he or Jeremy would want to be seen with a woman in the middle stages of pregnancy, so she'd have to think of someone else. Someone she could trust to keep their mouth shut. Someone who had probably already guessed her condition and who could be persuaded to keep quiet about it. Now who could she think of like that?

She found Inspector Rolleston irritatingly impudent. He had no manners and she had no time for him. She glanced at the photograph he showed her. "I can assure you I would remember if I ever saw such a villainous face. It's horrid. Please take it away."

"Can you tell me anything more? Anything else you remember about that day? Who was on the door for instance?"

"I really can't recall. It's so long ago now. There was a lot going on and I'd hardly be likely to notice a doorman would I?"

"His name's Alfred Elsworthy. He's sixteen and was employed here as a porter."

"Really? Well, if he worked for the family he'd be honest, loyal, reliable and thoroughly trustworthy. If you think he had anything to do with the murder you are quite wrong. Now, I have a headache coming on so, if that's all." She waved him away.

He touched his forelock. "Thank you anyway, Miss Fitzroy."

She sighed as she watched him go. They're clutching at straws, she thought. Completely out of their depth.

*

When Daisy was called into Mr Lawrence's office again her stomach churned. Had he told Inspector Rolleston about Jack hanging around outside the hotel? Were the police now looking for him?

He smiled when she walked in. He should smile more often, she thought, it suits him. "You wanted to see me?"

"Please." He indicated the chair where she should sit. "What I'm about to say to you is a matter quite delicate and confidential. I must first be assured that no word of our conversation will go outside of this room."

That surprised Daisy. "Of course. You have my word. Utmost discretion. It goes without saying."

"It's about Miss Clara. You have noticed, you said yourself, she has been quite poorly of late."

Daisy nodded. Now it was becoming clear.

"Arrangements have been made for her to visit a friend on the coast where she will stay until she regains her health. The thing is, she requires someone she knows well to be with her." He swallowed as though trying to find the words. Daisy thought how handsome he looked when he blushed. "She has asked me to enable you to go with her."

Daisy gasped. "Me? Go to the coast? What about my job here?"

Lawrence sighed and sat back. "Well, we will miss you of course. I'm not sure how we'll manage but…"

Daisy's mind whirled. Her go to the coast with Miss Clara? The thought of leaving London while the police investigated Felix Benton's death might seem appealing, but then if she wasn't here… she'd never know what was going on. Anything could happen. Then there was her job. She couldn't afford to lose that. "I don't know, sir. I'd have to give it some thought. I mean this is very sudden. My family… I don't know what to say."

"It would only be for a few months until… until Clara was quite well. She needs someone with her who understands her… err… situation. Someone who will not take advantage, or spread vicious rumours to sully her reputation." He became quite agitated. "My sister's reputation is paramount. You must see that."

"Yes, sir. Of course. But still…" Daisy's mind raced. Then she had another thought. One that might solve her other problem. "There is someone," she said.

"I have a sister. Her husband is away, working up North and she's looking for employment. She has recently lost a child and, being a married woman, is far more likely to be aware of any difficulties your sister may encounter due to her... err... ill health. I'm sure she would appreciate the chance to see the coast and would be far more use to your sister than I would be."

Relief flitted across Lawrence's face. This wasn't going to be as difficult as he had imagined. "Your sister? A married lady? Well, it certainly sounds like a viable proposition. Of course I would need to see her and Miss Clara would have to agree." He smiled, then frowned as though struck by another thought. "She'd have to be discreet and understand the need for complete confidentiality."

"Of course, sir. She's well able to keep..." She was going to say keep her mouth shut, but thought better of it. "...Be discreet. I'll vouch for her if it puts your mind at rest."

"Very well. I'll speak to Miss Clara. I must admit I value your presence here and would struggle to replace you."

"Thank you, sir." Daisy's heart swelled at the compliment.

It was late afternoon before Miss Clara called Daisy to her room.

"Mr Lawrence tells me you have a sister who could accompany me to the coast where I am to visit friends in order to recover my health. Is that so?"

"Yes, Miss Clara. Her husband is working away at the moment so she is able to take on a temporary position."

Clara huffed. "I wanted you to accompany me, but it seems that my brother values your services more highly than he values my health."

"I'm sure he didn't mean anything like that," Daisy said. "He just wants what's best for everyone. My sister is far more capable than I would be to assist in your particular circumstances."

"Is that so?"

"She's a married woman who's lost a child. I think that qualifies her to have knowledge and experience of situations I would be hard pressed to understand."

Miss Clara was obviously not appeased. "I swear he cares more for this hotel than he does for me."

Daisy saw tears glistening in her eyes. She put it down to her condition and the hormones. She recalled Jessie being very on edge when she was pregnant. "I'm sure that's not the case, Miss Clara."

Miss Clara sighed. "Very well. I'm leaving in the morning, on the ten o'clock train. Tell her to meet me at the station. No, better still, you bring her to the station in time for the train. I'll decide then if she's to come with me. If I decide not then you will accompany me. Is that understood?"

"Yes, Miss Clara."

"What's her name?"

"Jessie. Jessie... Ferguson." Daisy hadn't told Mr Lawrence that Jessie was only sixteen and married to the brother of the dead man in the paper. The name Benton was splashed across all the pages. She'd have to warn Jessie not to say anything.

Miss Clara sighed again. Daisy saw the helplessness in her eyes. She was in a position she hadn't asked for, struggling to cope, fearful of what lay ahead of her and unable to do anything about it. For the first time since she'd met her, Daisy felt sorry for Miss Clara Fitzroy. She had no more control over her life than any of them did.

Chapter Thirty One

Daisy caught the omnibus to Silvertown. She found Jessie in the kitchen arguing with her mother. The newspaper lay open on the table.

"Look what the cat's dragged in," Nora said when Daisy walked into the room.

"Miss High-and-Mighty. Too good for the likes of us," Jessie said. "Slumming it are you?"

Daisy knew she deserved all she got. She'd stayed away as life was easier if she did so. She didn't want to get mixed up in their rows and disagreements but she needed Jessie's help now. "I'm sorry," she said. "It's been difficult what with—"

"Aye. Difficult to drag yourself away from the cosy billet you've found for yourself. What brings you 'ome now? Trouble is it?"

"No. It's good news. Miss Clara's looking for someone to go to the coast with her and stay for a couple of months. I thought of Jessie." She took her hat off and unbuttoned her coat. "I'll have some tea if you're making one."

Nora turned to put the kettle on. Jessie glared at her. "You thought of me? What you setting me up for now? Ain't you done enough to ruin my life? Can't you leave me alone?"

Daisy sank onto the chair next to her. "I know you've been through a lot. I thought a trip to the seaside might make you feel better. A chance to get out of London. Get away for a while. And you'd be well paid."

"Paid? How well paid?"

"Well, there are conditions. Let's have a cup of tea and I'll tell you all about it. You can make up your mind then."

Over tea and some of Nora's fresh baked scones with jam, Daisy told them about Miss Clara, her condition, the place she was going and the part Jessie would be required to play. She emphasised the need for discretion.

"I can keep me mouth shut, if that's what you mean," Jessie said. "I ain't no grass nor blabbermouth."

"Miss posh Clara up the duff," Nora said. "Fancy that." Daisy didn't miss the satisfied smirk on her face.

"You'll have to say you're eighteen," Daisy said, "and your name is Mrs Ferguson."

Jessie frowned. "Mrs who? Why?"

"Well I couldn't tell him you were Mrs Benton, could I? Not with what's in all the papers."

Jessie looked chastened.

"And your husband's working up North."

"What, like our Jack and Dan?" Nora said. "Or is it a different North?" She glared at Daisy. She must have guessed the lie, but Daisy wasn't about to enlighten her further.

"We have to meet Miss Clara at the station for the ten o'clock train. I'll go with you. She has the last word, but as long as you do your best to make a good impression. I've told her about the baby, so she'll be sympathetic." Daisy wasn't at all sure of the last bit, but she needed Jessie to agree or she'd have to go and that was the last thing she wanted. Anyway, it would be good for Jessie to get away. See a different side of life.

Jessie still looked reluctant. "How long will I be away for?"

"A few months at most. You'll be staying in a grand house, all found and you won't find Mr Lawrence ungenerous when it comes to pay. By the time you come back you'll have enough to set yourself up doing whatever you chose."

"What do you think, Ma?"

"You're doing nowt sitting around here. You've a good head on your shoulders. Might be a chance to make somat of yourself."

Jessie nodded and relief washed over Daisy. That settled they spent the rest of the evening talking about what was in the paper.

"Can't believe owt you read in the paper," Nora said. "I see they're looking for a lad worked at the hotel. Was 'e in it do you think?"

"No. Definitely not," Daisy said. "He's just a lad."

"So was Felix when 'e started thieving," Nora said. "Could be 'im an' that lad were in it together."

Daisy shook her head. Gossip and speculation were another reason to get Jessie out of London before she remembered Daisy taking the necklace. Thankfully the paper only mentioned jewellery, nothing specific. Giving her the opportunity to get away and earn good money might help heal the rift between them too.

Now it depended on Miss Clara being agreeable, which was never a foregone conclusion.

The next morning Daisy met Jessie at the end of the road in time to get to the station for the ten o'clock train. She was pleased to see that Jessie had made an effort. She wore the outfit she'd had made for her wedding, her best shoes and carried a not too tatty suitcase. She'd brushed her hair into a bun at the back of her head, under her hat and put some lipstick on. She was playing a part. Daisy had given her the chance to be someone else and it was clear she was determined to take it.

"Well done, Jessie," Daisy said when she met her. "Remember, Mrs Ferguson, you're eighteen."

Jessie smiled. "Don't worry, sis. I won't mess this up. Thanks for giving me a chance."

Daisy's heart fluttered. Everything was going to be all right.

When they arrived at the station Mr Lawrence and Miss Clara were waiting for them. Miss Clara looked Jessie up and down. "She's a lot younger than I thought she'd be," she said.

"I'm eighteen," Jessie said. Same as you, Daisy thought.

"We'll have to get her some new clothes." Miss Clara wrinkled her nose. "Still, I suppose she'll do."

Daisy relaxed, Jessie grinned and Lawrence heaved a sigh of relief. Once he'd got them settled in the private compartment he'd booked so they wouldn't be disturbed, he offered Daisy a lift back to the hotel. "I can't tell you how grateful I am," he said. "Knowing Clara's in safe hands. It's a weight off my mind."

Mine too, Daisy thought as her heart fluttered like a bird about to take flight.

*

On the train Clara took out the Jane Austen novel she planned to read. Jessie sat staring out of the window at the passing buildings as the train pulled out of London.

"Have you ever been to the coast before, Mrs Ferguson?" Clara asked.

"Once. A long time ago," Jessie said her voice warm with the memory. "It was magical. There was a pier that stretched right out into the sea. You could walk right over the water."

Clara smiled. "I doubt there'll be such a thing where we're going."

Jeremy had sent her a set of instructions and rules when he booked her place at The Grange. She took it out of her bag. "From now on you're to refer to me as Mrs Smith," she said. "You'll be Miss Jones. It's a condition of residence to ensure anonymity. I hope you understand."

Jessie's eyebrows went up but she said, "Yes, Mrs Smith."

"You will call me 'ma'am'."

"Yes, ma'am." Jessie smiled. She's quite pretty when she smiles, Clara thought.

"The place we're going to is a retreat. Privacy and discretion are to be our watchwords."

"So I understand, ma'am."

Clara smiled. At least the girl has something about her. "The rules are very strict. Here." She passed Jessie the paper and watched her face as she read it.

The *No men allowed on site with the exception of Doctor Klein and Doctor Woodleigh* had made her smile. At over six months gone she wasn't going to welcome an advance from any man, no matter how handsome or rich he was. Anyway, she'd learned her lesson where men were concerned.

No visitors was another rule. However, *In an emergency and at Doctor Klein's discretion, an appointment for a meeting in the gatehouse may be made. Mixing with other residents is discouraged to maintain anonymity. Residents may walk in the extensive grounds or along the private stretch of seafront. Gentle exercise is encouraged. Facilities include a library and spa which can be booked by appointment. There is also a small chapel for quiet contemplation.*

Meals will be served in suites at the following times: Then the times were set out. *Menus will be supplied daily. The Ethos of The Grange is calm tranquillity and individual reflection.* Clara read that to mean they should think about what they had done to get themselves in the sort of mess where a retreat was needed.

Jessie nodded and handed the paper back to Clara. "All very straight forward and clear, ma'am."

Clara began to warm to her. Perhaps bringing her instead of Daisy wasn't such a bad idea. She was certainly more biddable than her sister. "What's your first name?" she asked.

"Jessie."

"Jessie Ferguson? Well, I shall call you Jessie, when I'm not calling you Miss Jones."

When they arrived they were greeted by Doctor Klein, a well-upholstered middle-aged man with a fleshy face, and wispy, dark curls turning grey. Clara thought he looked fatherly and was immediately reassured.

"Welcome, Mrs Smith, Miss Jones." He shook their hands. "I hope your stay here will be restorative." His voice betrayed a slight German accent. "Allow me to introduce Mrs Merryweather who will be looking after you." He indicated the plump, matronly lady standing next to him. Clara wondered if that was her real name or an alias like theirs.

"Welcome," she said. "Your trunk has arrived and been unpacked. Come with me and I'll show you to your rooms."

They followed her up the stairs to a set of rooms on the first floor. The room they entered was a small sitting room. Two comfortable armchairs sat either side of a fireplace, the fire already lit but barely warming the room. It reminded Clara of the nursery in the house where she grew up. A small round table and chairs stood near the window, the exact same sort of table she'd sat at for nursery tea with her dolls, her brothers and Nanny Gibbs when she was five years old. That felt like a long time ago. She was pleased to see a writing desk with an upright chair against the wall. At least she could write home.

The suite contained two bedrooms, one large where the contents of Clara's trunk had been unpacked into a single wardrobe and a smaller room containing a single bed and a chest of drawers with a wash bowl and water jug on top. A small bathroom opened off the main bedroom.

Clara walked to the window and looked out. She gazed over the immaculate lawns, a short stretch of promenade and a shingle beach. Mist hung over the sea. Pearl grey clouds drifted across a charcoal sky.

"I hope you'll be comfortable," Mrs Merryweather said. "If you need anything please ring." She indicated a bell rope hanging beside the fireplace.

"Tea. I'd like some tea please, after our journey."

Mrs Merryweather's eyebrows rose. "Lunch will be served at one o'clock," she said.

Clara's face fell. Mrs Merryweather must have seen her dismay. She relented. "I'll send the girl up with some tea," she said. "Now, if there's nothing else I'll leave you to settle in."

"Thank you."

Mrs Merryweather hurried out. As she closed the door Clara saw the *Rules of The Grange* pinned to the back of the door. I am five years old again, she thought. Then she remembered how much Lawrence had had to fork out for her place there and realised how lucky she was.

Chapter Thirty Two

The following week Daisy decided to visit her mother to see if she'd heard from Jessie. She'd recommended her on an impulse as a way of getting out of going herself and was now wondering whether she'd made the right decision. Jessie hadn't written and she had no address to write to Jessie but she thought her sister might write to Ma.

When she arrived Nora had just finished doing the washing so Daisy helped her peg it out in the backyard to dry. The day was unusually warm for early March and, had the backyard been anywhere else, it would have been quite pleasant. As it was the air was filled with soot and smoke from the factories and the pungent smell ever present.

"I don't know why I bother," Nora said. "Takes ages to dry and when it does it carries the stench from the factories. Your dad's always complaining."

"Have you heard from Jessie?" Daisy asked. "I wondered how she was getting on."

"I 'aven't 'eard and I don't expect to. Jessie never was one for writing much. She ain't turned up on me doorstep. I take that as a good sign. Here, pass us a peg."

Daisy handed her a peg out of the basket on the floor.

"I do hope she's behaving herself. Miss Clara's not the easiest of people to please."

"You don't have to worry about our Jess. She knows which side 'er bread's buttered. She'll toe the line as long as she's being paid. I'd 'ave thought your Mr Lawrence would have heard if there was owt wrong."

"He hasn't said anything."

"No news is good news, so they say." Nora pegged up the last of her husband's shirts. "Are you staying for a cuppa?"

"Please."

In the kitchen Nora made the tea while Daisy sat at the table. "One good thing," Nora said, "Felix Benton didn't kill that tart at your place. I didn't reckon 'im for a killer. Thief, conman, cheat, twister, liar, pick-pocket, yes, but not a killer."

Daisy couldn't believe her ears. "What? Where did you hear that?"

"It's in the paper. Don't you read owt?"

"Where?"

Nora got the paper and showed Daisy the headline, *Dead man no longer suspect in Fitzroy Hotel Murder.* Daisy gasped and read on. The piece said Felix Benton, the man whose body was found floating in the Thames, had been ruled out and was no longer a suspect in the murder of Miss Deverill at The Fitzroy Hotel. It repeated the story of the body being found and the jewellery in the dead man's pocket being associated with the murder. It said further inquiries were being made and the matter of the murder of Miss Deverill remained under investigation.

Daisy's head swam. She couldn't believe what she'd read. Felix said he'd done it. "There must be some mistake."

"Not according to the paper. 'Course you can't always believe what you read, but that looks pretty clear. Unless you know owt about it?"

"No. No, of course not." A vivid memory spun through Daisy's head: the feel of Felix behind her, pulling up her skirt, saying what he was going to do to her. She even recalled his actual words: *I killed that tart. I 'ad her an' all, before I topped 'er, just like I'm going to 'ave you.*

Why would he say that if he hadn't done it? To impress her? Humiliate her further? Frighten her? Was he bragging about something he wished he'd done to intimidate her? It didn't make sense.

Her heart pounded and her hands shook as she put the paper down. "I have to go," she said. "Just remembered I have a few errands to run."

"So you want me to let you know if I hear from Jessie?"

"Yes. Please. It would put my mind at rest."

Nora nodded. "There's nowt so strange as folk," she muttered as Daisy hurried out.

Daisy rushed to catch the omnibus but first she bought a paper from the boy at the end of the road. "Anything interesting?" she asked him. If anyone knew about the goings on in Silvertown it would be the newsboys who heard all the gossip.

"Yeah. Felix Benton is innocent as a new born baby." He chuckled. "An' I'm the King of England."

She flicked through the paper on the bus, looking for any other items of news that might pertain to the story. There was nothing else.

She didn't go straight back to the hotel. Matilda had said that morning that she was going to the pictures with George Perkins that evening, so Daisy thought he must be coming off duty soon. If she made her way towards the police station she might catch him on his way back.

She saw him as she walked slowly up the road leading to the police station at the end of his beat. She fell into step with him. "Constable Perkins," she said. "What a lovely surprise."

"Miss Carter. Good to see you too." He nodded a greeting and touched his hat.

She appreciated he was on duty and may not want to talk to her, but it was worth a try. "I believe we're going in the same direction," she said. "May I walk with you?"

He hesitated. "All highly irregular," he said. "Still, I'm almost off duty so I suppose it will be all right. I trust you are keeping well."

She walked alongside him. "As well as can be expected with all the to-do at the hotel again. I understand that the man found in the Thames is no longer thought to be responsible for the death of one of our residents. I must say I find that quite disturbing."

"Disturbing? How so?"

"Well if he didn't do it then the murderer is still at large. I fear for the safety of myself and my staff. Are you sure there's been no mistake? I was convinced the man had done it. It made sense, him being a thief and a well known criminal."

Constable Perkins tipped his helmet to a lady passing who bid him good afternoon as they walked along. "No mistake," he said. "It's the fingerprints, see. His didn't match the ones found in Miss Deverill's room. He wasn't there."

"But surely… I mean being a burglar he may have been wearing gloves." The thought of Felix Benton wearing gloves to commit his crimes was outlandish even for Daisy to believe.

"No. His fingerprints were found in Mrs Fortescue-Jones's room and one or two others, but not Miss Deverill's. The fingerprints found in Miss

Deverill's room belonged to someone else. They didn't match any of the staff or the family." He gave a smug grin. "Unlike people, fingerprints don't lie."

Daisy felt chastened. "I'm sorry to hear that. I fear we may all be at risk if he strikes again."

They were approaching the station and Constable Perkins slowed. "I don't think you have anything to worry about. I shouldn't be telling you this but the latest thinking is that Miss Deverill was killed by someone she knew, someone she'd invited into her room, possibly someone she'd been with earlier. We now think it was personal, so you and the rest of the staff have no need to fear he will come back and strike again."

"Unless someone saw him," Daisy said. "He may want to come back and silence them." She shuddered.

"I understand you and most of the staff were at the procession, so you have nothing to fear on that count either."

"All of us except young Alfred," Daisy said. "You don't think…" She gasped.

"All I can say is that we are looking for Alfred Elsworthy and would like to speak to him. If you know of his whereabouts…"

"No," Daisy said. "That's the thing. He's gone and nobody's seen him. He didn't even stop to collect his pay. Don't you find that suspicious?"

Constable Perkins nodded. "If he saw who was with Miss Deverill he may be at risk. All the more essential that we find him before anyone else does."

They'd reached the police station. "Good day, Miss Carter, Daisy. Please don't worry yourself more than necessary. We have the matter in hand and you can rest assured we will do everything we can to find

Mr Elsworthy. Good day." He smiled and walked away.

Daisy huffed. Those damned fingerprints, she thought they'll hang Jack yet.

By the time Daisy got back to the hotel Matilda was getting ready to go out. "You look nice," she said. "Is that a new dress?"

"No. An old one, but I've added the lace collar and cuffs. What do you think?"

"I think you look beautiful and George Perkins is a lucky man."

"It's me who's lucky," Matilda said. "He's so clever and knowledgeable. I think he'll make detective one day."

"I'm sure you're right," Daisy said. "Have a good evening."

"We will. He's taking me to see Harry Houdini at The Alhambra."

"The famous escapologist? That should be entertaining. I believe he escaped from handcuffs in Scotland Yard."

"Yes. George thinks he's amazing."

Downstairs in the kitchen the rest of the staff were speculating over the news item in the paper. Barker had noticed it, even though it was on page five and he usually only read the sports pages.

"So, that geezer didn't do it," he said. "Police think it was someone else."

"I knew it," Mrs T said. "I thought that all along. Burglars don't kill people. If they see someone coming they run. Doesn't make sense to stay and get in worse trouble."

"Your right, Mrs T," Barker said. "Police think it's someone she knew."

"Woman like that. In her profession." Mrs T sniffed. "Probably one of her clients. Thought he'd get somat for nowt. When he couldn't have what 'e wanted 'e killed her."

"Police'll be looking into 'er personal life," Barker said. "Says 'ere they're gonna leave no stone unturned." He pouted. "Friend of Mr Jeremy weren't she? I 'spect they'll want a few more words with 'im."

Chapter Thirty Three

Clara soon settled in at The Grange. As the weather turned warmer she took walks either in the grounds, or along the seafront with Jessie who turned out to be a reasonably tolerable conversationalist, considering where she came from.

If the weather was cooler she'd sit and read while Jessie did some embroidery. She wrote to her mother telling her that she'd arrived safely. She made up stories about the people she hoped to meet and the parties she'd be attending. She mentioned several planned outings. *A trip along the coast is planned,* she wrote, *so it would be best to write to me care of the hotel. Lawrence will know where I am and can send your letters on.*

Then she wrote to Lawrence and Jeremy. *Please write and share your news or I shall die of boredom. Counting the days until I can come home.*

One day she went to reception to ask for an extra pillow as she found lying down in her condition uncomfortable.

"Mrs Smith isn't it?" the girl said. "What room would that be?"

"Room seven."

The girl made a note. Another girl appeared with the morning post, collected from the gatehouse.

"Are there any letters for me?" she asked. The girl shuffled through them. Clara noticed they were all addressed to Mrs Smith, only the room numbers differed. Saves remembering names, she thought, but the anonymity reassured her.

As time went on, March turned to April, the days lengthened and trees put on their spring coats. Being out of town and away from the hustle and bustle of London, Clara came to enjoy simple walks by the sea, the air sharp with salty spray. Some days the sea lapped the shingle beach, calm as a mill pond, on others the wind whipped the waves to crash onto the shore. Clara often stopped to stand at the railings and simply stare out, watching the seagulls floating on the breeze or screeching and swooping over the water. The vastness of sea and sky brought home to her how small and insignificant they all were with their worries and trivialities.

In the grounds of The Grange snowdrops gave way to daffodils and swathes of purple crocus. Apple blossom decked the trees with clouds of white. Tulips, Roses and Peonies came into flower filling the beds with colour. The scent of lavender drifted across lawns green and smooth as a billiard table.

Clara read books, wrote letters, played the piano in the music room, although reaching the keys became difficult. She booked treatments at the spa where a large German woman massaged her back and feet.

"We need get these knotens out," she said and rotated Clara's shoulders even harder.

She taught herself some new card games and filled her sketch pad with drawings. She even undertook to do a little embroidery although it wasn't her favourite pastime.

As the burden she carried got heavier she cursed the promise she had made to Jeremy about not doing away with it at the beginning. How do people manage, she thought, with this terrible lump having to be carried around? She swore, even when she married she'd never have children. It was too debilitating and seriously curtailed any chance of a social life.

It was only the presence of Jessie that kept her sane. The girl had spirit and a sense of humour. As the weeks went by she warmed to her. She asked her about her home life and her husband, but Jessie smiled and shook her head.

"Nothing to tell," she said and refused to comment further.

Clara sighed. Of course she shouldn't have asked. It was quite inappropriate. She'd only asked out of boredom, but it put the girl in an impossible situation. What would her mother say if she knew she was talking to servants as though they were friends? She'd say it was 'quite beyond the pale'.

Clara sat and looked at her rapidly increasing bump. "I suppose I'll end up talking to you," she said. "Really, I wish you'd just get on with it and I can be rid of you."

Chapter Thirty Four

The vision of Felix's body lying on the ground and Jack standing there with a brick in his hand stained Daisy's mind. She couldn't shift it. It kept going round and round like a carousel. Jack didn't mean to kill him, she knew that. He was protecting her. Felix would have killed her if it hadn't been for Jack. Guilt, like a stone, weighed inside her about that.

At Easter she had an afternoon off so she went to see her mother hoping she would be able to tell her the latest gossip about Felix's death, now that the dust had had time to settle.

The day was warm and the hotel quiet as people enjoyed spending their time out of doors making the most of the spring sunshine. Daisy caught the omnibus to Silvertown. When she arrived she found her mother in the kitchen as usual.

"Have you heard anything more about Felix's death?" she asked as casually as she could manage while drinking a cup of tea. "I haven't seen anything in the paper."

"They say 'e drunk 'iself to death," Nora said. "Got drunk, fell down, knocked 'iself out and lay on the marsh until 'e died. Wouldn't surprise me."

Daisy frowned. That didn't sound right. Perhaps Nora had confused him with someone else. "Drunk himself to death? Is that what they're saying?"

"What it said in the papers." She paused and drew her brows together. "I kept it back. It's here somewhere." She went to a drawer and shuffled through it. Eventually she brought out a folded newspaper. "Here, you have a look." She passed Daisy the local paper. Felix Benton being a Silvertown resident there was a full report on the inquest into his death.

Daisy's bewilderment grew as she read it. It said Felix Benton had last been seen in The Dog and Duck Public House on the edge of the marshes. The landlord had refused to serve him as he appeared to be already intoxicated. However, when his body washed up on the shore, an empty whisky bottle was discovered on his person. The landlord confirmed that it had been stolen from the storeroom of The Dog and Duck. It was presumed that he had drunk it and, highly intoxicated, fallen into a gully. There were signs of concussion from a wound on the back of his head possibly caused by hitting a rock as he fell. The body had lain there undiscovered for several months until the flood water lifted it and carried it into the river. The medical report gave cause of death to be hypothermia due to exposure. Intoxication was a contributory factor. The coroner recorded a verdict of Death by Misadventure and the case was closed.

Daisy was stunned. Hypothermia? He was on the marshes? Surely Jack hadn't taken him there? She thought they'd left him somewhere near the docks. How could he have got to the marshes? None of it made sense. She wished she could ask Jack. She missed him more than ever. He seemed so far away.

She read the report again not believing any of it. If Felix had been seen after Jack left him then he was still alive. Jack didn't kill him. *Concussion from a wound on the back of his head* she read again. Jack certainly did that, but he wasn't dead. The words kept repeating themselves in her brain.

Felix had got to the marshes, east of the docks, found a pub, stolen a bottle of whisky and drunk it.

That's what killed him. A chaos of confusion filled her head.

The case was closed. No one was to be held responsible. The police weren't looking for a killer. Jack had run away to America for nothing. He hadn't killed anyone. If only she could let him know that she'd feel better. She knew it would play on his mind – the guilt. Now she had the means to relieve him of it but no way of letting him know.

Still, Felix was dead and she had to admit Jack had contributed to that, so perhaps going away had been the best thing after all. Plus, they were still looking for Miss Deverill's killer and Jack's fingerprints could well be in her room.

Daisy soon found that Matilda was the best source of information about what the police knew and what they were thinking about the case. Her frequent gasps of: "George thinks this," "George thinks that," or "George says this," and "George says that," rather than being annoying were a useful guide to their progress, although Daisy did wonder if she had a mind of her own.

"George says they're looking for a military man," was her latest pronouncement over lunch.

"A military man? Anyone in particular?" Daisy asked, aware that Jack had seen Miss Clara with a soldier on Coronation Day.

Matilda shrugged. "No. It's just the way she was killed. Her neck was broken, like they train soldiers to do in the army. That's what they think anyway." She beamed as she told them this latest titbit, thrilled to be the centre of attention. Daisy thought how much she'd changed since meeting George. The shy, retiring mouse who never said a word was gone and in its place a flower blossomed. Daisy was glad for her.

"I suppose that makes sense," Hollis said. "I mean, not everyone knows how to twist a head and break a neck. I certainly wouldn't."

"It's not as easy as it looks," Barker, who'd seen service in his younger days, said. "It's a knack. Not everyone can do it."

"I wouldn't mind having a go," Mrs T said. "There's few people I could mention…"

They all chuckled. Daisy thought about Felix. He was a bully and a thug, but a trained killer? And to kill a woman? That would go against the grain. Felix had threatened to kill her, but that could have been bravado. The drink talking. He might beat one up, but to kill with a twist of the neck? That takes a special skill. Perhaps the police were right. Felix didn't do it. Someone else did.

"I see they're still looking for Alfred," Barker said. "There's a picture in the paper. An artist's impression. It looks just like 'im."

"There are posters out too," Kitty said. "And flyers offering a reward."

"Yes. Mr Lawrence has been persuaded to offer £100 for information on his whereabouts," Daisy said, a note of disapproval in her voice. "If that doesn't help find him nothing will."

"I saw that police inspector coming out of Mr Lawrence's room," Hollis said. "He said he thought Alfred Elsworthy was the key to the whole case."

"No wonder they're looking for 'im. Poor lad's going to solve the case all by 'iself." Barker shook his head.

They all laughed.

"I hope they find him," Annie said. "I liked Alfred."

Chapter Thirty Five

One morning in late April, when the sun streamed in through the window in Clara's room, she felt a pain. Then, a little while later she felt another. She got up and walked around. Another stab of pain. She lay on the bed and called for Jessie. Was it beginning, the end of her discomfort? How soon would it all be over?

Jessie rang the bell and Mrs Merryweather appeared. She smiled as she examined Clara.

"It's a start," she said. "It'll be a little while yet. Have some tea and I'll come back in an hour or two."

"An hour or two! How long is this damn thing going to— aarrhh…" Clara howled.

"Good girl." Mrs Merryweather grinned. "You're doing fine. Miss Jones will take care of you. It'll be over before you know it." She nodded to Jessie. "I'll be back to see how she'd doing later."

Clara felt like a prize cow. She'd seen a cow give birth on one of the farms on the estate, before her grandfather… No she wouldn't think about that, but a vision of a bellowing cow in the cowshed filled her mind. That's what I look like, she thought, a bloody, broody, bellowing cow.

After a light lunch of scrambled eggs and smoked salmon, which Clara picked at, she was taken to the delivery suite downstairs.

That evening, after several hours of screaming, shouting, bellowing, cursing and howling, and in the calming presence of Doctor Klein, Clara's baby was born. She watched the nurse pick up a squiggly, wriggly, skinny, bundle of skin and bone and heard its pitiful cry.

"Is it all right?" she asked as sudden fear gripped her.

"It's a boy." The nurse smiled and wrapped him in a blanket.

"Let me see."

The nurse looked at Doctor Klein. He nodded and the nurse passed the bundle to Clara. As soon as she saw him, in that moment, her life changed forever.

The deepest feeling of pride and love filled her whole body as she held him in her arms. A great swell of emotion rose up inside her. This tiny scrap of fragile humanity was hers, part of her. He was perfect. A perfect little person, real and quite amazing. And so helpless. His vulnerability melted her heart. She'd given him life, brought him into the world. Now she had to take care of him. She wanted to protect him, keep him safe. She gazed at his screwed up face and saw the future ahead of him. "He's beautiful," she whispered. "Perfect."

"I'll take him now," the nurse said leaning over to retrieve him.

Suddenly Clara remembered her reason for being there, the arrangement she'd made to have him given away so she'd never have to see him again. Never see him grow up, or see the man he would become. Never be part of his life, or have him part of hers. Never know what might become of him or what his life would be. Never have a chance to be there when he needed her. It all felt very wrong.

The child in her arms snuffled. A tiny sound, like clearing his throat ready to speak, but he couldn't speak up for himself could he? He'd have no choice in the matter.

"No." She hugged him to her chest.

The nurse looked at Doctor Klein. He waved her away and pulled a chair up to the side of the bed next to Clara.

"I've changed my mind," Clara said as he sat down. "I want to keep him."

The doctor smiled. "Only natural," he said, "after you have given so much effort to have him. You want to keep him now, but this is not real, Mrs Smith." His kindly face creased into a smile, compassion glistened in his eyes. "When you recover and go back to your real life you will not want him then. You will feel differently. You will blame him for ruining your life, your reputation. It is not his fault, but you will blame him."

"No. Never. I'll never do that."

The doctor sighed. "You will come to resent him simply for existing. Although he has done nothing wrong. You may even come to hate him."

Clara looked at the innocent child sleeping in her arms. The doctor's words washed over her.

"If you keep him your reputation will be in shreds, your life ruined, you will lose your place in society and you will blame him. Even though he has done nothing, you will blame him."

Clara bit her lip, trying to hold back the tears threatening to stream down her face. "I won't," she whispered.

Doctor Klein touched her cheek, his eyes full of kindness. "You are no more than a child yourself. You have your whole life ahead of you. A life full of dresses and parties. You will go back to your loving family, friends, your social whirl. You will have liaisons, get married, have more children. You will forget him. You with your easy life." He looked at the child. "For him it will not be so good. The illegitimate son, the bastard. His life will be hard. Everyone will know, will talk about him, snigger at him. Is that what you want for him? A life of ignominy?"

"No. Of course not."

"Then let me find him a good home with a family who will care for him."

"But how will I know? How will I know if they really care for him?"

Doctor Klein took a breath. "Life is a chance we all have to take. If he is strong he will survive."

"And if he is not?"

The doctor shrugged.

Clara's determination grew. "What happens if I refuse to give him up?"

"This is not a prison. It is a place of retreat and reflection. I cannot force you to give up your child. I can only advise you with the voice of experience." His tone was one of reproach. "You are tired. You must sleep. When you wake you will feel differently. Give him to me now."

"No." Clara hugged him tighter.

The doctor motioned to a nurse who opened the door and called Jessie, who had been waiting outside, into the room. "Your maid will take the child."

He took the sleeping baby from her and passed it to a shocked Jessie.

"Oh. He's beautiful," Jessie gasped, her hazel eyes lighting up as she took the child into her arms.

"Come. Follow me." Doctor Klein strode out and Jessie followed.

The nurse helped Clara into a wheelchair and took her back to her room where she fell into a deep, dreamless sleep.

Clara awoke to pale morning light filtering through thin curtains. Rain spattered the windows and a light mist clouded the sky. It looked a dismal day. Memories of the previous evening sifted through her mind. She recalled Doctor Klein's face as he spoke to her. His words about feeling different when she awoke echoed through her head. Did she feel any differently? She didn't think so.

She gazed at her empty arms even as her breasts swelled in readiness for nursing the absent child. That would go after a day or two Mrs Merryweather had assured her. What did she know about the loss of a child? She tried to visualise the life ahead of her, at home, with Lawrence and Jeremy. It felt strange and unreal. Could she really carry on as though nothing had happened? Pursue a life of pleasure, fun and parties, a social whirl devoid of responsibility?

She didn't think so, not while the image of the child, his screwed up, trusting face and vulnerability filled her mind. She felt a surge of protectiveness towards him. If not her, who would protect him? Who would ease his path in life?

She thought of her father. What would he say? He'd tell her to face up to her responsibilities. That was his way. He'd never shielded his children from the realities of life. They'd had to make their own way. Then she thought of her mother. Elvira would be shocked, distraught, devastated at the loss of opportunity for her daughter, madder than a raging bull, but she was a mother. Clara felt a glimmer of hope that she would at least try to understand.

She heard a whimper from the next room and Jessie shushing. He was awake, they were both awake.

She called for Jessie to bring in the child. Perhaps if she saw him it would all become clear.

She heard Jessie shuffling about, probably putting on a wrap, lifting the baby, distressed at having woken him.

"I'm sorry," Jessie said. "I tried to get him back to sleep."

"It's all right. I just want to look at him."

Jessie laid him in Clara's arms. The great swell of love she'd felt the day before returned tenfold. He opened his eyes, blue as the sky. A thin fluff of blonde hair covered his head. Would her family make her give him away? It was what she had agreed. It was madness to even think about keeping him in her situation, her circumstances, with no ring on her finger and no man by her side. Unmarried women had been put away for less. She'd be letting Lawrence and Jeremy – the whole family down. Her head told her she'd have to give him up, and best to do it straight away. Her heart told her otherwise.

She passed him back to Jessie. "You can take him for now," she said.

Jessie took him back to her room.

A great swell of sorrow welled up inside Clara. It was all her fault. His birth, her position, the trouble she caused, all down to her. She let out a sob, buried her head in the pillow and cried herself out.

Much later two nurses came to give her a wash and tidy her up. "I must look a mess," she said, aware of the tear stains on her face and the dampness on her pillow.

The nurse smiled. "It'll be the hormones," she said. "You'll feel better when you've had something to eat."

Clara wished it was as easy as that.

After a light lunch, served on a tray, Doctor Klein came to see her. Jessie had taken the baby downstairs to the nursery to be fed.

"How are you feeling?" he asked, taking her pulse.

"Like I've been hit by a coach and four at full gallop," she said.

"That's good. A sense of humour." He put his stethoscope to her chest. "You are in excellent health," he said, removing it. "Any problems elsewhere?" He nodded at her lower half.

"No."

"Good. A couple of days and you will be able to go home."

"With the child?"

He shrugged. "Like I said. This is not a prison. It is not my decision to make."

"Do any of the girls here ever change their minds?" she asked. "Have any of them kept their babies?"

"It happens. Whether they live to regret it I cannot say. My only concern is for the child. That he should have the best life available to him. Whether that is with you or someone else, I cannot say. Only God knows that." He sighed as he left and Clara felt guilty all over again.

"Do you think I'm selfish, wanting to keep him?" she asked Jessie when she returned an hour or so later. "Doctor Klein thinks I'm very selfish."

"You don't know that," Jessie said.

"I do. I can see it in his eyes when he looks at me. He's thinking, 'another spoiled brat used to getting everything she wants and with no idea about the consequence of her actions or how they affect other people.' But I'm not like that, really I'm not." She paused as the memory of picking up Captain Sebastian Shawcross in the park, with no thought of the consequences, ran through her mind. "Not now anyway."

"I could look after him," Jessie said. "On your behalf, I mean. I could be employed to look after him for you."

Clara perked up. She chewed her lip. "I don't know," she said, but then a plan formed in her mind and another idea entered her head. "I need to speak to my brother," she said. "Pass me the writing pad."

While Jessie cradled the baby in her arms, singing softly to him, Clara wrote to Lawrence, *Please send Daisy Carter. I have a job for her.*

Chapter Thirty Six

The hotel soon became a spectacle for passers-by to stop and stare at. People came into the tea room with the newspaper and questioned the waitresses, trying to glean any clue that might help them earn the reward. It became quite tiresome and the girls were directed to refer enquirers to the police.

"Never sold so many tea cakes and iced buns in me life," Mrs T said. "It seems bad news is good for business."

"If I knew owt I'd claim the reward meself," Kitty said. "That's what I tell 'em."

The bookings too were up. "Got to find that £100 from somewhere," Barker said.

None of the staff were very happy about the arrangement. "Poor Alfie," they said. "Sold to the punters as an attraction, like the bearded lady or the two-headed goat. That Mr Lawrence should be ashamed of 'imself."

Daisy was the only one who stood up for him. "I'm sure he's doing his best," she said. "He'll be doing what Inspector Rolleston asked him to do. He won't like it any more than we do."

"No, but he'll like the extra business," Barker said. "'E won't be saying no to that."

One morning, on her way to Mr Lawrence's office to pick up the schedule of arrivals and departures, Barker stopped her. "Letter 'ere for you. Foreign. Come from overseas."

Daisy's heart leapt as she recognised Jack's handwriting. "Thank you," she said and suddenly the day looked brighter. She slipped the letter into her pocket. She'd read it later, when she had time to savour its contents.

In the office Mr Lawrence asked her sit. Her heart dropped a little.

"I have a favour to ask," he said. "Well something I... Miss Clara... has asked. She..." He stood up and paced the room. "It's really quite irregular, but... well..." His smile appeared as if by sheer force and determination. He swung back into his chair behind the desk. "She wants you to visit her. I have no idea why. She doesn't say."

"Has she had..."

He shrugged. "I've no idea."

Thoughts whirled in Daisy's brain. Of course if she had given birth it wouldn't be mentioned. Secrecy was the whole reason for going away. She'd hardly write about it. Daisy said the first thing that came into her head. "I expect she wants some clothes altered."

Mr Lawrence looked relieved. "Yes. I expect that's it." He passed her an envelope. "This is the address and directions that you must follow. There's enough there to pay for the return ticket and some lunch or a few extras you might need. You should have time to catch the ten o'clock train. I can't tell you how much I appreciate your help. Thank you, Daisy." He smiled and his eyes lit with warmth.

Daisy was lost for words, and breath. "Thank you, sir," she mumbled and stumbled out of the room. She was going to the coast on the ten o'clock train. Whatever could that be all about?

She caught the train by the skin of her teeth. She'd thrown a few things into a bag, not sure how long she'd be expected to stay. All the while thoughts ran helter-skelter through her brain. Was it Jessie? Had she let

230

herself down? Miss Clara wasn't the easiest person to get along with and Jessie had a temper. She knew that. Or was it something else? Had she let slip who she really was, the wife of the brother of a now notorious villain connected to the Fitzroy Murder? She'd swing for her if she had. The last thing she wanted was to be going to see Miss Clara. No. The last thing she wanted was losing her job because of her hot-tempered, thoughtless sister.

On the train she relaxed. Whatever was done, was done. There was no undoing it. She'd just have to make the best of it when she arrived.

She watched the miles fly by, buildings giving way to sunlight creeping over open fields. Then she remembered Jack's letter, still in her pocket. She opened it. The first thing she noticed was the return address. Somewhere in New York. They must be settled, she thought, to have sent a return address. Her heart filled with hope as she read:

Dear Daisy, I hope all is well with you. I just thought I'd let you know that me and Dan are all right. We have both found work in the Embassy Theatre here in New York. I am a stagehand and Dan is a call boy. There is a girl he is sweet on and he is happy. It is good here with lots of opportunities.

Tell Ma I love and miss her and Jessie. Tell her not to worry about us. We are doing all right.

I love and miss you too,
Your loving brother, Jack

As she read she saw his face, imagined him bent over the paper writing it, the dark curl of his hair, the concentration on his face. And Dan, dear sweet, gentle Dan.

A lurch of sorrow swirled inside her. Suddenly they seemed a long way away. She sniffed and looked out of the window. Tears sprang to her eyes. They were here, in her heart, she thought, and that was all that mattered. And they were safe. She could tell Ma about the letter. Make up some story about a chance to go to America and keeping quiet as they didn't want to upset her, or be talked out of it.

She read it through again. Short and sweet, but at least she could write back. Tell Jack about Felix's death and how he wasn't responsible. Even send him the newspaper cuttings she'd saved from her mother's newspaper, so he need no longer feel guilty about it. Felix could have got drunk and fallen down at any time. It wasn't Jack's fault. She checked the date on the letter. It had been sent three weeks ago. She sat back and watched the world rush past. Jack and Dan were safe.

A little while later she read the *Directions and Instructions for visiting The Grange.* How bizarre, she thought, how very strange.

When she arrived she was greeted at the gatehouse by a girl who took her name and checked a list hanging by the door. "Mrs Smith is in the garden," she said and pointed Daisy in the right direction. The first person Daisy saw was Jessie pushing a baby carriage across the lawn.

"What are you doing here?" Jessie's face fell. "You ain't come to replace me 'ave you? I ain't done nothing wrong. 'Onest. I bin good as gold, remembered all you said. Why are you here?"

"Your guess is as good as mine," Daisy said. "All I know is Miss Clara asked for me and Miss Clara usually gets what Miss Clara wants." She gazed into the baby carriage. "Is that...?"

Jessie nodded. "I'm looking after 'im. Sweet little thing ain't 'e?"

Daisy felt a stab of grief at the warmth in Jessie's voice. Clearly she'd become attached to the child, which wasn't in the plan at all. "I thought they were meant to take him away," she said. "Not have you look after him."

"That's what I thought an' all," Jessie said. "But it seems Miss Clara has other ideas. She wants to keep 'im."

"What? She can't. The whole point of coming here was—"

"To get rid." Daisy didn't miss the bitterness in Jessie's voice. "Well, she's changed her mind."

"But she can't. I mean..." Shocked, Daisy didn't know what to say. Even Miss Clara wouldn't be so stupid as to believe she could keep her illegitimate child and retain her reputation and place in society. "She can't. Not after all everyone has done for her. She can't just do as she pleases."

Jessie shrugged. "You know Miss Clara. Law unto 'erself she is."

"Where is she? I'd better go and have a word. I really can't believe she'd be so stupid."

"I can." Jessie giggled. "Miss Clara thinks she can have everything she wants."

Daisy stomped off. She'd heard of women losing their marbles when they had babies. Something about hormones. But even so. After all Mr Lawrence had done for her. It just wasn't right.

She found Miss Clara sitting in the summerhouse reading a book. She looked tired and Daisy saw the extra weight she still carried. Not quite back to normal yet then, she thought. She wasn't sure whether to humour her or tell her straight. She chose the latter.

"You sent for me," she said. "Is everything all right?"

"Ah. Daisy," Miss Clara brightened. "I'm glad you came. Please sit."

Daisy sat. "I've seen Jessie," she said. "She tells me you plan to keep the child. I'm not sure Mr Lawrence... your family... after all they've done for you I don't think—"

"Oh. Please don't fuss. I get enough of that from the people here." She put her book down and turned to Daisy. "It's not fair," she said. "Why should I have to give up my child? If Jeremy, or God forbid Lawrence, had fathered a child out of wedlock do you know what would happen to it?"

"No."

"It would be looked after on the estate by a tenant or a farmer's family. It would be accepted and recognised. Everyone would know its origins, but there'd be no shame in it. Some such children even inherit. It would be looked after and cared for, not given away like a packet of tea to anyone willing to take it." Her voice broke and tears filled her eyes. "Why should my child be different? He's a Fitzroy and I want him brought up as a Fitzroy. Is that so awful?"

Seeing her distress Daisy felt sorry for her. She was right. If she were a man, things would be different. She had a point, but nevertheless, keeping the child was out of the question. "Is it so hard?" she said.

"Think about your family, your life at home, your future, what lies ahead... You will forget about him..."

"No. I'll never forget." She jumped up and paced the floor. "Nothing anyone says will change my mind. I sent for you because I have a task for you to undertake. Will you do it?"

Daisy decided to humour her. "If I can."

Miss Clara sat again. "You must tell no one what I'm asking of you. Promise?"

Daisy shrugged. "I promise. Silent as the grave me." She thought of all the secrets she already kept. Would one more weigh any heavier?

"On your mother's life?"

Daisy nodded.

"Do you believe in love at first sight, Daisy?"

Daisy shrugged. She thought of all the lads she'd known in what would have been her 'courting years' had she been inclined towards marriage. Some were more eligible than others, but there wasn't one who'd moved her enough to make her change her life. Not one she would readily give her heart to. "I'm not sure I do, Miss Clara," she said.

"Well, I do." Miss Clara passed her a folded piece of paper. "I want you to find this man. I've told no one of him, his name or his position. I'm entrusting it to you in the utmost secrecy. I want you to find him and tell him he has a child. It's up to him what he does about it, but it's his right to know."

Daisy opened the paper and read:

Captain Sebastian Shawcross, Gloucester Rifles.

She stared at Miss Clara. The enormity of the secret crushed her. "I don't know, Miss Clara. I..."

Miss Clara closed her hand over the paper. "Do it for me, please. You promised."

Daisy thought of the child, Mr Lawrence, Mr Jeremy, the Fitzroy family. She owed them her loyalty too. "It's a big thing you're asking."

"I know. That's why I chose you, Daisy Carter. Because I knew I could rely on you. I wouldn't trust anyone else."

Daisy sighed. Miss Clara was right. They did share a bond with all they knew about each other, the shared secrets, the shared experiences, the family loyalties. A bond unwanted, but nonetheless acknowledge. She smiled. "I'll do my best," she said and wondered what on earth she'd let herself in for.

Once that was settled they talked pleasantly enough about the arrangements that had to be made, Jessie, the baby, the hotel, the Fitzroy family. No mention was made of the murder or anything sordid. Being taken into Miss Clara's confidence gave Daisy a jolt of confidence of her own. It made her feel valued and appreciated. A stab of pride made her catch her breath. I hope I can find this man and not let Miss Clara down, she thought.

When she returned to the hotel Daisy left the letters Miss Clara had given her for Mr Lawrence and Mr Jeremy on Mr Lawrence's desk. Miss Clara had written to both her brothers telling them of her plans to keep the child and asking them to make the necessary arrangements. Daisy didn't want to be around when they opened them.

Chapter Thirty Seven

Once she'd finished her work the next day Daisy turned her mind to Miss Clara's request. She wasn't sure where to start, or how to go about it. She did think of asking Barker, who was a font on all knowledge when it came to the military, but he wasn't the sort to give away information without knowing the reason for it. He had a knack of reading minds too, which made him good at his job but not someone you'd approach with a secret mission if you wanted it to remain secret.

She'd read the papers. Since the signing, the previous May, of the Treaty of Vereeniging, ending the war in Africa, troops had been returning home. That meant he could be in the country at least. One thing she did know about him was that he took part in the King's Coronation procession. Miss Clara had told her about meeting him in the park, the invitation to the boating party, going back to her room in the hotel and what followed.

"I'm not proud of it," she'd said. "No doubt you think I got everything I deserved. I know Lawrence does."

Daisy was horrified. "No," she said. "No one deserves that."

Miss Clara again swore her to secrecy. "You must treat what I've told you with the utmost confidentiality," she said. "Speak to him personally. It's not the sort of thing you can put in writing." She'd paced the room, wringing her hands as she thought it through. "He'll probably need some persuading that it's the truth, not some low-life trick to get money out of him. Tell him I'm asking for nothing. I just wanted him to know." She stopped and gazed out of the summerhouse window. "Tell him…" she bit her lips, "tell him the child will be well looked after." A tear rolled over her cheek. "Tell him…" She stopped.

Daisy sat and waited. After a few minutes Miss Clara turned to look at Daisy. "Watch him. Let me know his reaction. You must make him see that it is the truth. The child can only be his. I'm not some…" She shook her head turning away. "Just tell him."

Daisy had nodded, although her heart was heavy as stone.

She sighed at the memory. She'd go to the library if she could get away that afternoon and see what she could find out about the Gloucester Rifles. There must be somewhere she could go to find him.

Crossing the lobby on her way back to the kitchen she saw Barker reading the newspaper. He held it up so she could see the headline. *Missing Witness Found.*

"They've found 'im," he said. "Our Alfie's headline news."

Daisy picked up a copy of the paper from the pile that had just been delivered. She hurried to the kitchen to read it. Downstairs, everyone had heard the news and crowded round as she read it aloud:

"Alfred Elsworthy, the missing witness in The Fitzroy Hotel murder case, has been found. He turned himself in to a local police station in Beckton where he has been living. It is understood that he is suffering from amnesia due to a serious head injury inflicted at the time of the murder. Thanks to his picture appearing in this newspaper, his memory is gradually returning. The police are working with doctors to further restore his recollection of the events at The Fitzroy Hotel on Coronation Day in the hope that it will lead to the arrest of the man responsible for the death of Miss

Dolly Deverill. Alfred Elsworthy is in custody helping the police with their inquiries."

"Poor lad. They ought to bring 'im 'ere," Mrs T said. "That'd jog 'is memory. Somat familiar."

A short while later Inspector Rolleston appeared with Constable Perkins and Alfred Elsworthy.

"There. What did I say?" Mrs T gloated. "He'll be all right now. It'll all come back to 'im."

Inspector Rolleston coughed. Constable Perkins motioned to the staff to gather round.

"Now, lad." Rolleston pulled himself up to his full height. "Who do you recognise here?"

Alfred grinned. He pointed to the cook. "Mrs T. I'd remember her anywhere." He glanced at the others. "And Miss Carter, she's... erm. ...head of housekeeping." He glanced around again. "There's a maid. Kitty. Can't see her here."

"She's upstairs cleaning the rooms," Daisy said.

"Well remembered, lad," Rolleston said. "Seems your memory's working all right now."

Alfred grinned.

The inspector turned to go.

"Won't you stay for a cup of tea?" Daisy asked. "I'm sure Alfred and Constable Perkins would appreciate it."

Inspector Rolleston hesitated. He glanced at his coat, still wet from the rain. "Well, thank you, miss. That'd be most welcome."

Daisy showed them into the sitting room. Tea and scones might loosen their tongues and she could find out what more Alfred remembered.

Over tea and buttered scones Alfred began to tell Daisy what he remembered but Inspector Rolleston stopped him. "Careful, lad," he said. "Don't want it in all the newspapers, do we? Keep it for the statement at the station."

So Alfred didn't say any more but Daisy was able to gather than he had been picked up on a road near the river, badly bruised and taken to hospital where he woke up with no memory of how he got there. "I didn't even know my name, until I saw the picture in the paper," he said. "That brought it back, well, some of it. The rest is still a bit hazy, but it's coming."

"What do the doctors say?"

He glanced at Inspector Rolleston.

"They say it'll all come back eventually," Rolleston said. "He'll be our star witness when we catch the bug— begging your pardon, miss... culprit." He sipped his tea.

Daisy smiled. "I'm glad you're all right, Alfred," she said. "You'll be welcome here anytime."

Chapter Thirty Eight

Two weeks after the baby was born Clara was ready to go home. She'd written to her brothers setting out the arrangements she wanted made for her and the child she'd decided to call Herbert, after her father, and Edward due to his being conceived on the day of the Coronation. He was to be known as Harry Fitzroy.

Over the weeks the exchange of letters had become bitter, but Clara was determined to have her way. In the end Jeremy was sent as peacemaker. Clara arranged for him to meet with her and Dr Klein at the gatehouse. She insisted Jessie and the baby accompany her. She was convinced that, once Jeremy saw his nephew, he would support her wish to keep him and bring him up as a Fitzroy. At least she'd have more chance convincing Jeremy than Lawrence, so her hopes rode high.

She found a suitable dress she'd had Jessie take in for her and brushed her hair up, pinning it into soft curls. She wanted to show Jeremy that she was fit and well and thinking straight. This wasn't a passing fancy, as Lawrence had called it in one of his letters. She was serious and wanted to be taken as such. All the same her heart fluttered faster than hummingbird wings. She had to be strong, not for herself, but for the child she'd just brought into the world. Doctor Klein had assured her that the huge swell of maternal love she felt would fade in time, but he was wrong. Every time she looked at the child she saw their future together. Nothing was going to tear them apart, no obstacle would be too large to overcome.

They met in the small garden at the back of the gatehouse. May sunshine dappled the lawn, summer roses scented the air. A soft breeze whispered through trees and birds chirped their merry songs. When Jeremy arrived she was glad to see him. She'd forgotten how handsome he was, how caring. He greeted her with a kiss on her cheek. "I see motherhood hasn't changed you," he said. "Still as headstrong, impulsive and stubborn as ever."

Love for this charming, intelligent man she was lucky enough to have as a brother filled her heart.

Doctor Klein greeted him with caution. They shook hands.

Clara was anxious that Jeremy should see the child before any decisions were made about his future. She beckoned Jessie forward with the child in her arms.

"Look at him, please, Jeremy."

"I've seen a baby before, Clara. I don't need to see him."

"You haven't seen my baby, Jeremy. Please."

Jeremy sighed and glanced at the child wrapped in a blanket. He gently pushed the blanket off his face to get a better look. He sighed again and nodded to Jessie who took him away, back to the nursery. They sat around a decorative, white enamelled garden table to have tea. At first Clara enquired about the hotel, how Jeremy was getting on, the weather, anything to generate a little light-hearted, general conversation to begin with, until they all relaxed. Then the heated discussion about Clara's future began.

Doctor Klein was ambivalent. He shrugged his shoulders. "We are not in the business of keeping people against their will," he said. "If a certain path is chosen I can only advise on the hardships and difficulties associated with that path. I cannot prevent anyone taking it. We all have free will."

"Can I persuade you to change your mind, Clara?" Jeremy asked.

"No. My mind is settled on keeping him. Nothing you do or say will change that."

"Are you sure you've thought this through, Clara? You know how impetuous you can be. A child is for life. You're whole future will be irrevocably changed, damaged even."

"I know. I'm prepared for that. It's what I want, Jeremy. He's my child. Part of me. I can't... I won't... give him up." Determination raised her voice and clenched her jaw. She glanced at Jeremy and her face and voice softened. Her eyes filled with tears. "I thought at least you'd understand."

Jeremy sighed. "I do, Clara. That's the problem. It's just as I thought. I've known you long enough to be aware of your stubborn determination to do whatever you want, regardless of whether or not it is in your best interest. So, I've spoken to Lawrence."

A band of dread tightened around Clara's heart. Of course Lawrence would have the final say. He was head of the family. Her stomach churned.

Jeremy put the teacup and saucer he was holding on the table and glanced at Clara. "If you must attempt this foolishness we have decided it would be best for everyone if you were to return to Maldon Hall. Mama of course has to be been informed. Lawrence is there today preparing the ground, so to speak. A place will be found for the child and your maid in one of the farm cottages. This is a temporary arrangement until things can be settled and a proper future for you both mapped out. It is the best we can do."

Clara threw her arms around his neck and kissed him. "Thank you, Jeremy. Thank you."

243

Jeremy smiled, his eyes twinkled. "It's a temporary arrangement. We still have to get Mama's support. Heaven knows what she will say."

"She will do whatever Lawrence tells her to do," Clara said. "She may not like it, but she will do it."

"That's settled then," Jeremy said. "I will make the arrangements. Be ready to leave in the morning. I will send a carriage. Your maid and the child will follow later in the day. You cannot arrive together."

"Thank you. I knew I could rely on you."

Jeremy chuckled. Then he sighed. "It's not an easy thing you're doing, Clara, but I have a feeling it's the right thing to do." He grinned. "And that little chap looked like he had a mind of his own too. Cute little thing. Can't blame you for wanting to keep him."

Clara kissed him again and her heart soared. All she had to do now was convince Lawrence and Mama. At least Jeremy was on her side.

Bathed in morning sunlight Maldon Hall looked just as magnificent as always. The rambling Georgian house, surrounded by manicured lawns, stood at the end of a long tree-lined drive. The familiar surge of nostalgia hit Clara as the carriage made its way up to the front door.

Happy childhood days, carefree laughter and naive enthusiasm, she thought. Now I have to face Mama. I've let her down. Lied to her in letters full of eligible dates and imaginary parties. How will she ever forgive me? I've managed to thwart her ambition. I'm a ruined unfortunate destined for ignominy.

Try as she might to think of herself like that Clara couldn't do it. Had she no shame? All she knew was that she was still a Fitzroy. Her father's daughter.

Nothing she did could change that. She'd walk in with her head held high, just as she always did, as though having a child out of wedlock was the most natural thing in the world.

A white-gloved footman opened the carriage door. She stepped out, took a breath, braced her shoulders and walked up the steps into the spacious hall. Her luggage was taken in and packed away with the quiet efficiency expected from servants who had a long history of working together.

Her mother and Aunt Doris stood waiting for her. Elvira moved towards her, arms outstretched and embraced her. "My poor, poor child," she said. "Why on earth didn't you tell me?"

"I'm sorry, Mama," Clara said and realised she really was.

"Well, I suppose it's done now. We just have to deal with it." Her voice held no warmth and Clara felt as bad as she'd ever done. "You've arrived in time for tea."

Tea was served in the drawing room.

"I'm sorry," Clara said. "I've let you down."

Elvira patted her hand. "Don't worry. Lawrence explained it all to us." She poured the tea. "He's a much better advocate than you might suppose. He should have taken up the Law. He'd be very good at it."

"I'm very grateful to him."

"You have good reason to be, but save your gratitude. You're going to need it."

Clara realised how difficult this must be for her, after all her hopes and plans. She felt wretched. "I know I'm a disappointment."

"No. Don't say that. Never say that." Elvira passed her a cup of tea. "You are a Fitzroy. We look after each other. Isn't that right, Doris?"

Aunt Doris, who had been sitting in silence, perked up. "Yes, Elvira," she said.

"Good. Now, what's done is done. You will stay until things are sorted out." She glanced at Clara and her face softened. "It's good to have you home," she said.

"It's good to be home," Clara said.

After tea Elvira suggested Clara go to her room for a rest before lunch. "You must be exhausted," she said.

Clara smiled at her concern. "No. I'm fine, really. I'd like to see where Mrs Ferguson and young Harry are to stay."

Elvira blanched at the mention of the child's name but quickly recovered. "Are you sure you wouldn't like a little lie down first?"

"No, Mama. I'm perfectly fit and well. I want to see where my child will be living."

Elvira huffed and took a breath. "Well, I suppose, if you must."

"Yes. I must."

"Of course, darling." Elvira's face bore the expression of one whose patience was wearing thin. "They're to stay with the Craddocks. Since their boys have left they have the room."

"The gamekeeper and his wife? Do they know who he is?"

"The child of a friend, I believe they were told," Elvira said as she guided Clara out. "You'll need a coat and some boots. I'll have the buggy brought round." Clara saw the ice beginning to melt. A great weight lifted off her shoulders. It seemed that Lawrence had

246

successfully persuaded her mother to indulge her. That was a start.

Thomas, the head groom from the hotel who now worked for the family, brought the buggy round. He raised his cap when Clara appeared. "Good morning, Miss Clara," he said.

"Thomas. Thank you." She climbed into the buggy. "I'm to visit Mrs Craddock," she said.

Thomas nodded, climbed up to the driving seat and whipped the horse into a trot.

When they arrived at the cottage a smiling Mrs Craddock opened the door. "Good morning, Miss Clara. Good to see you 'ome. I dare say Mrs Fitzroy's missed you, what with Mr Herbert…"

"Yes. Thank you, Mrs Craddock. I've come to see where Mrs Ferguson and the child she's bringing will be staying. I hope it's not inconvenient."

"Bless you 'course not. Come in." Clara followed her into the small front parlour. "Can I offer you a drink? I have some fresh made lemonade if…"

"No. Really, I'm fine." She glanced around. The room was small but well kept and orderly. Highly polished horse-brasses shone on the chimney-breast matching the highly polished brass fender around the fireplace. Magazines and papers were tidily stacked on a side table beneath a glass-fronted cabinet containing china ornaments. Once assured of Mrs Craddock's pride in housekeeping, Clara asked to see the room where the child would sleep.

"This way." Mrs Craddock led her up the stairs.

"Has anyone told you anything about the child?" Clara asked.

"An orphan, Mr Lawrence said. Taken in out of the kindness of Mrs Fitzroy's 'eart. Always was a good woman, Mrs Fitzroy. Bin good to us an' all."

So that's to be the lie, Clara thought.

Upstairs the room was bright with morning sun. Clean, white lacy curtains billowed in the breeze through the open window. A single bed, neatly made, stood beside a cot that Clara supposed had held both the Craddock boys when they were babies. That too was neatly made up. She took off her glove and ran her hand over the mattress, feeling for any sign of damp. Then she opened the top drawer of the chest that stood alongside the other wall. A knitted shawl and a few items of baby clothes lay in the drawer. Everything was clean, neat and tidy.

"I put a few of me odd bits and pieces in, if you don't mind," Mrs Craddock said. "Milly in the dairy's boy just grew out of them. Hardly worn, so I thought…"

Clara smiled. "You did well, Mrs Craddock. I'm grateful. I will of course be sending outfits for the child, but it was a nice thought."

"Well, we're pleased to 'ave 'im. I must say place 'as bin quiet since the boys left." Clara wasn't surprised. She remembered the Craddock boys. A few years older than her they were always getting into mischief.

Clara nodded and made her way out and down the narrow stairs. "I expect you miss them," she said. "How are they?"

"Oh they're doing well. Both got jobs on a farm near the coast." Clara heard the pride in her voice. Yes, she thought. Harry will be all right here until I can make other arrangements.

"Thank you, Mrs Craddock. I'll call again this afternoon with Mrs Ferguson and the child." She sighed and glanced again at the cosy cottage before climbing back onto the buggy for the ride back to the house. It was a start.

Chapter Thirty Nine

It took Daisy a while to find out where she could get the information about the Gloucester Rifles she needed. She tried several places without success. She had no authority for her search and due to the secret nature of the mission, going to Whitehall was out of the question. She tried the barracks at Chelsea where she knew soldiers were billeted. "The Gloucesters?" the chap on the gate said. "They'll be in the West Country. Not sure where. You could try the Military Library." He gave her the address.

"Thank you."

Another week went by before Daisy could get out to visit the library. Nearly a month had passed and Miss Clara was getting impatient. At least Jessie is settled looking after the child. That's one thing I can be pleased about, Daisy thought.

When she got to the Military Library she wasn't sure where to look. She wandered into the section on Military History where she found an elderly man perusing the shelves. She stood alongside him and glanced at the books.

"Are you looking for anything in particular?" he asked.

"The Gloucester Rifles," she said. "My aunt's cousin is recently back from Africa, but they've lost touch. She's quite poorly and I need to contact him. I'm at a loss as to know how to find him or where to go."

The old man smiled, and walked to a pile of magazines and papers. He picked them up, selected one, rifled through the pages until he found what he was looking for. He passed it to her. "Here you are. Latest news from the Glorious Gloucesters."

"Really?" Daisy's spirits lifted. That hadn't been as difficult as she'd imagined. "Thank you." She took the paper and read the article. It said that the 1st Battalion had returned from Africa to their barracks in Bristol. There was no indication of any future assignments. Daisy made a note of the address, left the paper and thanked the man again. Now all she had to do was find a way to get to Bristol, find him and persuade him that he was a father. How hard could that be?

She pondered on the problem until later that evening when Mrs T made cocoa for her, herself and Barker. They were discussing the events of the day and the plans for tomorrow, when Matilda burst into the kitchen flapping around like an excited chicken. "You'll never guess what George told me," she said, almost exploding with excitement.

"Go on," Barker said, unimpressed.

"He said someone's been arrested for Miss Deverill's murder. You'll never guess who." Her eyes shone brighter than the beacons lit for the King's Coronation.

"Go on then, who?"

"You'll never guess in a million years."

Barker and Mrs T looked at each other.

"Spit it out, girl, before you choke," Mrs T said.

"It'll be in all the papers tomorrow so I don't suppose there's any harm in telling you – that's what George said."

"Good for George," Barker said. "Only 'urry up. I've got to go back to work in six hours' time."

Matilda beamed. "Viscount Westrow."

"What?" Daisy didn't understand what she was saying. "What about him?"

"He's the murderer."

Stunned, they all stared at each other in disbelief. The silence stretched to every corner of the room. Daisy struggled to take it in.

Barker huffed. "You and George been drinking 'ave ya? Thought you'd 'ave a little joke?"

Matilda glared at him. "It ain't no joke. George told me." Her voice rose with indignation. "Alfred remembered seeing 'im. They took 'is finger marks, then they arrested 'im. George says they've got 'im bang to rights."

Barker shook his head. "What would a toff like 'im be doing with a trollop – begging your pardon – person – like her?"

"Other than the obvious?" Mrs T raised her eyebrows.

Barker stroked his chin as though weighing it all up. "'E 'as been 'ere, Sir Richard. Friend of the guvnor, Mr Herbert, he was, but I still can't think why he'd want to kill someone like 'er."

Daisy didn't know what to think.

"Blackmail," Mrs T said. "Got caught with 'is trousers down. Wouldn't be the first."

Daisy recalled Inspector Rolleston calling earlier that evening.

"Yes," Barker said. "Then Mr Lawrence rushed out with a face like thunder. Called for a cab to Mr Jeremy's club."

"Surely you don't think…"

"Wouldn't put it past 'im."

"I dunno…"

The speculation went on well into the night. Daisy was just relieved. If Sir Richard was guilty it let Jack off the hook. It wasn't his fingerprints they'd found in Miss Deverill's room.

The next morning the papers confirmed the arrest. Sir Richard's name was spread across all the headlines, together with the name of The Fitzroy Hotel. The revelation sparked renewed interest in the hotel and the girls in the tea room were rushed off their feet. On Mr Jevons's instructions questions about the case were batted away with non-committal answers. The trial was set for a month's time.

Various possible scenarios were put forward and debated by the hotel staff. Barker set up a sweep-stake on the outcome.

*

Elvira Fitzroy seldom read the newspapers. They were of course delivered daily as they had been throughout Mr Herbert's lifetime. Elvira read the Court Circular and the Society pages, but very little else. Clara was similarly inclined, caring only for the fashion magazines, so Jeremy's arrival, carrying the paper under his arm, caused quite a stir.

"I wasn't expecting you," Elvira said rising from the breakfast table to greet him. "I hope it's not bad news."

"It depends upon how you look at it," he said kissing his mother's cheek. He smiled at Clara. "I trust you are keeping well, Clara."

"Yes, thank you," Clara said, aware that she owed him more than a polite acknowledgment. She felt sure he was the one who persuaded Lawrence to allow her child to be brought to Maldon Hall.

"Lawrence sends his regards."

"Won't you join us?" Elvira said as a maid appeared with a fresh pot of tea and another cup and saucer.

Jeremy nodded to the girl and waited while the teapot was replaced. Once the girl had gone he spread the newspaper on the table. "I don't suppose you've seen this," he said. "Lawrence came to see me last night. He thought you should know."

Clara stared at the headline: *Police Arrest Viscount Westrow.*

Elvira fumbled for her reading glasses. "Jeremy, you know I don't read the papers. What does it say?"

"It says the police believe Viscount Westrow murdered Dolly Deverill at The Fitzroy Hotel on Coronation Day."

"What? Our Viscount Westrow?"

"Well, there's only one, Mama."

"What nonsense." Elvira turned her attention to pouring the tea. "I refuse to believe such dreadful tittle-tattle."

Clara picked up the paper and read it, becoming increasingly bemused as she did so. "I suppose it could be true," she said. "After all, he had known her in the past, hadn't he?"

"Yes. And I believe that might be the reason for it," Jeremy said. "Dolly told me she'd seen him around that time, in a club in town. He hadn't recognised her, but she'd recognised him. I think she may have invited him to the hotel, then told him who she was, either to humiliate him or to threaten to expose him to his peers and make their previous association public."

"Do you really think she'd do that?"

"She had nothing to lose, he had a great deal. It would have cost him his reputation."

"But, it's all speculation, isn't it?" Elvira said. "Anyone can accuse anyone of anything, if they're trying to get money out of them. They can make things up."

"Their earlier liaisons weren't made up, Mama. I believe Dolly had proof."

"He propositioned me, Mama," Clara said, feeling an unexpected bitterness at the memory. "That's the sort of man he was." What had happened to Dolly could easily have happened to her too. "If he's guilty I hope he hangs."

"Clara!" Elvira banged the teapot on the table. "Sir Richard was a friend—"

"No, Mama, he wasn't," Jeremy told her. "He was a blood-sucking leech who attached himself to Grandfather and bled him dry. We're well rid of him. I believe Clara had a narrow escape."

"And much good it did her." Elvira glared at Clara as though she was personally responsible for all the ills in the world. "I can't listen to any more of this nonsense. I'm going for a lie-down. I hope when I have recovered we will be able to speak of pleasanter things." She stood, glanced at the paper, said, "You shouldn't read such rubbish," and strode out.

Jeremy shrugged. "Poor Mama. Her world has been turned upside down. She'll never believe ill of anyone who has money. It's as if only the poor can sink to horrendous deeds. Apparently, great wealth makes us immune to unconscionable behaviour."

"Do you really think he did it?" Clara asked. "I mean, killed Dolly?"

"The police seem to think so. He was definitely there. They have proof of that."

"Then I'm glad they caught him," Clara said, but she couldn't help thinking about what had happened to her on Coronation Day and whether the man she was with had anything to do with Dolly's death.

Chapter Forty

With all the uproar and the hotel being so busy, Daisy couldn't get away to Bristol for several days. She wanted to look as businesslike as possible so she put on her best navy suit with a high-collared white blouse and a straw boater with a navy band and bow. She booked a return ticket on the train and packed an overnight bag in case she had trouble gaining entrance to the barracks to see the captain.

Knowing that it might be difficult she thought about what Jack would do, him being expert at gaining entry to places he had no business to be and prepared accordingly. She also took the dress Miss Clara had asked her to destroy and the uniform button, in case it might prove useful.

All through the journey she rehearsed what she would say. She gazed out of the window as the train rushed through the countryside, but she was oblivious to the fields bathed in June sunshine, picturesque villages and woods carpeted with fragrant bluebells. Anxiety churned within her. What if she failed? What if she found him and he didn't believe her? Or worst still, supposing he accused her of making it up to blackmail him? The thoughts rushed through her brain faster than the train she was travelling on.

She arrived at the station just before twelve o'clock and caught a cab to the barracks. A young lad stood in the sunshine, looking bored, by a sentry box at the gate. She noticed a scattering of cigarette butts on the floor around him and guessed he'd been there quite a while. She strolled up to him.

"Good day," she said. "My name is Miss Carter. I've come to see a..." She took an official looking paper out of her bag and consulted it. It was actually the headed paper they printed the menus on in the hotel restaurant. "Captain Shawcross."

"Do you have an appointment?"

"No. But I must speak to him most urgently. It's a family matter." She took out a packet of cigarettes which she'd 'borrowed' from Hollis and offered it to him. He took one and she produced a lighter, also 'borrowed' from Hollis, to light it. He drew on the cigarette and she tucked the rest of the packet into his breast pocket. A trick she'd seen Jack use to turn anticipated resistance to friendly co-operation.

"I'll have to check," he said.

"I'll wait."

In the box he picked up a handset, dialled a number and cranked a handle. She couldn't make out the conversation as it was muffled.

"All right, Miss," he said when he came out. "You can see Major Carstairs." He pointed. "Straight ahead. First door you see."

She smiled. "Thank you." She hurried along. So far so good.

She tapped on the first door she came to and opened it. Two soldiers sat at desks in the small room. They stood when she entered.

"Miss Carter to see Major Carstairs," she said.

One of the soldiers moved to another door, tapped on it and opened it. "There's a Miss Carter to see you, sir," he said.

A voice came from within the next office. "Show her in."

Major Carstairs, a plump man in his late forties, rose as she entered. Sparse grey hair attempted to cover his head and his face wore a matching moustache.

"Miss Carter? Private Dodds tells me you've come to see one of my officers."

"Yes, Captain Shawcross."

"What do you wish to see him about?"

"It's a family matter. A private and confidential family matter."

Major Carstairs pursed his lips. "If it's a matter of discipline..."

"No. Nothing like that. But I must speak to him most urgently. I've come a long way."

The major surveyed her for a few moments. The minutes felt like hours, but eventually he said. "Very well, I'll have him sent for. You may wait outside."

Daisy's heart beat a tattoo in her chest. She was surprised no one heard it. "Thank you," she said, much relieved.

She found a bench outside the outer office and sat, waiting. Bunches of men moved around the path in front of her. Then she saw one of the men from the outer office returning with a tall, blonde soldier in a captain's uniform. He strode along with an air of arrogant confidence, but the smile on his face showed unexpected warmth. Well, Daisy thought, very handsome. No wonder Miss Clara was so taken with him.

They went into the office, neither of them gave her so much as a glance. A few minutes later she was invited into the major's office.

"Well, Miss Carter, here he is." Major Carstairs glared at her.

"Thank you, Major Carstairs, but I need to speak to him in private."

The major looked at Captain Shawcross. "I don't know what you've been up to, Shawcross..."

"I've never seen this young lady before, sir. On my life, sir," Captain Shawcross bore a look of quiet conviction.

"I must speak to you alone," Daisy said. "It's a family matter. Nothing to do with the Service."

The major, whose patience was obviously wearing thin, tutted. "You'd better take her to the recruiting office, Captain, and get this matter sorted out. It's most irregular."

"Yes, sir." Captain Shawcross saluted and ushered Daisy out. They crossed the road to another building where he showed her into a small room, empty save for a desk and some chairs. He motioned for her to sit. "I have no idea what this is about," he said, his tone one of rising irritability, "but it had better be important."

Daisy was in no mood to apologise. She hadn't asked to be here either. "I'm here on behalf of Miss Clara Fitzroy, late of The Fitzroy Hotel, Bloomsbury, now resident at Maldon Hall, Nettlesham."

His face turned ashen. He sank onto a chair. "Miss Clara Fitzroy?"

"Yes. I believe you visited her on the day of the Coronation." She took the sprigged lavender dress out of her bag and showed it to him. "This may help jog your memory. And there's this." She held out the tunic button she'd found caught in the fastenings of the dress.

He took it. Swallowed and dropped his head into his hands. His body slumped in the chair. Several minutes passed before he spoke. "Miss Clara Fitzroy of The Fitzroy Hotel?" he said.

"Yes."

He took a breath, lifted his head and turned to look at Daisy. "I behaved abominably," he said. "I made a mistake. I thought…" He shook his head. "You don't want to know what I thought." He sighed and tears filled his eyes. "I can't tell you how badly I've felt since I found out I'd…" He shuddered. "I've thought of nothing else for months. I can't believe…"

Daisy'd never seen anyone look so wretched.

"I acted like a complete bounder, a cad of the worst order. I'd been drinking, we both had, and I was high on the excitement of the day, but that's no excuse. How she must hate me. I'll never forgive myself. I wouldn't blame her if she…" He ran his fingers through his hair. "What on earth must you think of me?"

Daisy said nothing. It wasn't her place to think anything of him. She was just the messenger.

He sat for a while, twisting the button in his fingers, as though reliving the moment. "How is she? Miss Clara?"

"She has a child. Your child. A boy. A son."

His eyes widened. A stricken look filled his face. "No," he breathed.

Daisy stood. "She said you'd say that. Said I was to persuade you of the truth of it. Well, it is true, and the child is yours, there's no denying it. But she said to tell you she wants nothing from you. She just thought you had a right to know."

His brow furrowed.

Daisy continued. "She wanted me to tell you that the child will be well cared for."

"The child? Have you…"

"Seen him? Yes. And I must say he has the look of you about him."

Captain Shawcross swallowed. "Where is he now?"

"He's being cared for on the Fitzroy Estate, by a nursemaid."

"You mean she…"

"Decided to keep him? Yes."

He nodded. "And Miss Clara's family?" He rose and paced the room, then stopped and stood staring at the ceiling as though looking for answers there. "Her brothers?"

Daisy bit her lip. "As you would expect. Mr Lawrence and Mr Jeremy Fitzroy care deeply for their sister and don't want to see her hurt."

"But no doubt that principle doesn't apply to me?" He started pacing again, this time with a troubled look on his face. "I daresay I deserve everything they want to do to me, but it was a mistake, an honest mistake. The party, the drink, the invitation…" He shrugged.

"There's no fear of that. Miss Clara has refused to give them your name."

"She has?"

"Yes."

He looked puzzled. "And yet you're here."

"She swore me to secrecy, on my mother's life."

"She did that?"

Daisy picked up the dress, put it back in the bag and took the button from his fingers. "She wanted me to tell you. I've told you. Now, if there's nothing else." She moved towards the door.

"No. Wait, please. I'm sorry. This is such a shock. I never thought…"

No, Daisy thought, you men never do.

"I don't know what… what you expect me to do."

"Miss Clara expects nothing from you."

"That's not good enough," he said, his face flushed, his fists clenched, his voice rose. "You can't just come here, drop a bombshell like that and expect me to do nothing." He glared at her.

Daisy shrugged. She didn't know what to say.

"I want to see the child. This child you say is mine. I have a right to see him. Take me to him."

Daisy panicked. She hadn't been prepared for this. "I don't know. I'm not sure…"

"Wait here. I have some arrangements to make but you will take me to him. Is that clear?"

Daisy's heart trembled. What would Miss Clara say? She hadn't anticipated him wanting to see the child, but she didn't really have a choice. "Yes, sir," she said.

Chapter Forty One

At the station Captain Shawcross checked the times of the trains. He found they could get the London train to Reading, then pick up a connection to take them to Nettlesham. Daisy wanted to telegraph ahead to let Miss Clara know they were coming but the captain prevented her.

"If things are as you say, then there's no need to alert them of our imminent arrival," he said.

They had a short wait for the train and the captain bought them tea and cakes in the small station buffet. They hardly spoke, each lost in their own thoughts. Daisy glanced at the station clock, surprised that it was gone four. She hadn't realised how long she'd been in the barracks.

By the time they reached Maldon Hall it was gone six.

"Captain Shawcross has come to see Miss Clara," Daisy told the butler who opened the door. "Please let her know that we have arrived."

Daisy's heart lifted with her responsibility over as the captain went with the butler and she was able to escape to the kitchen where Mrs Wilkins, the cook, offered her tea and sandwiches after her journey.

Clara was playing whist with her mother and Aunt Doris when Meadows, the butler, announced Captain Shawcross's presence. She gasped and the blood drained from her face.

"What's the matter, dear?" Elvira asked. "You look dreadful. Who is this Captain Shawcross?"

264

Clara quickly recovered, despite feeling quite faint. "He's the brother of a girl I was at school with. Lily Shawcross. You remember, Aunt Doris? We met him in the park last year."

"Did we?" Doris's face puckered. "How good of him to call."

"I expect he has news of Lily," Clara said. "I'll go and see."

Elvira looked sceptical, but didn't say anything.

"Ask him to wait in the library," Clara said. "I'll be with him shortly."

She rushed up to her room to powder her nose and tidy her hair. Captain Shawcross here! She couldn't believe it. She'd asked Daisy to find him, not bring him to see her, but was that such a bad thing? Wasn't that what she'd wanted all along – to see him again? She'd fallen in love with the child as soon as she saw him, but wasn't that a reflection of her feelings for its father? She could hardly breathe with excitement.

Once she was satisfied that she looked her best, she took a deep breath and went to meet him.

He was everything she remembered. Tall, dignified, handsome but with a certain dash of spirit and humour, although the latter appeared somewhat lacking today.

"Miss Clara," he said, bowing his head. "I owe you the deepest, abject apology. I can only say how sorry I am. I could barely live with myself when I realised what I had, albeit unwittingly, done. I shall never forgive myself."

"And yet, here you are," Clara said. "Looking none the worse for your transgression."

He had the grace to look shamefaced. "What can I say? I behaved abominably and can only ask for your forgiveness. I made a grave error that will colour the rest of my life."

"And mine I fear."

He swallowed. "Indeed – so I believe. Is it true? There is a child?"

At the mention of the child Clara's show of bravado crumbled. Her heart crunched at the vision of him in her arms, so small, fragile and trusting. Tears sprang to her eyes. Lost for words she nodded.

"May I see him?" His voice softened.

"Of course." She rang the bell and a maid appeared. "Ask Thomas to bring the buggy round and fetch my coat. We are going to visit Mrs Craddock."

"Yes, Miss Clara." The maid bobbed a curtsy and left.

Clara braced herself. She wasn't quite sure what Captain Shawcross wanted. Supposing he wanted to take the child away with him? That would be more than she could bear. Perhaps sending Daisy to find him hadn't been such a good idea after all.

Thomas brought the buggy round and Clara and Captain Shawcross stepped out into the still evening air.

Mrs Craddock opened the door as the buggy drew up outside.

"Is anything wrong?" she asked, a wary look on her face.

Clara sprung down to greet her. "I'm sorry to disturb you so late, but we've come to see Mrs Ferguson and the child," she said with a bright smile.

"Jessie's not here. I haven't seen her all day. I don't know where she is." A worried expression creased the stout woman's brow.

A chill ran down Clara's spine. A stone of dread gripped her. The smile dropped from her face, her heart dropped to her stomach. "What do you mean you haven't seen her all day? It's past seven. The child should be in bed." She pushed past Mrs Craddock and ran through the cottage glancing in every room calling, "Jessie, Jessie, where are you?" in mounting panic.

Upstairs the empty cot stood abandoned in the empty room. Clara rushed to the chest of drawers and pulled open one empty drawer after another. "She's taken him," she screamed, panic swirling in her brain. "Taken my baby and all his things." She glared at Mrs Craddock who stood in the doorway, wringing her hands. "When did you see her last?"

"This morning. She was here when I left for the market. I've been in town all day."

"And Mr Craddock? Was he here?"

Mrs Craddock shook her head. "He was out at dawn. Long gone."

Clara's spirit leeched out of her. Jessie had gone and taken Harry with her. Her knees buckled. If it hadn't been for Captain Shawcross stepping forward to catch her she would have been on the floor.

As the horror of what had happened crystallised in her brain a cauldron of rage bubbled inside her. Tears like a damn bursting coursed down her cheeks. Her face was granite.

"I'm sorry, Miss Clara," Mrs Craddock said, still wringing her hands. "I had no idea. She was so good with him. Doted on him she did. Called him her little cherub."

"It's not your fault, Mrs Craddock. You couldn't have known."

She took a breath. How stupid she'd been. She pushed the captain, who still had his arms around her, aside so she could dash down to the buggy. He followed her. "It seems you've had a wasted journey," she said over her shoulder. "Back to the house, Thomas, fast as you can." She lifted her skirts and jumped into the buggy. Captain Shawcross leapt up beside her as it pulled away. Only his excellent sense of balance prevented him falling to the ground.

Blinded by tears Clara could think of nothing but gaining retribution, both for her humiliation in front of the captain and the loss of her child. She turned to him. "I'm sorry," she said, her voice glacier cold. "It seems the nursemaid I employed has stolen our child, but we'll get him back. I'm going to call the police."

"If there ever was a child," he said.

"What?" Aghast, Clara couldn't believe what she'd heard. The cauldron of rage started to boil. "You have the audacity to say that to me, at a time like this? To accuse me of, what – lying? After what you did to me?" She stared at him in disbelief.

"I'm sorry. It's just…"

The cauldron boiled over. She slapped his face. "You are not the man I thought you were." Her eyes blazed, white hot with fire. All her hopes and dreams shattered like crystal into a thousand pieces around her.

Back at the house she jumped from the buggy as it drew to a halt. "Meadows, get on the telephone to the police and send Daisy Carter to me, immediately." Her tone on the last word would have struck terror into a lesser man's heart.

"Yes, Miss Clara." He scurried away.

Captain Shawcross, a look of sullen determination on his face, followed Clara into the room where she paced the floor until Daisy Carter appeared.

"Is something wrong?"

"I'll say. Your sister has stolen my baby. You recommended her. You told me she was reliable. You vouched for her. I trusted you. Now my child is gone and it's your fault." Clara spat the words out.

Daisy sank onto the sofa, her eyes and mouth wide.

Word of the kidnapping had obviously spread through the house. Elvira hurried into the room. "My dear, Clara. Is it true? The child's been taken?"

"Yes, Mama." A fresh slew of tears assailed her. Elvira put her arms around her daughter and pulled her close to comfort her. She glanced at the captain. "And who might you be?" Her tone was one of righteous indignation.

Clara raised her head, sniffed and said, "That poor apology for a man is Captain Sebastian Shawcross, Harry's father."

If looks could kill the captain would have dropped to the floor under Elvira's gaze. "You!" she said, her tone a mixture of incredulity and horror. "You should be horse-whipped."

"You're right, and I'm sorry," he said, "but I understand the child's been taken. It would be better to spend your energy trying to find him, rather than seeking retribution for something in the past that I deeply regret." He spoke with a cutting edge and an unmistakable air of authority. "I suggest your man here organises a search of the grounds in case she's still in the area. She may be closer than we think." He turned to Daisy. "Now, Miss Carter. Miss Clara said the girl is your sister. What can you tell us about her? Where would she take the child?"

Daisy sat, mortified at the scene before her. The captain she'd brought back from Bristol had spoken to Mrs Fitzroy as though she was a naughty child, Miss Clara, normally the epitome of self-control, was sobbing on her mother's shoulder and it was all her fault. She'd recommended Jessie because she didn't want the job herself. She'd assured Miss Clara of her respectability. A tidal wave of guilt washed over her. The captain was saying something but she couldn't take it in.

He hunkered down beside her. "Miss Carter. Your sister. Where would she go? Would she take the baby home?"

"Home?" Visions of Silvertown flashed through Daisy's mind. She shook her head. "No. She wouldn't go there."

"Where then? Is there somewhere special to her? A favourite place? Somewhere she'd feel safe?"

Clara spun round, seemingly recovered. "She told me she'd been to the coast once. A magical place. With a pier."

They looked at Daisy. "Oh yes. There was a place. The pastor took us. Jessie didn't want to come home."

"Where?" The captain's voice strained with impatience.

Daisy racked her brain. The minutes ticked away. "Southend," she said. "We went to Southend."

The captain's brow furrowed.

"It's north of the river," Daisy said.

"Take the carriage," Elvira said. "It'll be quicker." She nodded to Meadows who stood by the door, his face implacable. He obeyed instantly.

"I want to come with you." Clara picked up her skirt to go for her coat.

The captain stopped her. He shook his head. "It's best you stay here." He spoke with kindness. "She may have a change of heart, realise how foolish she's been and bring him back."

Clara's face lit up. "Do you think so?" Her eyes shone with hope.

"Miss Carter will accompany me." He turned to Elvira. "Tell the police to alert their colleagues in Southend. We will meet them at the pier. That's the most likely place we will find her."

As soon as the carriage was ready they were on their way. Captain Shawcross sat beside Thomas on the driving seat. Daisy sat in the coach, feeling wretched, as they hurtled along. It became clear that Thomas, as well as being an excellent driver, had driven the road many times and knew the shortest route. By the time they crossed the river the light was fading. An hour and a half later they drew to a halt in front of the pier in Southend. The police were already there, waiting.

Chapter Forty Two

The pubs, shops and bars along the promenade were ablaze with light that spilled out onto the road. Street lamps gave off a golden glow. The warmth of the day lingered. The front was busy with walkers enjoying the view across the estuary. The tide was high. A police officer approached his hand extended. "Sergeant Pendle," he said.

"Captain Shawcross." They shook hands.

"We've had a report of a young girl by herself with a baby on the pier. Bit late for a baby to be out. Would she be the one you're looking for?"

"Miss Carter knows her. If you don't mind?" Captain Shawcross nodded at Daisy.

"Go ahead. We'll follow at a distance, in case you need us." Sergeant Pendle handed the captain a lamp. The lights on the pier hardly penetrated the darkness, although the moon was high and stars sparkled like a handful of casually thrown diamonds across a black velvet cushion of sky.

Daisy joined the captain and together they walked along the pier. She heard the rushing of the waves beneath them. A cool breeze brushed her face. She stared into the darkness, looking for Jessie. About twenty minutes passed before she saw her standing by the rail gazing out to sea, the baby in her arms and a large bag at her feet. They stopped a little way off.

"Can I talk to her?" Daisy whispered. "She'll listen to me."

The captain nodded. "A few minutes, that's all."

With her heart in her mouth Daisy strolled up to her sister. "Hello, Jessie," she said.

Jessie turned, glancing around.

"It's all right. It's just us."

Jessie gazed out across the water.

Daisy leaned on the rail. "Do you remember coming here with the pastor?" she said. "What a lovely day we had."

Jessie smiled but didn't speak.

Daisy glanced up at the sky. "Look, a full moon. I love moonlight. Don't you? And the stars. So many stars."

Jessie looked up.

"Can I see the baby?"

Jessie pulled him closer. Then she smiled and turned so Daisy could see his face. "It's my little Charlie," she said. "Don't you think he looks like Charlie?"

Daisy's heart faltered. "So he does. Can I hold him?"

Daisy went to take the baby but Jessie pulled him away. "I'm waiting for Charlie," she said. "He'll be here soon."

A knot of fear tightened in Daisy's stomach. They stood in silence for a while, Daisy's heart racing. She didn't want to hurt Jessie any more than she had already.

"Does Charlie know where you are?" she said eventually.

A shadow of doubt flitted across Jessie's face.

"We could send him a note." Daisy took a notepad and pencil out of her pocket. "Here, give me the child. You can write to Charlie." She smiled and tried to sound more cheerful than she felt.

Jessie hesitated.

"I expect he's waiting to hear from you," Daisy said.

Jessie thought for a moment. Then she handed the baby to Daisy and went to take the notepad. As soon as the child was safe in Daisy's arms Captain Shawcross and Sergeant Pendle appeared at Daisy's shoulder. Two policemen appeared out of the darkness and grabbed Jessie to drag her away. "My baby, my baby!" she screamed and Daisy's heart broke.

"I'll take him."

Through her tears Daisy saw the captain. She handed the child to him. As he took the bundle the infant squirmed and whimpered, no doubt annoyed at being disturbed. Captain Shawcross held him closer, the ghost of a smile touched his lips. He moved the blanket aside to see the child's face. "It's alright, my boy," he whispered so quietly, Daisy hardly heard him but she didn't miss the look on his face and the wonder in his eyes. "So, this is my son?"

Daisy nodded. "Jessie thought it was her baby," she said. "What will happen to her?"

He sighed. "He looks none the worse for his ordeal," he said, "but abduction is a serious offence. They'll take her mental state into consideration. She hasn't harmed the child. It's all been a terrible misunderstanding."

He shuddered as though someone had walked over his grave. "Let's get this little one back to his mother." He paused. "I'll do what I can for your sister," he said softly. "She didn't mean any harm. We all make mistakes."

Sergeant Pendle took them to the police station and called a doctor. There was paperwork to do. One of the constables brought them some tea.

"He's fit and healthy," the doctor said after he'd examined the baby, and had him changed and fed. "And none the worse for his adventure."

"What will happen to Jessie?" Daisy asked.

Sergeant Pendle stroked his chin, deep in thought. "Well," he said. "We'll keep her here overnight and she'll be up before the magistrate in the morning. No doubt the Fitzroys will want to see her charged."

"She doesn't appear to be violent or a danger to anyone," the doctor said, "just confused and disorientated. It's treatment she needs, not punishment."

"Can I see her?"

"Best not to," Sergeant Pendle said. "It'll only upset the both of you."

"But she's my sister."

"I know. It's hard, but we'll look after her. Please don't worry."

Easier said than done, Daisy thought. Poor Jessie. Why did everything have to go wrong for her? She wasn't unaware of the part she'd played in the tragedy either.

Daisy dozed on the ride home, the baby asleep next to Jessie's bag on the seat beside her.

Captain Shawcross sat opposite but neither of them spoke. Daisy's heart was heavy with dread. She felt a great emptiness inside her. What on earth was she going to tell Ma?

*

As the carriage drew up outside Maldon Hall a glorious summer dawn broke over the trees, sending shafts of sunlight across the emerald lawn.

"They're back," Clara called, rushing out to greet them, followed by Meadows and one of the maids. Captain Shawcross got out first. Daisy handed him the sleeping baby. "Thank God," Clara said taking the child from him. She scowled at Daisy. "I'll deal with you later."

"The doctor says he's fine. No harm done," the captain said. He followed her into the morning room where Elvira was having her coffee.

"Look, Mama, he's back." Clara turned to the captain. "I can't thank you enough," she said.

"It's Miss Carter you should thank," he said. "She was the one persuaded her sister to part with him. Without her it may all have ended very differently."

"Well, he's home now and he can stay here until I can arrange for another nursemaid to care for him."

The child started to cry. "There, there," Clara said, rocking him gently in her arms.

"He's probably hungry," Elvira said. "There's milk and bottles in the kitchen." She nodded to Meadows, standing in the doorway, who stepped forward to take him. "See that he's attended to."

"Ma'am." The butler took the child and left.

Elvira's glacial glance swept over the captain. "I expect you could do with some refreshment, Captain Shawcross, after your journey. You must be quite famished. Won't you join us for breakfast?"

"Breakfast would be most welcome," he said.

"I'll go and see to it then. I expect you two have some things to discuss."

Left alone with the captain Clara's resolve deserted her. His presence seemed to fill the room. She felt like a naughty schoolgirl summoned to appear before the headmistress. She'd sent Daisy to find him. Now he was here she had no idea what to do with him.

"Miss Clara. I owe you another apology. I doubted your word. That was unforgiveable. I don't know what I thought…"

Clara turned away to gaze out of the window with her back to him, lest her face betray the anguish she felt seeing him again. "That's easy. You thought I was a low prostitute trying to trick you to get money, or worse."

The captain shuffled his feet his discomfort clear when he spoke. "I can't deny the thought crossed my mind but I see that I was wrong. I am sincerely sorry. I see now that there is a child and I am responsible for it. I don't take that responsibility lightly. I am ready to acknowledge it and do whatever you want. I am only sorry it came to this."

She spun round, a ferocious fury coiled inside her. "You're sorry? Well that's fine and dandy then." Tears sprang unbidden to her eyes.

He stepped towards her. "Clara. What can I do? What can I say to make things right between us? I came here because I have feelings for you. I've thought of nothing or no one except you since that day. It was the thought of seeing you again that brought me here. I had hoped that you might…" He bowed his head and turned away. "I'm sorry. It's foolish of me. How can you look at me with anything other than disgust? Of course there can be no hope. Not after…"

Clara stared at him her heart pounding.

He took a breath, squared his shoulders. "I'll go if you wish. I will of course provide for the child…"

"Go? I'm not asking you to go." She bit her lip. This was going all wrong. "I want you to stay." She forced a smile to her lips although her insides were churning. "You're not the only one who's been foolish. My brothers tell me I'm foolish beyond measure. Perhaps we have something in common after all." She touched his shoulder and turned him towards her. "I'd like to get to know you better," she said, "in happier circumstances." The breakfast gong sounded. "Won't you join us?"

"I'd be happy to." He offered his arm and they went into breakfast together.

Clara helped herself to some scrambled egg and toast while the captain sat down to a hearty breakfast of bacon, sausages, kidney, eggs grilled tomatoes and toast.

"So, are you the brother of a girl Clara went to school with?" Elvira asked once he was seated. "Or is that another of Clara's little stories?"

He looked at Clara.

"Mama! Please don't embarrass me." Clara grimaced.

Captain Shawcross laughed. "I have a sister, but I doubt she was at school with Miss Clara, unless she too was schooled in Cheltenham."

"No, she wasn't. Tell us about your family," Elvira persisted. "Where exactly do you come from?"

"My family have a modest estate in Gloucestershire. Mostly farm land. A few sheep and cattle. I have a sister, but no brothers."

"Exactly how modest?"

"Mama!"

He was saved any further explanation by the late arrival of Clara's Aunt Doris. "I'm sorry I'm late," she said. "I couldn't find my glasses."

"Doris. This is Captain Sebastian Shawcross." Elvira raised her eyebrows. "Harry's father."

"Really? Oh. How lovely. How do you do?"

The captain rose. "How do you do, Mrs…"

"Templeton," Clara said. "You remember, Aunt. You met him in the park."

"Did I? How lovely. I hope I'm not too late for the bacon. I do enjoy a couple of rashers."

"Sebastian was telling us how he got Harry back. Weren't you, Sebastian?" Clara said.

"It was Miss Carter who got the child back. I was merely an onlooker."

"I'm more interested in your intentions, Captain Shawcross." Elvira speared a devilled kidney on her plate.

Clara's heart sank. Why did her mother always have to be like this? Then she remembered her previous ambitions for her and how she'd scuppered her dreams of a good marriage. She pushed her plate away. "I find I'm not hungry after all," she said and rose to go.

Seeing her, the captain rose too. "Excuse me," he said, crumpling his napkin and going after her.

"Tut tut. These young people today," Clara heard her Aunt Doris say as she left the room.

She went out of the front door stepping into the fresh air and morning sunshine, her mind in turmoil.

The captain followed her out.

"I'm sorry," she said. "Mama worries about me."

"As every mother should," he said. "I'd like to see the boy again, before I go."

Clara brightened, her bad mood evaporating. "Of course," she said.

"And about Miss Carter."

"Yes?"

"You shouldn't be too hard on her. She took great pains to find me, even paying her own fare to Bristol and braving the wrath of my superiors. Not everyone would have done that. She's very loyal to you. That's rare in a servant. You're lucky to inspire such loyalty. Don't throw it away."

Clara nodded but anxiety swirled inside her. She thought about Daisy. All the little jobs she'd done for her without complaining. How she'd come to depend on her. How she'd confided in her, trusted her and the secret she'd kept, despite everything. And he was right. Loyalty was often hard to come by.

"She was the one who recommended her sister to me." As she said it Clara thought back to the weeks in The Grange when Jessie had walked with her, waited with her and on her, looked after her and looked after Harry. She'd liked the girl. Was she being unfair?

"She couldn't have foreseen..."

"No. I was the nearest to Jessie. I spent a lot of time with her. She loved..." Her heart crunched as she thought about Jessie. She'd loved Harry. If she didn't foresee it, how could she expect Daisy to? "What will happen to her?"

"That depends on you. If you wish she will be charged with abduction and put in prison."

"Or?"

"Or you could say it was a misunderstanding and see she gets the hospital treatment she needs. We all make mistakes, Clara."

Clara smiled and nodded. "And we all deserve a second chance," she said. "Even you."

He put his arm around her, leaned towards her and kissed her gently on the lips. "Thank you," he whispered.

Clara blushed. No kiss had ever tasted so sweet.

*

Daisy was pleased to be going back to the hotel. She'd expected a telling off from Miss Clara over what Jessie had done but it wasn't as bad as she'd anticipated. In fact Miss Clara had been fairly complimentary about her efforts to find Captain Shawcross and she didn't hold her entirely responsible for Jessie actions either. The captain must have been true to his word and put in a good word for her, she thought. There could be no other explanation.

Miss Clara wasn't pressing charges against Jessie either, as long as she agreed to stay in hospital for treatment until the doctor passed her fit again.

"It's a delayed reaction to the loss of her own baby," he said. "Treatable with therapy and medication."

Daisy's heart lifted as she walked back into the familiar kitchen. She'd only been away a couple of days but it felt like a lifetime.

"So you're back are you?" Mrs T said. "Nice break was it?"

"Sort of," Daisy said. She hadn't told where she was going or why. As far as they knew she was visiting a sick relative. They didn't know about Miss Clara's baby either, but Daisy wasn't sure how long that would stay secret.

"I suppose you'll be wanting tea an' all."

"Yes please."

"There was letter for you," Barker said. "Foreign. I put it on the mantel in the sitting room."

Daisy rushed to get it. Her hands trembled as she tore Jack's letter open. He thanked her for her letter and was pleased to hear her news. *It'll make things easier,* he wrote, *but I still feel bad about it.* That made Daisy angry. Didn't he realise that if he hadn't been there something dreadful would have happened to her? She read on: *The good news is that we will be coming home for Christmas.* Daisy gasped with joy. *I've been working with The Great Bandini, a magician and illusionist. I manage his props and Dan is my assistant. We'll be travelling with him on a three month tour of Europe, starting in Paris, then Antwerp, Oslo and Copenhagen, finally coming to London in December. I'm looking forward to seeing you, Ma and Pa and Jessie. Give them my love and Dan's. Love always, your affectionate brother, Jack.*

It was the best news ever. She couldn't wait to tell Ma. It would help to soften the blow when she told her about Jessie. She glanced around the cosy sitting room. It's good to be home, she thought.

Chapter Forty Three

Viscount Westrow's trial opened at the Old Bailey on a cloudy July morning. Determined not to miss it Clara planned to return to London the day before.

"I don't know why you want to watch such a deplorable spectacle," Elvira said. "To see an old friend in such circumstances. It's horrid."

"He's not a friend. You forget, I knew Dolly Deverill. I may not have approved of her lifestyle but she didn't deserve what he did to her. I want to see him punished."

"Hmm. I do believe you're enjoying this, Clara. It's quite distasteful."

Lawrence also wanted to watch the proceedings. "Whatever happens it will reflect badly on the hotel," he said. "I suppose I'm better off hearing it first hand, rather than relying on the exaggerated nonsense they'll print in the newspapers."

"The prosecution have asked me to give evidence about Dolly's previous relationship with the accused," Jeremy said. "So I'll be there."

On the day the trial opened Clara and Lawrence travelled together and climbed the stairs to the public gallery of Number One Court at the Old Bailey. A tremor ran through her as she gazed down at the dock, the witness box and the seats that would contain the barristers and other court officials. Gradually the courtroom filled as the reporters, clerks and ushers took their places. Barristers in wigs and gowns filled the benches, playing out a well-practiced ritual. Another shiver ran through her as the men of the jury were led in, the court assembling in silence. Whispered murmurings, fitting for the solemnity of the occasion, ran through the public gallery.

Clara let out a gasp when Sir Richard was led in between two uniformed officers. He looked slightly dishevelled but still carried himself well. He appeared smaller than she remembered and she wondered why she'd been so intimidated by him. He stared straight ahead, his eyes filled with disdain.

An usher called 'All Rise' and the court rose as one. The scarlet gowned judge walked in and took his place on the bench in front of the crest that showed his authority from the Crown. Clara gripped the rail in front of her so hard her nails bit into flesh. She glanced at Lawrence, his face set as he watched. Let the show begin, she thought.

The usher swore the jury in and the trial commenced. One of the barristers rose and addressed the bench. "Mr Edward Eversham, Q.C. speaking for His Majesty's prosecution, My Lord."

The other barrister rose, "Sir Desmond Childerhouse, Q.C., Milord, for the defence."

The judge, Lord Chief Justice Bowden-Brown, a weary looking man in his early fifties, nodded. "Then let us begin," he said.

Sir Richard spoke only to confirm his name and address and then the charges were read out. Edward Eversham opened for the prosecution, setting out the circumstances of the case and outlining the evidence they would produce. Clara thought they had a pretty good case.

Sir Desmond Childerhouse opened by assuring the jury that all the prosecution's evidence was purely circumstantial and he hoped to prove, beyond any reasonable doubt, that Viscount Westrow was innocent of all charges.

The first witness to be called was Inspector Rolleston, who was asked to tell the court about his investigation. Wearing a smart suit, white, winged-collar shirt, and with his hair neatly brushed, Clara thought he looked far more efficient than when he interviewed her at the hotel. He told the court, often referring to and reading from his notebook, about being called to the hotel, finding the body of a woman he first believed to be Miss Dolly Deverill, but who he later discovered was in fact a Miss Hillary Grenville. He added all such evidence as he'd been able to establish through questioning the staff and hotel guests.

Apart from querying the time of the call, Sir Desmond had no further questions, given that the inspector was only called after the event and everyone on the premises at the time of the murder had given statements to the effect that they'd seen and heard nothing untoward.

The chief medical officer, Doctor Julian Graves, was called next to give evidence about the cause of death. His evidence was detailed and contained medical technicalities that went over Clara's head. The only thing she understood was that the woman she knew as Miss Dolly Deverill had died from a broken neck.

Further questioning established that, in Doctor Graves's expert opinion, the perpetrator was most likely to be a man with experience in the military. Sir Desmond tried and failed to shake Doctor Graves's view.

"It's not an easy thing to snap someone's neck," the doctor said, "unless one's been trained to do so."

The last witness before lunch was Inspector Haverstock, the fingerprint expert from Scotland Yard. He gave an extensive account of the fingerprints found in the room and the process of identifying them and matching them to the accused.

"Those finger marks could have been left at any time, couldn't they?" Sir Desmond asked.

Mr Eversham rose. "Milord, I have a written statement from the chambermaid who cleaned the room that morning stating that the room was thoroughly cleaned and the brass bedstead polished."

"A chambermaid who'd lose her job if she said otherwise," Sir Desmond said, offhandedly.

"Milord!" Mr Eversham appealed to Judge Bowden-Brown.

"Yes. Sir Desmond, that remark was uncalled for. The jury will disregard it."

Inspector Haverstock continued. "The finger marks were found on the brass bedstead and on a silver clasp on the dress the deceased was wearing," he said. "Two separate sets which suggest that the deceased was grabbed around the waist from behind and the perpetrator leaned over the bed after she was killed, holding onto the brass bedstead."

Clara pictured it in her mind. Poor Dolly, she thought, she didn't stand a chance.

"My Lord," Sir Desmond turned to the bench. "That is pure speculation."

"Quite so." Judge Bowden-Brown nodded. "The jury are asked to disregard the inspector's last remark."

After lunch Jeremy was called. He spoke of the deceased prior relationship with Sir Richard when he brought her to London, as an innocent girl named Hillary Grenville.

Sir Desmond objected. "My Lord. This is hearsay and gossip. It has no place in this court."

"It goes to motive, Milord," Mr Eversham said. "The deceased, known today as Miss Deverill, cannot speak for herself. Mr Fitzroy has been a close friend for many years and should therefore be able to speak on her behalf."

"Fair enough, Mr Eversham. The witness will be allowed to proceed."

"Thank you," Jeremy said. He took a breath. "Dolly, Miss Deverill, told me that she'd seen Sir Richard recently. He didn't recognise her but she knew him. I believe she intended to confront him and threaten to make his previous behaviour public. When she did so he killed her."

Sir Desmond looked pained as he began his cross-examination. "Your belief has no place in this court. You cannot say what happened unless you were there, which you clearly weren't." He went to walk away, but then had a second thought. "You say the deceased met recently with my client. Where would that have been? A club? A bar?"

"She said it was a well-known diners' club."

"And was my client intimate with the deceased at that time? Given her profession?"

Jeremy's discomfort showed on his face. "I really couldn't say."

"So, he may have been?"

"I suppose."

"At which time his finger marks may have been left on the clasp of her dress?" Sir Desmond grinned. "No need to answer."

Clara's heart went out to Jeremy.

"Is it true that your family have had a business relationship with my client going back some years?"

Mr Eversham jumped up. "My Lord, the witness's business affairs are hardly relevant."

"On the contrary," Sir Desmond said. "I intend to show that this witness's testimony, and indeed the whole case, is a result of bad blood between the Fitzroy family and my client going back generations."

"I hardly think this is the place to air historical grievances that have no bearing whatsoever on the murder of the woman known as Miss Dolly Deverill," Mr Eversham said. "The Fitzroy family are not on trial."

"No, but their motives might be."

The judge sighed. "Very well, Sir Desmond, I will allow some latitude, but I won't have any muckraking in my court."

"Thank you, Milord. So, Mr Fitzroy, is it true to say that you and your family lay the blame for the dire state of your finances and loss of status at my client's door?"

Jeremy pulled himself up to his full height. "You mean is he a crook as well as a murderer? I would say so."

A gasp ran through the gallery.

"Milord?"

"Yes, Sir Desmond. The jury will disregard the witness's last remark. Any further questions, Sir Desmond?"

"No, Milord."

Jeremy was dismissed.

"Call your next witness, Mr Eversham."

The prosecution called Alfred Elsworthy.

Clara and Lawrence both perked us as Alfred was led to the witness box and took the oath. Small, pale faced with his dark hair smarmed down Clara thought he looked about ten, rather than sixteen.

"He looks scared to death," Lawrence said as Alfred glanced wildly around. He leaned forward and smiled encouragement. Clara smiled too but Alfred still looked frightened out of his wits.

Mr Eversham approached the witness box. "It's Alfred isn't it," he said, a twinkle in his eye and kindness in his voice. Alfred swallowed and nodded. "Can you tell me in your own words what you remember about the events of 9th August 1902?"

Alfred's voice was almost lost in the vastness of the courtroom. Clara leaned forward, straining to hear him. "I was on the door. Mr Barker had gone with the others to watch the Coronation parade."

"Yes. And what did you see that afternoon?"

"There wasn't many people about, what with the procession an' all, but I saw Miss Clara. She came in with a soldier. They went to her room."

Clara grimaced. "Did the world need to know that?" she muttered.

"Then what happened?"

"Shortly after I saw the woman what died. She came in with 'im." He pointed at Viscount Westrow sitting in the dock.

"The woman? You mean Miss Deverill?"

"Yeah. She was nice. She give me sixpence once for running an errand."

"And then?"

"Erm." He thought for a moment. "Then the soldier what was with Miss Clara come out. 'E was in a hurry. Didn't give me nothing." He frowned.

"And after that?"

"He came out." He pointed again at the dock. "Viscount Whatsisname. Looked a bit miffed, but he give me half-a-crown to 'elp 'im get somat out of 'is carriage. When the carriage come up 'e opened the door and said the parcel was inside. I reached in to get it, that's the last thing I remember. Next thing was, I woke up in 'ospital. Couldn't remember nothing then. Not even me name."

"Thank you." He turned to Sir Desmond. "Your witness."

Sir Desmond strode up to the witness box, thumbs hooked inside his gown, a look of incredulity on his face. "That's a pretty story," he said. "Now let me be clear. You say that when you woke up in hospital you had no memory of the events leading up to your being there?"

"Yeah. That's right."

Mr Eversham jumped up. "My Lord, I can produce several witnesses to the fact that Mr Elsworthy was found on Tollgate Road on 9th August 1902. He had been badly beaten and sustained sufficient injuries for him to be taken to the hospital in Beckton."

"Thank you, Mr Eversham. Duly noted. Please continue, Sir Desmond."

"And your memory didn't come back until you saw your picture in the paper and the one hundred pounds reward?"

Alfred's face creased into a frown. "It wasn't 'cos of that."

"But you did collect the reward from your employer, Mr Lawrence Fitzroy?"

"Yeah. Right gent is Mr Lawrence."

"And you are still in his employ?"

"Yeah."

"You spent some time helping the police with their inquiries, is that correct?"

"Yes, sir."

"I put it to you, Alfred, given the length of time that has elapsed since the incident and because of your lapse of memory you weren't so much helping the police with their inquiries, as they were helping you concoct a story for us all to hear."

Mr Eversham jumped up. "My Lord, Sir Desmond is inferring that the police used undue influence on the witness to elicit information that would support their case against the accused. Mr Elsworthy's doctor will confirm that it is quite possible for people with amnesia to regain their memories over time. Such memories can be triggered by something they've seen or heard."

"Possible, but not probable," Sir Desmond said. "My Lord, I think the matter of police influence is something the jury can decide upon for themselves, given that the incident took place almost twelve months ago. I think I'd be hard pushed myself to recall with such accuracy the story we've been told today after such a long period of time."

"Milord, Sir Desmond's memory is not in question here, but Mr Elsworthy's is."

"Quite so, Mr Eversham. I agree with Sir Desmond. The jury can decide upon the efficacy of the witness's evidence. Do you have any further questions, Sir Desmond?"

"Yes, Milord." He turned back to the witness box. "Mr Elsworthy, do you really expect us to believe that the time you spent helping the police and the lure of the reward, a substantial inducement I'll warrant, played no part in the story you told us?"

Alfred looked bewildered. "It's the truth."

"And can you swear, under oath, with one hundred per cent certainty, that the person you saw with Miss Deverill on that day, nearly a year ago, was my client, Viscount Westrow and that you can clearly recall those events without undue influence being placed upon you?"

Alfred glanced around, looking haunted. He bit his lip.

Mr Eversham sprang up. "Asked and already answered, Milord. Sir Desmond is trying to intimidate the witness."

Judge Bowden-Brown sniffed. "Yes, Sir Desmond. We've got your drift. Now move on."

Sir Desmond stared at Alfred. "No further questions, Milord."

"Mr Eversham?" The judge glanced at the prosecution barrister.

Edward Eversham shook his head

"Very well." He looked at the clock. "I see time is running late. We will resume tomorrow." He banged his gavel and court was adjourned.

After court Clara went with Lawrence to meet with Mr Eversham, the prosecution barrister. None of them were optimistic.

"How do you think it went?" Lawrence asked.

Mr Eversham pouted. "Sir Desmond, as you saw, is a formidable opponent. He's relentless in court and his reputation is well deserved. I fear he has done enough to cast reasonable doubt upon the case."

"So what will happen now?" Clara asked.

"I have no other witnesses. Sir Desmond has effectively discounted the fingerprint evidence we were relying upon to place Sir Richard in Miss Deverill's room on that day. The only actual witness who can place Sir Richard at the hotel has a memory that is, at best, tenuous and is in your employ. He will use that against him."

"Poor Alfred," Clara said. "He did his best, but I'm afraid he was out of his depth."

"Sir Desmond will play on that fact. He will use the rift between your family and Sir Richard to impugn his evidence. He will show Sir Richard as an upstanding member of society who has been brought before the court on a spurious charge dreamed up by disgruntled former business associates."

"You mean Sir Richard will get away with it?" Clara was aghast.

Mr Eversham shrugged. "He has wealth, position and friends in high places. The members of the jury will have more in common with him than with the witnesses. He will make them believe that you have orchestrated a vendetta against him because of your prior association and that he is innocent of the crime of which he has been accused. That is what I would have done. We have no one other than Mr Elsworthy who saw him at the hotel on that day, unless..." He frowned. "It's a bit of a long shot..." He picked up his papers. "Leave it to me," he said. Clara and Lawrence were left staring as he rushed out.

Chapter Forty Four

The next morning a despondent Clara and Lawrence climbed the stairs to the public gallery at the Old Bailey. "We need to prepare ourselves for a vicious attack on our character," Lawrence said. "Sir Desmond will do his best to discredit the Fitzroy name and Mr Eversham can do nothing to stop him."

"I can't bear the thought that that toad, Viscount Westrow, will get off scot free," Clara said. "If only there was something we could do."

"Mama will be incandescent with rage when she reads the reports in the newspaper," Lawrence said. "Unfortunately they have a way of reporting that skews the facts to make more salacious reading."

"Do you think it will affect the hotel much? I mean, it's our only business now. Our only source of income other than the rents from the farmers on the estate and they pay hardly anything."

Lawrence guffawed. "The hotel will become a place for people to come and gawp. Murder brings out the worst in people. If Sir Richard gets off, and I'm assuming he will, then they'll all think the worst of us. Sir Desmond will make it look like a conspiracy we've come up with to get our revenge on him for alleged previous wrong-doings. It won't be pretty."

A stone of dread formed in Clara's stomach as she took her seat. Hadn't her family suffered enough? "I don't suppose I've helped much when it comes to preserving our reputation," she said. "I'm sorry."

Lawrence squeezed her hand and smiled. "Whatever doesn't kill you makes you stronger," he said. "We'll get thought this. We always do." And

Clara thought again how lucky she was to have two such adorable brothers.

Once the court had assembled and Judge Bowden-Brown taken his place at the bench, the case continued. Judge Bowden-Brown reminded the jury that they were still tied by the oath they had taken.

Mr Eversham stood up. "If Your Lordship pleases, I have another witness to call. He was present at the time and his evidence will be instrumental in proving our case."

Sir Desmond, looking complacent, shrugged.

"Call your witness, Mr Eversham and let's get on with it," the judge said.

"Call Captain Sebastian Shawcross," Mr Eversham said, and Clara nearly fell off her seat.

Captain Shawcross took the stand and was duly sworn in. "Captain Shawcross, can you please tell the court of your movement on 9th August 1902, the day of the King's Coronation?"

"Certainly. I took part in the procession to the Abbey, then, having a few hours to spare during the actual service, I went to meet Miss Clara Fitzroy in Hyde Park. I had been invited to a boating party organised by her brother, Mr Jeremy Fitzroy." He gazed up at the gallery and Clara caught his gaze. She smiled, although her heart nearly jumped out of her chest.

He continued. "From the park we went to The Fitzroy Hotel where I spent a pleasant few hours. I was due back on parade later that afternoon so I left. On my way out I saw the accused with the lady I now know to be the deceased. They were going into her room."

"And you are sure it was the gentleman you see today sitting in the dock?"

"Oh yes. I noticed him particularly as he was bare-headed but wearing Regimental Guard's dress uniform. I noticed the insignia of a Major General on his shoulder and I was surprised a man of his age and rank needed to resort to the kind of service I thought she offered, but you never can tell, can you?"

"You thought the hotel was a house of ill-repute?"

Clara groaned and hid her head in her hands.

"At the time. I know now that I was mistaken and I can't say how sorry I am."

"Thank you. No further questions." Mr Eversham sat down and Sir Desmond stood. "So, Captain Shawcross, you thought the hotel a house of ill-repute? What changed your mind?"

"I came to learn later that I had been mistaken."

"But at the time you were there, in Miss Clara Fitzroy's bedroom, you were still of that opinion?"

Mr Eversham stood up "My Lord, it is irrelevant what the witness thought of the hotel at the time. The reputation of the hotel is not on trial. Sir Desmond is following this line of questioning in an effort to sully the reputation of the Fitzroy family. It has no bearing on the case."

"Quite so, Mr Eversham. Sir Desmond, please confine your questioning to actual evidence of what the witness saw, not what he thought or his opinion."

Sir Desmond's face creased in annoyance. "Yes, Milord. So, Captain Shawcross, after you spent some time in Miss Clara Fitzroy's bedroom…"

Mr Eversham half rose. The judge noticed and nodded. "Sir Desmond." The tone of his voice carried a warning.

"Begging your pardon, Milord, just establishing the facts of the matter." He turned back to the witness box. "When you left Miss Clara Fitzroy's room you say you passed the accused in the hallway. You were in a hurry to get back on parade. You had tarried a little too long perhaps? How long did this passing the accused take? Did you stop perhaps for a moment or two? Or were you rushing past, eager to get back to your post?"

"I saw them from the end of the corridor. I walked towards them, perhaps twenty or so yards. The young lady was fiddling with her key to open the door. The accused looked up at me as I approached. He turned away as I passed, but I had time to register his features."

"Come now, Captain Shawcross. You are telling me that a fleeting glance of a man in a darkened corridor nearly a year ago is fresh enough in your mind to recognise him today with one hundred per cent certainty?"

"I have every reason to remember that day. The details of it are impressed upon my memory as though it were yesterday. It was a very special day. I was taking part in the King's Coronation procession, a great honour and a privilege. I'd even go so far as to say a once in a lifetime experience. Then I'd been invited to a boating party by the most beautiful girl I'd ever met. Any man would remember a day like that. I saw the accused with the young lady. No question about it."

"You didn't think to come forward before with this information, given the reports in the newspapers and the search for witnesses?"

"After the Coronation I was shipped overseas. I have only recently returned."

Sir Desmond paced the courtroom as though struggling for answers. "Are you in a relationship with Miss Clara Fitzroy?"

Mr Eversham rose. "Captain Shawcross's relationships are irrelevant, Milord," he said.

"Not so. I am trying to establish whether this witness has a relationship with a Fitzroy as it goes towards influence. The last witness was in the employ of the Fitzroy family. This one may well be in a relationship with one of them. If that is the case the jury are entitled to know so. It goes to motive."

"I'll allow it," the judge said. "But be careful, Sir Desmond."

Captain Shawcross pondered before responding. Clara held her breath. What would he say?

"I am not currently in any relationship with Miss Clara Fitzroy." The captain's words were measured. "I hope that will not be the case in the future. During the time I have known Miss Clara she has acted impeccably and I resent the slurs on her character being propagated by the defence. She is a person with the highest morals and since renewing my acquaintance with her I have found her to be not only courageous but also deeply compassionate. I would deem it a privilege to be allowed to get to know her better."

Clara sat wide-eyed, unable to believe what she'd heard.

Sir Desmond was apoplectic. "So, it is possible that you are here today at the request of the Fitzroys, possibly in an effort to impress in a way that would enhance your suit."

Now the captain was incensed. "I can assure you that I have no need to impress anyone. I am an officer in His Majesty's Service and I speak as an officer and a gentleman. I know nothing of the Fitzroys apart from Miss Clara, who has impressed me with her honesty and integrity. My personal life and the personal life of the Fitzroys have nothing to do with the fact that I saw the accused going into the deceased's bedroom on the day she was killed. You have my word and my oath on that."

A murmur went round the courtroom and along the public gallery. Clara sat stunned. She still didn't believe what she'd heard.

After Captain Shawcross's testimony Clara felt the mood of the court change from one of hostility to one more open to fair assessment of evidence. Mr Eversham had no further witnesses to produce so Sir Desmond prepared to present his case for the defence. He called several witnesses to attest to Sir Richard's character and his presence at an event held earlier in the day, but as none of them could testify to his whereabouts at the time of the murder Mr Eversham made short work of them.

Sir Desmond turned to the dock. Sir Richard sat stony faced. He shook his head.

The defence rested and the court was adjourned for lunch.

Chapter Forty Five

When the court reconvened Sir Desmond gave his closing argument in defence of Viscount Westrow. He dismissed the fingerprint evidence as misleading, the witness testimony of an employee of the hotel as prejudiced and took great pains to emphasise the good character and status of the defendant. He made a great deal of the bad blood between the viscount and the Fitzroy family, going back for many years. "You have seen for yourselves the acrimony between the Fitzroys and the defendant," he said.

He reminded the jury that much of the evidence the prosecution relied upon to prove their case was provided by employees who depended on the Fitzroy family for their livelihood and again remarked on the amazing coincidence of a sudden return of memory.

"Viscount Westrow is a man of honour," he told them. "Put here today by the vindictive, maleficent, actions of a resentful, unforgiving, family who blame him for their misfortune. They have used the death of a woman of ill-repute, known to them and living in their hotel, to concoct a story and fabricate evidence to support it. Their actions and attempts to blacken the viscount's name have allowed the actual murderer to go free. If anyone should be punished it is the Fitzroy family, not the man sitting in the dock.

"You can only find Viscount Westrow guilty of this horrendous crime if you are one hundred per cent certain of his guilt. If you harbour any reasonable doubt you must find him not guilty."

Mr Eversham stood up. The courtroom filled with the palpable silence of anticipation. People in the public gallery leaned forward to hear better. Clara sat with her fingers crossed.

"Gentlemen of the jury," Mr Eversham said. "Sir Desmond has woven a web of myths and misinformation surrounding the Fitzroy family in an attempt to deflect your attention from the evidence. He has offered only conspiracy theories masquerading as truth. He hopes to bamboozle you with smoke and mirrors like the best circus flimflam man. His sole defence is the antagonism between the Fitzroys and Viscount Westrow. This is not evidence, this is gossip and tittle-tattle of interest only to muckrakers and scandalmongers. It has no place in a Court of Law.

"The Fitzroy's opinion of the defendant is irrelevant, as was much of Sir Desmond's evidence. Nothing he produced gave any satisfactory proof of the defendant's innocence. His defence is that he has been charged due to a case of mistaken identity, but we have the word of an officer and gentleman that he saw the defendant at the scene of the crime. This is indisputable.

"Viscount Westrow declined to give evidence in his own defence. That of itself is not an indication of guilt, but it does give one pause to wonder.

"Let us look at the actual evidence. His fingerprints were found in the bedroom, on the bedrail and on the buckle of the dress the deceased was wearing at the time of her murder. Fingerprint evidence has proved reliable and efficacious in previous criminal prosecutions. The cause of death was a broken neck. The medical officer has testified as to the difficulty of breaking someone's neck. It is his expert opinion that, in all likelihood, the killer had undergone military training. That gives us means.

"We've heard that the defendant had a prior relationship with the deceased which, if exposed, would bring his name into disrepute and sully his reputation. In the words of Syrus 'a good reputation is more valuable than money.' Sir Desmond tells us that Viscount Westrow is a valued member of society. He had much to lose. That gives us motive.

"Two eye-witnesses have placed him at the scene. Now you may feel a little unsure about the young man on the door, who admits to his failing memory, but there can be no doubt in anyone's mind that Captain Shawcross, an officer in the service of the King, has told us the truth. He has no reason to do otherwise. Viscount Westrow was with Miss Deverill when she died. That shows opportunity. Means, motive and opportunity. The cornerstones of criminal detection. Viscount Westrow has been proved to be in possession of all three.

"This is the evidence upon which you must base your verdict. Not the hotchpotch of rumour and innuendo produced by the defence. I put it to you that you have no option, based on the evidence placed before you, but to find Viscount Westrow guilty as charged, beyond a reasonable doubt."

Mr Eversham sat and Judge Bowden-Brown began his summing up. In his directions to the jury the judge, using his judicial discretion, outlined the legal requirements needed to reach a guilty verdict in English Law. "In order to find the defendant guilty of murder you must be convinced that he did, with malice aforethought, kill Miss Hilary Grenville, also known as Dolly Deverill, in contravention of the law. If you find that the defendant did kill Miss Grenville, also known as Deverill, other than with malice aforethought, but rather in a spontaneous act in response to some provocation, you may find him guilty of the lesser charge of manslaughter."

The jury retired to consider their verdict.

*

Over the next few days everyone at the hotel was on tenterhooks. The staff had followed the reports of the trial in the newspaper, their spirits rising and falling as the evidence was produced then dismantled.

"Poor Alfred," Daisy said. "It must have been an ordeal. I'm glad I'm not in his shoes."

"I wouldn't have minded," Mrs T said. "I'd tell 'em exactly what I thought."

"It looks as though he's going to get away with it," Hollis said. "From the reports in the paper."

"Well, he's got money and plenty of it," Mrs T said. "His sort always get away with it. If it had been one of us…"

"Miss Clara hasn't been out for days," Daisy said. "Frightened of missing the verdict."

Mrs T laughed. "Still, she's not been lonely has she? Not sure what I think of that Captain Shawcross." She banged the dough she was kneading onto the table, sending up a flurry of flour.

Daisy knew more about Captain Shawcross than anyone. "Oh, I think he's good for Miss Clara," she said. "She's calmed down a lot since she met him."

As time went on and no verdict was forthcoming they were convinced that the case would be thrown out. "Told you he'd get away with it," Mrs T said. "His sort always do."

"You don't know that," Daisy said. "You have to trust in the system. They'll find him guilty, no doubt about it."

The opinions in the kitchen were evenly split, although they all thought Viscount Westrow guilty as charged. "If you ask me he's got away with too much for too long," Barker said. "I remember when Mr Herbert had the hotel – the tales I could tell you about his father and Sir Richard. Make your toes curl, they would."

The morning of the fourth day Mr Lawrence, Mr Jeremy and Miss Clara rushed out to the Old Bailey to hear the verdict.

When they returned Daisy, looking out of the window of one of the upstairs rooms, saw the commotion and hurried down to see what the fuss was all about.

"They found him guilty," Mr Lawrence said, his face shining with delight. "Guilty of manslaughter. Life imprisonment. This calls for champagne."

Reckless with relief he sent a couple of bottles down to the kitchen so the staff could join in the celebration. Miss Clara, Captain Shawcross, Mr Lawrence and Mr Jeremy celebrated in the hotel bar. They all drank to Dolly Deverill's memory. "May she rest in peace," Miss Clara said.

"Manslaughter, not murder," Mr Jeremy said. "Still, he'll spend the rest of his life in prison."

He was the most relieved of all.

Chapter Forty Six

The trial being reported in all the newspapers brought a fresh influx of guests and visitors to the hotel. This time the more salacious papers called it, *The Toff and the Tart Murder.*

"Better than The Fitzroy Hotel Murder," Daisy said, "but it doesn't stop people coming to see the scene of the crime."

"Everyone loves a murder," Barker said. "It's the drama of it. Livens up their dull lives."

"Hrmph," Mrs T said. "Anyone would think no one was ever done away with afore. Ghoulish I calls it."

"Who'd of thought murder would be good for business," Hollis said. "Still, I'm glad of the extra tips."

"Me an' all," Barker said.

"All right for some," Mrs T said. "All I get is extra work."

"I wouldn't mind," Kitty said, "but they keep looking at us as though we were part of a freak show, or murderers ourselves."

"Or tarts," Matilda said, the horror of it clear in her voice.

"Strange, though, isn't it? People coming to have tea where a murder's been committed."

"It's the journalists who are the worst," Kitty said. "Always asking questions. I wouldn't trust any of 'em."

"Muckrakers and tittle-tattle merchants. That's journalists for you," Mrs T said.

"Not that we're allowed to talk to 'em," Annie said. "I don't want to lose me job."

"Me neither," Kitty said. Still, Daisy knew Barker made more than a few shillings from the papers with anecdotes about Grandfather Fitzroy and his exploits.

"Nothing they couldn't get from any pub or club in London if they took the trouble to ask," Barker said, when Daisy confronted him. "Anyway, it'll soon be yesterday's news. No one will be interested then. Have to make the most of it while we can. Next week it'll be some other poor beggars' turn to have their lives pulled apart."

Daisy sighed. Barker was right. It wouldn't be long before people forgot and moved on, then things could get back to normal. Thank the Lord, she thought.

*

Summer faded to autumn, the trees put on their tapestries of orange, red and yellow and leaves crunched underfoot. Pale sunlight shone across dew-spattered lawns turning fallen leaves to carpets of gold. Bright summer days gave way to mellow mistiness and starlit evening. At Maldon Hall Clara spent time with little Harry, her affection for him growing daily. If anyone thought it strange that she should spend so much time with an adopted orphan child, no one said anything.

A widowed woman from the village replaced Jessie. In her forties she'd had children of her own, now grown. Her experience and gentle handling of the child reassured Clara. She got on well with Mrs Craddock too, being of similar age.

"He's a bonny lad and no trouble at all," she often said and Clara's heart swelled with love and pride. She'd never seen herself as a mother, but now she was one she relished the achievement. Her son mesmerised her. She'd sit and watch his face and his little fists waving in the air. When he opened his eyes and smiled her heart leapt for joy. He'd come into her life and given it meaning. She felt more alive than she ever had before. She loved more, feared more and hoped more, because of his existence.

Sebastian too came to visit often.

"I don't know how he manages to get away, him being in the army," Elvira said, but Clara was glad to see him.

They'd take long walks in the garden and she wasn't at all surprised when, on a starlit night beneath an August moon, he dropped to one knee and proposed.

"This is something I should have done a long time ago," he said. "Clara Fitzroy, you are everything a man could wish for, clever, beautiful and courageous. I've come to care more deeply for you than words can say. You mean the world to me. I know I don't deserve you, but would you do me the greatest honour and become my wife?"

Clara, threw her arms around his neck. "What took you so long?" she said, laughing.

"I didn't think I deserved you," he said and drew her into his arms kissing her with the greatest passion.

"Is it what you want?" Lawrence asked Clara, when Sebastian approached him for her hand in marriage. "You're not marrying him out of some sort of misplaced obligation?"

Clara grinned. "No. It's what I want. What I've always wanted. Marriage to a man I can love for who he is, not for his wealth or position."

"Then you have my blessing."

Clara worried what her mother would say when she told her the news of her engagement.

"I suppose a gentleman farmer is as good as you'll get," Elvira said, when she heard that Sebastian would be resigning his commission to take over the running of his family's Gloucestershire estate. "Given your circumstances." At least she grudgingly approved, that was something to be thankful for.

"London's loss is Gloucestershire's gain," Lawrence said,

"I'm not sure Gloucestershire is ready for our Clara," Jeremy said, "but I hope they'll both be very happy."

"He'll have me to answer to if not," Lawrence said.

"At least he's had the decency to recognise little Harry as his son and heir and managed to salvage Clara's reputation in the process. Good to know our nephew will bear the name Herbert Edward Fitzroy Shawcross."

"The wife of a gentleman farmer is a fitting position for a Fitzroy who's been brought up in trade," Aunt Doris said when she heard.

*

Daisy looked forward to Christmas and seeing Jack and Dan again, but before that, in the months leading up to Christmas there were two weddings due to take place. Daisy wasn't sure which brought her the most happiness.

Matilda married George Perkins on an unusually balmy day in mid-September in front of a small gathering of friends and colleagues in the local church.

Daisy helped with her dress, a light blue serviceable cotton creation with a lace collar and matching jacket that would be saved for use as her Sunday best after the event. She wore a wide brimmed straw hat festooned with fresh flowers and carried a spray of Michaelmas daisies.

Matilda's cousin and her husband were the only members of her family present. George's brother, Simon, younger than George but similar in build and looks, stood as best man. Their parents, his sister and her husband represented the rest of his family.

A dozen of George's colleagues attended and formed an arch with their truncheons as a guard of honour, outside the church as they left.

The reception afterwards was held in the upstairs room of the Marquis of Bath Public House. Daisy spotted some of Mrs T's pies among the refreshments.

"You'll miss her," she said to Mrs T.

Mrs T sniffed, holding a handkerchief to her nose, her eyes glassy with water. "Miss 'er jam tarts and iced fancies, more like," she said but Daisy wasn't fooled. She knew Mrs T had become fond of the girl she'd taken on at the request of an old friend. Daisy remembered how timid Matilda had been when she first arrived at the hotel. Looking at her now, she'd blossomed into a different person; a beautiful, joyful bride beaming with contentment.

Daisy moved around the small crowd chatting to everyone.

"Call me Stuart," Sergeant McBride, looking very impressive in full Highland dress including a tartan kilt, said, when Daisy spoke to him. "We're among friends here." Sergeant McBride and his wife had both welcomed Matilda into their circle of friends and promised to help her after the wedding to make a proper home for George.

"I expect you're glad George will be staying on," she said.

"Aye. He's bright lad." He touched the side of his nose as though about to impart a secret. "Scotland Yard have their eye on him. He'll go far," he said.

"Aw, we'll miss her," Kitty said. They all joined in throwing confetti over the couple as they departed in the carriage George had hired for their short honeymoon by the sea. Daisy had tears in her eyes as the carriage pulled away. She'd miss Matilda more than she could say.

After a short honeymoon, George and Matilda would be living within easy commuting distance of the police station and close to his sister, her husband and Matilda's cousin, but it did mean that Mrs T had to break in a new pastry cook.

"Poor girl doesn't know what she's let herself in for," Barker said.

"Matilda will be a hard act to follow," Kitty said. "The new girl will have her work cut out."

"What a lovely day," Daisy said later, over cocoa with Mrs T and Barker. "I'm sure they'll be very happy."

"Made for each other," Barker said and he was seldom wrong about anything.

*

The wedding of Miss Clara Fitzroy to Captain Sebastian Shawcross, on a bright November day, sharp with frost, was a much grander affair. The week before the wedding the entire Fitzroy family descended on the hotel, which was closed to other visitors, for the pre-nuptial celebrations. Despite the closure the staff were busier than ever. The atmosphere for the whole of the week was one of celebration and the staff joined in the merrymaking.

The day before the wedding Daisy travelled with Miss Clara to Maldon Hall. The wedding was to take place in the church where Herbert Fitzroy had been laid to rest. Daisy was there to make sure everything was just right for Miss Clara's special day.

She spent the morning preparing Miss Clara's outfits. Her wedding dress consisted of several yards of the best satin silk. The bodice thickly beaded and the skirt heavy with pleats that fell into a deep frill with a train at the back. Miss Clara would wear a velvet cape, edged with ermine for the journey to the church. The jewellery she wanted to wear would have to be checked along with her underwear and shoes. Nothing was to be left to chance.

Daisy was as nervous as Miss Clara. She hoped everything would go well for her.

Once Miss Clara was dressed in her bridal outfit, her hair curled and pinned into a tiara with a veil, she called Daisy into her room. Daisy found her standing in front of the mirror studying her reflection. She turned around when she saw Daisy. "I have to thank you for this," she said. "If you hadn't found Sebastian for me none of this would have happened."

Daisy's heart swelled. It wasn't often Miss Clara showed her appreciation. "I only did what you asked," she said, but couldn't keep the pleasure out of her voice.

"And I have you to thank for getting little Harry back too," Miss Clara said, her eyes lighting up at the mention of her child's name. "I'll never forget your kindness, Daisy. You've been good to me and I haven't always been as kind as I might have been to you."

Daisy smiled, savouring the rare admission. "You did what you thought was right," she said. "I can't blame you for that."

"How will I manage without you," Miss Clara said. "I have something for you, a small token of my gratitude. I hope you like it." She handed Daisy a small leather box.

Daisy gasped when she opened it. A cluster of diamonds in the shape of a daisy sparkled from a brooch inside the box. "It's beautiful," Daisy breathed. She couldn't believe her eyes.

"I hope you'll wear it and think of me," Clara said. "I know I'll never have a friend as good as you again." She stepped forward and planted a kiss on a surprised Daisy's cheek. "Thank you," she whispered.

A light flutter of snow swirled in the air as Clara arrived at the church. Frost, that had stayed all day, iced the gravestones and the bare branches of trees. She stepped out of the carriage into the brittle, frosty air, but inside, the church glowed with warmth. Candles flickered and the organ played soft music. Bunches of white Calla lilies and Lisianthus decorated the end of every pew and garlands of laurel and Christmas roses decorated the walls. Huge bouquets of honeysuckle and roses stood either side of the aisle by the altar steps. Pale sunlight shone in through stained glass windows pooling in rainbow patterns on the floor.

"You look amazing," Lawrence uttered as she took his arm. "I hope Captain Shawcross knows how lucky he is."

I'm the lucky one, Clara thought but merely smiled at her brother, his eyes shining with pride.

"Ready?" he asked.

"Ready," she said and a bubble of confidence grew inside her. She'd do her family proud.

Walking down the aisle on Lawrence's arm, she glowed with happiness. This was her day, the day she'd dreamed of.

She gazed from left to right as they made their way down the aisle. All her family and friends were there. Heavily pregnant, Amanda Melville sat with her husband, Gerald. Aunt Doris sat gazing around at the commemorative plaques of generations of Fitzroys on the walls while cousins Henrietta and Verity each sat lost in worlds of their own.

Jeremy had brought several of his lady friends who were good fun and sure to enliven the proceedings. Clara smiled at them as she passed.

The only person who wasn't happy that day was Sir Richard, Viscount Westrow languishing away in prison cell, but no one gave him much thought.

As Clara walked towards her husband and her future she thought of the first time she'd seen him, in the park, a tall, broad shouldered young man with the world at his feet. She recalled the way the sunlight shone on his shock of blonde hair, burnishing it to gold, the laughter in his eyes. She'd known in a heartbeat that he was the one for her. Now she would be spending the rest of her life with him.

How empty and futile her life would have been without him, she thought. Now a great adventure lay ahead of her. He turned his head as she walked towards him. She caught his gaze and the world stood still. A swell of love blossomed inside her. It felt so right. Together they would conquer the world.

The party after the wedding would go on for several days, but Clara knew nothing about it, neither did she care. That night, in her captain's arms she had everything in life that she'd ever wished for. She'd found her Jane Austen hero and was never going to let him go. Sometimes dreams do come true, she thought. He turned to kiss her and her heart beat even faster.

About the Author

Kay Seeley is a talented storyteller and bestselling author. Her short stories have been published in women's magazines and short-listed in competitions. Her novels had been finalists in The Wishing Shelf Book Awards. She lives in London and loves its history. Her stories are well researched, beautifully written with compelling characters where love triumphs over adversity. Kay writes stories that will capture your heart and leave you wanting more. Often heart-wrenching but always satisfyingly uplifting, her books are perfect for fans of Anna Jacobs, Emma Hornby and Josephine Cox. All her novels are available for Kindle, in paperback and in Large Print.

One Beat of a Heart is her seventh historical novel set in London.

If you've read and enjoyed this book I'd love you to leave a review so other readers can enjoy it too.

Sign up to my newsletter for news about my latest books, free short stories and historical trivia. I'd love to hear from you. http://bit.ly/kayauthor

Facebook page:
https://www.facebook.com/kayseeley.writer

Twitter: https://twitter.com/KaySeeley1

Acknowledgements

I couldn't have written this book without the support and encouragement of my family and writing friends. I particularly want to thank my daughters Lorraine and Liz for reading it and their helpful suggestions. Thanks also go to Helen Baggott for her valuable assistance and Jane Dixon Smith for the wonderful cover. Mostly I'd like to thank my readers for their continued support and encouragement. Hearing from people who've read and enjoyed my books makes it all worthwhile.

Thank you.

A Troubled Heart

It's 1905 and Verity Templeton travels to London, staying at The Fitzroy Hotel for the season. During a weekend with her friend Charlotte Huntington-Smythe she meets Brandon Summerville, handsome, arrogant, wealthy and the object of Charlotte's desires. She soon finds that things are not as they appear to be.

When she uncovers a secret from the past she doubts everything she's believed in. Her fight to find the truth brings more heartache. Can she forgive or will it destroy her hopes for future happiness?

A meeting with a suffragette changes her view of things and leads her into more danger.

Meanwhile Lawrence Fitzroy contemplates his own future and things go from bad to worse for Daisy Carter, the hotel Housekeeper when Carl Svenson is appointed as the new Under Manager.

A story of love, deceit, honour and a struggle for justice.

Follow the fortunes of the guests and staff at The Fitzroy Hotel in *A Troubled Heart*, the second of The Fitzroy Hotel Stories.

Available from April 2023

If you enjoyed this book you may also enjoy Kay's other books:

A Girl Called Hope

In Victorian London's East End, life for Hope Daniels in the public house run by her parents is not as it seems. Pa drinks and gambles, brother John longs for a place of his own, sister Violet dreams of a life on stage and little Alfie is being bullied at school.

When disaster strikes the family lose everything and the future they planned is snatched away from them. Can Hope keep them together when fate is pulling them apart? What will she sacrifice to save her family?

A Girl Called Violet

Violet Daniels isn't perfect. She's made mistakes in her life, but the deep love she has for her five-year-old twins is beyond dispute.

When their feckless and often violent father turns up out of the blue, demanding to see them, she's terrified he might snatch them from her.

She flees with them to a place of safety where she meets the handsome and charming Gabriel Stone. He shows her a better way of life, but is he everything he appears to be?

Violet decides to stop running and finds the courage to return to London to confront the children's father. There she finds a far greater evil than she ever thought possible.

How far will Violet go to protect her children?

A Girl Called Rose

Set against the turbulent years of The Great War, A Girl Called Rose is a deeply moving story of young love, heroism, sacrifice, human weakness and the enduring strength of family ties. The close, loving family life Rose has known is shattered when the country goes to war. Rose resolves to do her bit so, aged sixteen, she leaves home to train as a nurse in London. There she finds freedom, excitement and a different way of life.

A brief encounter with a soldier opens her eyes to romance, but is he the man she thinks he is?Can first love survive long separation or will Rose discover that her heart belongs to another? Can she make a difference to people's lives as she hopes?

The Water Gypsy

Struggling to survive on Britain's waterways Tilly Thompson, a girl from the canal, is caught stealing a pie from the terrace of The Imperial Hotel, Athelstone. Only the intervention of Captain Charles Thackery saves her from prison. Tilly soon finds out the reason for the rescue.

With the Captain Tilly sees life away from the poverty and hardship of the waterways, but

the Captain's favour stirs up jealously and hatred among the hotel staff, especially Freddie, the stable boy, who harbours desires of his own.

Freddie's pursuit leads Tilly into far greater danger than she could ever have imagined. Can she escape the prejudice, persecution and hypocrisy of Victorian Society, leave her past behind and find true happiness?

The Watercress Girls

Two girls sell cress on the streets of Victorian London. When they grow up they each take a different path.

Annie's reckless ambition takes her to Paris to dance at the Folies Bergère. When she comes home she takes up a far more dangerous occupation.

When she disappears, leaving her illegitimate son behind, her friend Hettie Bundy sets out to find her. Hettie's search leads her from the East End, where opium dens and street gangs rule, to uncover the corruption and depravity in Victorian society.

Secrets are revealed that put both girls' lives in danger. Can Hettie find Annie in time?

What does the future hold for the watercress girls?

The Guardian Angel

When Nell Draper leaves the workhouse to care for
Robert, the five-year-old son and heir of Lord
Eversham, a wealthy landowner, she has no idea of the
heartache that lies ahead of her. She soon discovers
that Robert can't speak.

Lord Eversham, a powerful man, remarries but the new
Lady Eversham is not happy about Robert's existence.
When she gives birth to a son Robert's fate is sealed.
Can Nell save him from a desolate future, secure his
inheritance and ensure he takes his rightful place in
society?

Betrayal, kidnap, murder, loyalty and love all play their
part in this wonderful novel that shows how the
Victorians lived – rich and poor. Inspired by her
autistic and non-verbal grandson, Kay Seeley writes
with passion and inspiration in her third novel set in the
Victorian era.

You may also enjoy Kay's short story collections:

The Cappuccino Collection
20 stories to warm the heart

All the stories in *The Cappuccino Collection*, except one, have been previously published in magazines, anthologies or on the internet. They are romantic, humorous and thought provoking stories that reflect real life, love in all its guises and the ties that bind. Enjoy them in small bites.

The Summer Stories
12 Romantic tales to make you smile

From first to last a joy to read. Romance blossoms like summer flowers in these delightfully different stories filled with humour, love, life and surprises. Perfect for holiday reading or sitting in the sun in the garden with a glass of wine.

A stunning collection.

The Christmas Stories
6 magical Christmas Stories

When it's snowing outside and frost sparkles on the window pane, there's nothing better than roasting chestnuts by the fire with a glass of mulled wine and a book of six magical stories to bring a smile to your face and joy to your heart. Here are the stories. You'll have to provide the chestnuts, fire and wine yourself.

Printed in Great Britain
by Amazon

33373833R00185